The Sorcerer's Drum

Also by Kelvin Christopher James

Jumping Ship and Other Stories
Secrets
Fling with a Demon Lover

The Sorcerer's Drum

Kelvin Christopher James

iUniverse, Inc.
New York   Bloomington

The Sorcerer's Drum

iUniverse books may be ordered through booksellers or by contacting:

iUniverse
1663 Liberty Drive
Bloomington, IN 47403
www.iuniverse.com
1-800-Authors (1-800-288-4677)

ISBN: 978-1-4401-4170-6 (pbk)
ISBN: 978-1-4401-4171-3 (ebk)

Printed in the United States of America

iUniverse rev. date: 6/10/2009

For my children

Contents

Prologue

Scant flesh barely holding skin to bone, the sorcerer faced his peers. Caught before their inscrutable regard, he closed his eyes as the one with the speaker's staff announced, "The consensus is banishment from our guild!"

The sorcerer chuckled wearily. "Banish…can you banish sunshine?" he asked. "Can you outlaw night? Fresh air and fire? Storms and subjugation? Hear me now, gatekeepers! With my will as free as light, I leave your shade. And with full intent to thwart your influence, I depart vengeful!"

Then the proud sorcerer spread wide his skinny arms and, climbing up the sinews of a passing breeze, he abandoned his society.

Chapter One
BEGINNINGS

This is a tree that knows all the stories.

Some say it is the gods' mischievous messenger, Eshu-Elegba, who dwells in such a tree. Others caution that whoever speaks knowingly of Eshu is but a fool, that mere talk can hardly trouble the *coolness* of this enormous baobab so tendered with the calluses of unhurried Time.

So respect this gnarled ancestor that towers over the sunrise corner of the headman's compound, its wrinkled bark knobbed with ever-swelling dents and gullies.

Honor this stance of wrestled knots that supports a canopy of twisted branches which spread an evergreen cloud over half the compound.

Admire this baobab's formidable and grizzled bole. A score of link-armed hunters cannot girdle it. Bucks of boys and brash young men have ventured up the trunk and were deterred by its hosts of impassable junctions. After rain showers, its tumbled raised roots sweat an aroma that leaves a taste of tempting at the back of women's throats, and makes them touchy.

This is an experienced tree informed by bird and breeze, by rain and see-all shine. And although a dozen or so fruit trees might raise their crowns over the home zangalas in the headman's compound, every soul of the surrounding village knows that the orishas of this ancient baobab rule…

In an inner room of his large zangala privileged to the shade of this grand baobab, Prince Khufu Bembo Chinua Dan sat upon his mahogany throne. Head hunched down vulture-like, his gaze fixed on his sweaty hands resting listless on each knee like broken wings. A cock's crow set off a raucous competition outside. "Midday," his mind vaguely registered; there was business that needed tending. His only move, though, was to clasp his hands together, pass one over the other as if washing them in their own damp anxiety.

"So for some domestic trifle, you summon me, waste half my day?" An amused tone complicated the chide that issued from the doorway.

Startled, Khufu looked to the threshold and met a stare rheumy with contempt. Such a look as could only be cast by the piercing eyes of Lathso, his blood uncle and personal babawalo. Khufu started up from his big chair. A whine to his manner, he said, "Your home is but a stroll beyond the river. What you mean half-a-day?"

Skin and spark to a skeleton, naked but for a ragged red boubou around his waist, Lathso reached his knob-headed staff into the spacious room, stepped slowly in after it. Then he stood and looked around, taking his time as if he hadn't just been quibbling about busy. He studied each familiar wall, high to the thick thatch ceiling, low to the polished red-clay floor. He contemplated the cleverly woven mural, the numerous fetishes and pendants leaning against the wall, resting on the windows' broad ledges, the musket in one corner, a war drum in another.

At last, still without formal salutations or so much as a glance at Khufu, he answered, "My time is my own to measure. Does not require your leave".

Headman Prince Khufu took in a sharp breath and drew himself up lordly. With both hands he grabbed the folds of his robe and pulled it close around broad shoulders. "Be careful, old man," he said harshly. "You take it too far when you belittle my affairs."

Lathso chuckled, planted his staff and leaned on it to peer out the doorway he had just passed through. "Threats even. Hnnn!" he murmured and at last turned a casual eye to regard Khufu.

Nephew or not, the sorcerer mused, if ever a royal deserved exile, this was he. An arrogant man of limited ability, Khufu's leadership fitted simple systems. Ram goat of a new herd at a small watering hole, he was suited only to the basics. Complications caused him anxiety. Still, thought Lathso, the faults of this prince might turn out useful to my own purposes. The skin of even an ordinary goat might be stretched into an uncommon drum.

He moved closer to the prince and like a cloud—though with not a single stink fly in evidence—a powerful stench of unwashedness floated farther into the room with him.

Khufu gasped, marshaled an urge toward the window and insisted with less heat, "You are my babawalo. You have fealty to me, to my office."

"Servant of Eshu-Elegba I am. Ostracized dabbler I may be. But certainly I'll not be dog to incompetents who threaten me with posture. Until there are matters that match my abilities, hail to the ancestors!"

The old man thumped the floor vehemently with the staff's worn, splayed end and turned to leave.

"Forgive me, Uncle", Khufu said, suddenly sheepish. "In truth, I have presumed upon your time. But you know how I depend on you. Don't be stubborn. You are here now. Please, won't you toss your divining chain for me? Someone has cast up a spell on me, someone who wants to bring me down. Three full moons now, the same dream attends me. I'm tired, tired beyond measure. I'm struggling along a muddy road." Khufu's words gained speed, a relieved rush speaking torment. "Mired to my knees and going deeper, sinking in mud, and something is behind me, I can feel its hot breath. Then all at once I'm scrambling up a slippery tree-trunk, striving and striving but making no progress. Then tired almost to my death, in an agony of slowness, I am suddenly edging across a sickening, sagging rope bridge narrowing and ever narrowing, and always this panther is stalking just behind. Right there he is! I can feel his hot breath laughing on my naked backsides and when I scream awake my oko is like a tiny worm resting on my balls. I can…"

Prince Khufu stopped as Lathso's preoccupied gaze at the smooth clay wall announced he was not listening.

Silence grew solid as a mask.

Khufu endured it as long as he could, then broke. "Please, Uncle. This may seem simple to you, a father of secrets, an elder wise above elders. But I am no more than a bested, banished prince…"

"…wrestling his worries around his ring-fingers," Lathso interrupted and stamped his grizzled heel. "Study Ifa's knowledge and perhaps you'll find a solution."

Intent only on winning the old man's sympathy, Khufu dumbly accepted the admonition.

All at once, Lathso sprang forward with surprising agility and with fingertips held together, he struck Khufu *smack!* on his forehead.

And the air in front of Khufu seemed to swirl, then glaze to present a reflection of his ebony face. The shiny, fretful, furrowed brow. The bulging, reddened eyes. The full, bow-shaped lips gone slack. Then as suddenly as it had congealed into being, the image diffused and disappeared.

With a calm belying the magic he had made, Lathso murmured, "That boy who brought your message, I cannot place him."

Breathless and abashed by the image just plucked from empty air, still groping for composure, Khufu replied, "He's family, Uncle. Ammaa's nephew. He journeyed here with a recent party—the last one, I think. He's trustworthy enough."

"Not for my business. Yesterday, after placing your message token on my sleeping pallet, he remained eyes and fingers studying my quarters."

"You saw…?"

"My dwelling watches itself."

What more might the boy have been up to? Khufu worried. "Don't be hard on him, Uncle," he said. "His is only a youth's simple curiosity."

"Simple matters cast long shadows, but enough, enough. Tell me more of your troubled dreams so that I might find meaning in them. Maybe my *opelé* chain can show what must be done."

Late afternoon showers spattered down with extravagant vigor, self-indulgent and robust as a mature husband on those first nights with a lusty wife. Prince Khufu stood at his window watching the downpour while he sipped from a cup of lukewarm cava. His lips puckered from the bitterness, a taste befitting his mood.

Four full moons had passed since the sorcerer had done his part. He had cast his opelé chain, recited the odu verses, reported what the seeds of Ifà said. Yes, Khufu brooded grimly, it made sense that first wife Tebika should be the source of those troublesome dreams. Willful daughter of the King and his favorite diviner, she had been wived to Khufu upon his exile by her father—two troublesome royals tossed the distance of a two-month caravan. The time in her company had brought Khufu to understand the marriage to be further punishment. An ironic judgment, because though wife she might be, Tebika had proved herself among the most competent enemies Khufu ever had encountered. Most constant vigilance was necessary to remaining one trick ahead of her ambitious plotting.

A seep of gratitude slipped into Khufu's thoughts as he admitted the value of Lathso's guidance through this thicket of troubles. Never would he have managed without that Father of

Intrigues. He promised himself to remember this fact and treat the old man with patience.

A gust of wind slanted some rain in through the window, splattering Khufu's forearms. Obscurely reminded of his pending duty, he wished he could muster the rain's zest. He hoped that a head lightened by cava would help.

Intelligent, nubile, but of common stock, this recently bought third wife presented a special challenge. Koita M'fela Kemnebe was her name, the best Ahmed El-Houssan, the itinerant trader, had immediately available. She was Bambaran, of dervish bloodline, barely fourteen and stubborn enough to have deflowered herself rather than submit to ritual, which determination had forced her sale—as a spoilt female—into justifiable slavery. Same determination that Khufu saw as an unwelcome challenge, for only her complicity would foil the first wife's plots.

Carnal beyond his thirty-four years, his penchant was for a certain female wantonness that came with maturity. A manner personified by his second wife, Ammaa. But Tebika's intrigues had given him no choice and response was essential.

'*How he tempts the game his way is the best measure of a man,*' his late father's jovial voice sounded in Khufu's head. He muttered aloud, "You should be here and see how sayings only sound life easy." For as necessary as was this particular play, it did not come naturally to him. Bluntness, not charm, had always been his best way. Khufu sighed and heavier than his robust bulk, heaved himself up. He was unaware that he fingered Eshu-Elegba's amulet for luck.

Cloaking his shoulders with a soft leather hide, he ventured out toward Koita's quarters. Beyond the baobab's cover a sky of gorged black clouds cast a false dusk. The excessive rain beat down on the compound's trees. Pellets of water stripped leaves, sent immature fruit thudding to the ground.

Tail between its scrawny legs, an ownerless dog whimpered as it scuttled in search of a sheltering den, an urgency of which Khufu's instinct approved. But mindful of status, he reined his pace to a steady gait and turned his thoughts to other effects of the deluge.

Such torrents might easily gorge the streams and change them into savage rampaging rivers. Yet, despite this harsh assessment, Khufu was confident that the village's irrigation system would stand. That the crops and gardens would survive.

Three years past when choosing the site for settlement, he had studied this tributary relative to the overall lie of the land. He noted where was clay, sand, rock, or loam. Where was forest, field, or scrubland. Then with thoughtful plans, he had constructed this sound aqueduct.

A pride in his soul that he worked to suppress halfway welcomed the testing floods. Yet this pride was pricked by a worry for the surrounding fodder lands. They most likely were being swamped and becoming a hazard for the herd animals. Khufu snorted abruptly. Then, as if to force away concern, he blew his nose hard. Surely the men assigned to that problem would manage. What's more, he counseled himself as he stopped before his destination's door, these were matters for another time.

He masked his face as would a kindly master and softly called, "Koita, I am here."

Came her instant reply, the voice slipping out soft and shy like a river snail from its plain shell. "Enter with welcome, my lord."

She kept her waiting home clean, simply furnished. A fiber mat softened with embroidered pillows. A small mora-wood stool. A cured hide that curtained off her bed. Pale smoke spiraled up from a censer on a three-stone stand that held a smoldering charcoal fire. Source, maybe, of an unfamiliar, but pleasant woody fragrance in the air.

Koita approached Khufu from the smoky gloom. She knelt and removed his yard slippers. Then she gently dried his mud-stained feet with a soft cloth held in elaborately tattooed hands.

Barely disturbing the quiet, Koita asked, "Where would you rest, my lord?"

Khufu chose the mat, and she arranged pillows behind his shoulders. As she did this, he could smell her fear—not unlike that of a trapped antelope. He was not surprised.

"What can I serve…"

"You might warm my gourd of cava for me," Khufu offered, with a smile.

She took the gourd, went to the fire. Khufu watched her. Although Koita moved gracefully, her build was not his preference. She was of slight stature. Her face in profile was angular, her brow high. She had a sharp nose, pouting lips, a small chin. The faded blue khanga that she wore gathered over her shoulders and draped over her chest obscured another flat disappointment. More dismaying, though, were her narrow hips that hardly seemed capable of birthing.

Still, she was all that he had to counter Tebika and her sorcery.

"Here, my lord. Does this suit you?"

Khufu took the still cool gourd, sipped. "It pleases," he answered.

Koita went and sat on the low stool. "Is there any other comfort…" she began, her speech awkward with the Fon words.

A gesture from Khufu stopped her. In Dioula, a tongue more similar to her Bambara, he began, "You should know that in this household we accept your close-held feelings with utmost respect. You shall not be forced to anything here. We are not barbarians. I only look forward to the day when you would consider me your prince, and welcome me as Khufu, your husband." He regarded her long, keeping a serious demeanor, again sipping his cava.

Then, with a chuckle, he added, "That will be, of course, long after you are comfortable with meeting my admiring eye." he smiled to her startled look, admixed of surprise and relief, "But for now I am happy to tell you of ourselves so that you may know us better."

Encouraged by her hesitant nod, Khufu began recounting the colony's brief history. He quickly lost himself in the tale of his triumphs and travails.

Scant three years past, close to two hundred souls had departed the capital of kingdom Dahomey with him, an exiled prince made headman to this village now grown to three hundred and more. The banishment itself was a mild portion of a royal uncle's spite. Crueler still was being wived to one more wicked than wildfire, then bound to these hinterlands with a caravan of those who had fallen afoul of the Oba's regal affections.

Among those undone were acquaintances tainted by association with the cast-off royals. Their relatives and pets. Their craftsmen and their wives. The families' slaves and their families. Accompanying for reasons of their own were adventurers seeking reputation. And lovers eloping. And those artisans and weavers and toolmakers and sandal-makers looking for new business. And, of course, the musicians, storytellers, dancers, and drummers. Still others joined our exile as spies and scandalmongers, and various miscast souls with obscure motives.

So absorbed he became in his story, or so quietly respectful was she, that Khufu only noticed the second time Koita took the gourd to re-warm his cava. "No more," he said and stood up. "Already I have overstayed. We will continue tomorrow."

Koita returned the gourd to him, bowed her head. "As you wish, my lord," she murmured, and knelt to fasten his slippers.

Khufu lifted his cloak about his shoulders, stepped out into the night's cool drizzle, which, somehow, now felt pleasantly refreshing.

Three more evenings Prince Khufu returned to Koita with his settlement stories. On each visit he brought her a gift—a bolt of indigo cotton cloth, a bowl of honey, a charm. No need to mention that this fetish was provided by Lathso and assured her pregnancy with a boychild.

Came the time for what she saw as fate and duty, Koita was indifferent. She was, after all, a bought slave subject to her master's wishes. Yet, to ease it for her, before the bedding Khufu had her drink some cava, and he was gentle.

Purpose fulfilled, Khufu returned to his quarters with a light heart. "Mmngh!" he grunted with satisfaction. He had performed strictly to Lathso's directions, was now confident about foiling treacherous Tebika. This just-conceived boychild was indeed perfect response to the princess's schemes!

The thought of his wily uncle sent an uneasy memory flitting across Khufu's gloating. The babawalo's counsel had come at the price of a promise: When Lathso deemed the boychild ready, Khufu would permit his apprenticeship to the old man, an exiled and acknowledged enemy of the dreaded Leopard guild of sorcerers.

Khufu shook his head to un-snag this troubling thought. No reason to worry, he tried to assure himself, Time should see him a way out of that bargain.

On a sunny morning ten full moons later, toward the end of the second, brief rainy season, bought-wife Koita M'fela Kemnebe awoke to sharp pains in her womb, and a slow stinging drip of soupy liquid mixed with coppery blood. She sent her servant-girl to Prince Khufu with a message: "My lord, your son has begun the journey of his destiny."

Innocent about childbirth, but determined to manage by herself, Koita summoned no assistance. In the background of her life, countless women had made babies, lending a familiarity to the issue. A hard job, yes. But to slave-wife Koita, hard work was her pastime. More, she felt close enough to no one here to seek their help at such an intimate matter.

Strong comfort to her resolve was the intuition that this child would mark the end of her being without value. No more would she have to endure the hostility that first wife Tebika directed her way (an animosity that only intensified when the princess, too, found her belly.) For slave-wife Koita, this first child—a boy, the prince had assured—would be her safeguard against a cruel future.

So she spread an animal hide on the ground, put a clean cloth over it. Then laid herself upon this thin pallet to await the birthing. For reassurance, she reached out one hand and touched her silver knife's blade, sharpened to a keen edge. Same knife whose sturdy handle, in her former life, she had used to rupture herself. A comforting thought now that it was ready to sever the cord when her baby emerged.

Her ignorance was betrayed, though, by hour upon hour of immense struggle. Horrible pains rode her. They prodded and shoved with wild vigor. They fell upon each other in rushing forward to render wickedness for exquisite intervals. Sometimes after the briefest rest, and without a spit of mercy, they pummeled her in the tender pouch bellying the baby. Sometimes they battered her low down her backbone and hips and buttocks. They rearranged her insides high between her thighs for no right or reason. All of a sudden, her womb had caged a spiteful pinch that frightened her baby into trying to tear its way out.

Such war, such riot and ruction were beyond everything Koita had expected. Sliding down a well of fear, she watched her belly roil and bulge in places to twice its painful size. Breathing hard, sweaty with patience, she swallowed her groans. Finally, as the sun sank from the sky, it seemed that the baby, too, would descend. But strain as she might, it would not come out. So at last Koita's self-muffled screams decided her faithful servant-girl to alert the master.

Appalled that it had not been done earlier, Prince Khufu immediately summoned the village midwives.

The three elders surrounded the now very weak young woman. Weather-beaten hands softened with wisdom, firmly touching. Eyes calm and sympathetic. Confident voices urging instruction and patience. Orders snapped to excited servants bustling at bringing hot water. Bustling to new demands for wet cloths. Swift for a soft dry one. Sharp but gently to pass over the special swaddle.

Tested though was their combined expertise, the old women excelled themselves. They saved both mother and a healthy son. Koita remained conscious only long enough to see her knife's keen blade used on the thick, slick, purple-veined navel-cord.

Mother passed into safe sleep, the midwives called a servant and sent the good news to Prince Khufu. Then, sharing congratulations and hard-earned refreshment, they rested under the baobab.

"What big hands and feet, hiii!" one woman noted. "He's going to be a strapping fellow."

Another laughed, sallied, "Me, I made notice of his privates. I have granddaughters who should be…"

"…forewarned," finished the third woman with a cackle. She took a long draught of the ginger beer.

The midwives' own labor was not yet done, though. Scarcely had they cleaned and swaddled Koita's newborn, their special skills were again requested.

Earlier that day, as soon as princess Tebika learned about Koita's birthing pains, she had sent a trusted slave on an urgent mission. Now, quiet as a shadow, the sorcerer Lathso slipped into Tebika's zangala, into her intimate sleeping room where she sat on a stool beside her weaving loom.

Dirty and naked but for his ragged boubou and the mischief in his smile, Lathso presented himself. "Great lady, here I am, servant to the serpent who steals darkness. No god's pet, no man's beast, the fool unwelcome at funeral and feast. How can I serve the royal princess?"

"Save your prattle for commoners!" commanded Tebika. "You belong to Lord Eshu, who consumes the will of his servants. I summon you because I have a task that meets your unique skills and none must know of it. I will repay you with favor, or gold, or any manner you might name. Only our business must remain private."

A sly smile on his face, Lathso squared with her proud regard. "Of course, royal princess," he said and shrugged his skinny shoulders high as he continued, "But with whom would an outcast as I share privacies? What might be this special task?"

Tebika glared, said firmly, "First, you respect my condition for secrecy."

Without yielding her eyes, Lathso bowed slightly. "You have my word."

Her voice lowered and hesitant, Tebika said, "I want my baby born right now!"

"Of course, royal princess," said Lathso. "Already I was preparing for your summons."

Tebika cast him a confused look. "How…?" she began.

"When I heard that Koita was giving birth."

"Well, what payment do you wish?"

"Your trust in our enterprise is enough, royal princess."

"Is this your word?"

"It is!"

"Well then. What do I do?"

"Prepare yourself," said Lathso. "I must confer with my medicine cloak." And on the balls of careful feet, the sorcerer prowled out the royal zangala.

He quickly returned with potions that Tebika swallowed without hesitation. Soon afterwards began the pains of her birth labors, pronouncing a premature end to the pregnancy connived from the husbandly duty of a complacent Khufu.

Done with his part, the sorcerer slunk away.

When the midwives arrived at Tebika's zangala, her labor was in last stages. So not long after Koita's delivery, the royal wife Tebika had birthed a small, though perfectly formed baby. According to the weary midwives, the cocoa-colored boy came into this world with his right fist clenched and his wrinkle-wise golden eyes wide open.

Prince Khufu was overjoyed. First years of the settlement, he had spoken tolerantly and smiled with each daughter—Ezene, then Mesphi—born by second wife and favorite, Ammaa.

And now two sons in one day!

In celebration, he ordered slaughter of lambs and yard chickens and guinea-fowl. He had his kitchens prepare yam-poi and plantain balls, and cassava fu-fu, and boiled millet, and groundnut cakes, and sago, and plenty ginger beer.

Family members, neighbors close or cool, passersby—anyone who entered his compound—were bidden to join the merriment.

Second wife, Ammaa was not only a wholesome and experienced mother of two bright and healthy daughters, she was a pure-hearted, nurturing soul. So two moons later, it was natural that when they were not being nursed by their mothers, the babies were cared for in Ammaa's zangala.

This warm sunny morning found them loosely swaddled in small hammocks being gently rocked by their fascinated sisters, Ezene and Mesphi. The old-hand female servants were indulgent with watchful eyes as they kept flying insects at bay with brisk whisks and fans. Ammaa came in from her kitchen, knelt beside Koita's child and was touching his face and making mothering noises when Khufu tiptoed in, "Isn't he marvelous?" he said.

"He is," agreed Ammaa and gave her husband a conspiratorial look as she rose. "They both are."

She hugged her husband.

As he returned her loving embrace, he whispered gleefully, "Now I have the means to foil our grand princess."

"Yes, my husband," said Ammaa, showing him a rueful face.

"Yes! Yes! We will talk later. Now I want to borrow them."

"You don't have to, husband," said Ammaa with a giggle. "They are forever yours."

Khufu took up the swaddled infants and holding them one under each arm like long pumpkins, he went into his own zangala. He carried his baby sons into a private room built around an intrusion of baobab roots. A place that contained his secrets and masks, his Fà. He laid the bright-eyed boys on his altar, did ritual *etutu* thanking his ancestors. Then prostrate in that sacred hollow, in reverent tones he sang out over his blinking sons, "Praise to the ancestors for these man children, the prides of my continuance. And please, O generous Spirits, pass along my thanks to my mother. May the ancestors regard her kindly. Yes, please. With respect of service to her, I name my firstborn and natural heir, M'nalo Sikivu Fanta Bembo. His brother from the royal princess, I name Izi Onamuli Fanta Dan."

From the night of Koita's successful birthing, her status in the household was elevated. Her zangala was enlarged by one room and stained with white clay. A house-slave's eight-year-old daughter was assigned to her as help-nurse. Then Khufu himself installed the gift of a woven bleached-raffia wall curtain depicting his bloodline.

All this irked Tebika to no end.

Some time later, in her zangala preparing accounts to purchase garden seeds for the next season's crops, Tebika brought up the matter. "You shame me, Khufu," she railed. "She's a bought breeder. I am a royal princess. Even the walls of the village are laughing at me."

He sucked his teeth disdainfully, his eyes sliding away from hers and up and out to the window's pale blue sky. Then he explained loftily, "We have to make her feel like family. Welcome her. Remember, her son is mine, of royal blood, as is yours."

The answer only flared Tebika's outrage. She long had accepted Khufu's antagonism towards her. She knew that he preferred avoiding her company altogether. Still, once they were together, something in her high-born blood smarted so much she became helpless to her carping.

"But your grandfather's raffia curtain?" said she. "A piece with so much honor, such great prestige? You yourself said you hold it closest. And you gave it to her, raised it on her wall! She, a family problem that cost you a lump of silver and a sick cow. Oh! How my father would writhe in shame!"

"Take counsel from Ifà, Tebika," Khufu replied sharply. "Be careful and mind your pride. The boys, yours and hers, are tied together by the wish of Eshu Elegba. Their navel-strings are twisted one with the other and buried under the baobab. This is their destiny. The ancestors will not be denied."

"But she is a slave!" complained Tebika.

"Enough!" said Khufu firmly, rising and striking the table with his fist, upsetting the counting blocks and seed bowls, several of which fell to the floor. "I will hear no more of this cavil. If you do not wish to speak of business matters, I will return to my privacy."

Long after Khufu had escaped her zangala, Tebika roamed restless around her three dim rooms quarreling with her furious self. She would not be demeaned by Khufu and share her household's status with a slave. Some lazy god had permitted the Oba to banish her to this backwoods. But that did not mean she would accept such a future. It better suggested that she play a cleverer game. Or did Oba expect a princess born of his favorite sorceress to curl up and transform from viper to lapdog? And as for this second rate husband of hers. He who speaks as if navel cords cannot be dug up, and their Fà untwined. As if one can't be fed to night scavengers and the other reburied in his mother's special shrine. Did not this husband of hers consider that a royal princess would resist his commonplace destiny?

Thwik! came the sound as the branch whisked back. But with a graceful shift of her shoulder, his mother eluded the strike. She paused, eyes searching the distance as she resettled the sling that carried him. The vista of dry grasses, scrubby bush, and stunted trees went on and on, ignorant of limit. Koita straightened her shoulders, moved on.

"Isn't it a twisted path of mysteries?" she mused aloud. "A prince you are. Born of a nobody and now the staff of her life."

She spoke their special language in a tone of warmth that embraced infant M'nalo Sikivu. A wholesome timbre that fitted in with the swing and sway of her gait. A way her words flowed around her bobbing head, held up so proud and straight. How her voice pitched high, then low to a gentle gurgling as if privately amused.

"Heart won't feel what eyes don't see," Koita said. "Let the others fret about me. About why I accept such a burden of menial chores for Khufu's family. Well do I know the puzzle weighing on their wrinkled brows. Why I come out here? they wonder. Only for you, my son. Only you might know the true answer. For they have never known freedom. So they won't ever learn the bittersweet solace of this openness. They will not understand how it is that only out here in the scrubland, free of the compound and first wife Tebika's hawk eyes, only here can I feel ease and peace. Only out here can I forgive them.

"Yes! That is what I gain, my precious boychild. They will never comprehend my rich reward of these hours alone with you. Because we have such a short time together. For as with my own people in Bambara, sons here belong to their fathers."

His mother paused, snorted the dust from her nostrils. The frown remained as she concentrated back to her task. Hands loosely clawed and swinging ready at her sides, she set again to foraging the sun-drenched land.

Familiar with this pattern, M'nalo knew that in the main she sought firewood. Although her eyes were ready for wild grain, or groundnut plants. Last trip this way, despite its clever speckled-feathers camouflage, she spied a sand-grouse nest. Took two of the three eggs she found.

Much else might turn up. Maybe a tiny burst of scarlet flowers that she'd pick and fix in her black braid. She might find an edible tuber or sour-sweet berries in season. Whatever was small enough to be scrounged on the way out, she put in the pouch carried against her belly. When she came upon her main interest—suitable firewood—she set her crescent chalk-mark on it, left it there for collection on her return trip.

From the close, rugged hills to their right, a woman's voice called after her strayful child. Koita hailed back, called that she would cast an eye about.

As she rolled her shoulder and resettled M'nalo's weight, he glimpsed a smile cracking his mother's strict face. Briefly as a baby would, he welcomed it.

Snug and safe in the sling tied around his mother's shoulders, same as countless days before, M'nalo swayed to a light breeze that was stingy at cooling their faces as she picked her way through the sparse forest. Off and on, she sang snatches of a prayer-song to the spirits that bring rain. After a time, she began murmuring her thoughts in a voice wistful with memory: "We women are linked so close with the moon. Yet its soft light never bathes the stony bed that is a woman's life. This was the hard plot my mother lay down upon. Same as did her mother before her. Same as do all women. We are doomed to make a way for sleeping within a thorny patch.

"Think of me five years ago. Handed over to the prince, your father, for purchase price of a cow and a silver-beaded amulet. The prince himself was not demanding. Still, even though he honored me with many welcome gifts, in my heart I always knew I was an unwished for wife, a *harafin*. For there I was. Sold into slavery among strangers. Sentenced to sufferance. And yet I have found a measure of comfort here.

"True, I have sorely missed the muezzin's call to prayer. Such a sound that reminds of beauty in what is harsh. Even more, I miss the security of my father's compound. And my mother's sly humor against men. And all of us ten years and more, women well enough, preparing food, weaving cloth, making clothes. My heart squeezes with longing for that sharing at our weekly baths. Pulling and dyeing, combing and washing hair, staining hands with henna. Oh yes! I miss the soft scent of night in my long-ago life. I can scarcely recall the stories sung into the clear Bambaran moonlight. For this I feel regret as sharp as the fear I have of these people to whom I have been offered up. They worship strange gods. They indulge in savage practices. May Allah, the merciful, forgive them.

"I have followed the example the Holy Prophet. I have now discovered reasons to be thankful. One thing you must know, my son. Your father is an honest man. Throughout those early, sandstorm days his patient kindness was an oasis. Because of him the most painful strangles of slavery's noose were loosened. Now my scrounging the scrubland has become a pleasant heart-load. A meditation more than bondage."

All the while she spoke, his mother continued working in a pattern M'nalo by now knew in his bones. Last foray out some days ago, she had walked a similar swath some thirty paces nearer to the sunset. Next time she would work the same distance nearer to the high iroko forests rimming the valley. So it would be through the hot, dry days. To the forests, then back again. Together, mother and child had followed these paths so many times. Together in comforting repetition, they would follow them as many more.

The day's heat mounting to its fiercest, his mother headed to a grassy knoll with a stand of coro trees and a spring. Other women might be there escaping the searing scowl of the sun. As was her custom, she too would rest for a while, pass a word with them before starting back to the village.

Slung naked to his mother's back, cradled in cloth and warmth, M'nalo swung to the rhythm of her walk and song. Still of that age when all was lit by the sunrise brilliance of new memory, his perceptions were wondrous and gilt-edged. Nothing missed his all-absorbing sharpness. Not the breeze's slight whistle through the curls of hair fringing his mother's black braid. Not the big eye of the bright sky interrupted by the twisted branches of the sun-toughened shrubs through which he was borne. Not the plants with tiny pale green clusters, and soft, brown undersides. Often his mother stopped to kneel and probe the soil at the base of these small-leafed plants. Sometimes she withdrew fat, aromatic nuts, or fragrant sprigs. Sometimes, though, she'd shriek and jump away, her startle a pleasant jolt to M'nalo's passage.

He especially anticipated their pause at the spring. Often there were other children freed from their mothers' strict attention. They would play hiding games, or catch beetles, or dig for worms, muddying the stream as they cooled their feet.

Released from his swaddle this time, though, M'nalo found no other children about. So, aimless and alone through the cool shade, he sought his own excitement.

A flicker of pale green with a red stripe from head to tail tip caught all his attention. A darting blink of color that stopped startle-still. Then the lizard moved again. Off M'nalo went in pursuit, prowling burst for burst, patient hands cupped ready. The quarry one enticing pounce away. Then the wily creature shot under a tuft of grass.

Like a shadow, stealthily, so stealthily, M'nalo crouched and slowly reached past what might have been a curled string of sluggishly shifting red and black and yellow beads. Delicately, he shifted the blades of grass. And there where the lizard had to be, he beheld a creature so small he had to squint hard. Then he blinked and squinted more.

Yes indeed! Before him stood a tiny white-haired elder wearing nothing but a bright red rag of a boubou.

He was gently smiling, although a chastening sparkle in his eyes matched words not spoken, yet somehow heard: "Hnnn! Mud-child! Hold. *Why do you frighten your brother lizard?*"

The question echoed enormously in M'nalo's little head as he could figure no answer. Speechless, his mind swirled away in a many-colored whorl...

...he woke to his mother's ministrations. A sip of cool water, an anxious palm soothing his forehead and cheek, and soon M'nalo's head cleared. His eyes made four with Koita's as wakefulness returned. Then motherly concern gave way to motherly vexation.

M'nalo hopped to his feet as she pinched his ear. "You know better than to poke under short grass? Don't you?"

M'nalo nodded his head in the slant of the pinching fingers. "Yes, mammy. Yes."

" You know that's where bead snakes set?" The question cost his ear an extra twist before she released it.

"Yes, mammy. I know," M'nalo replied, blowing on his fingers, using them to smooth away the smarting at his ear. Then, enthusiasm trampling the bud of his remorse, he burst out, "But, mammy, it was not a real lizard. It was an elder..."

Patient through the telling, Koita listened to her son's exuberant tumble of words. When he was done, she was silent for a moment, her face troubled. Then she said, "My child most precious, be wary. Perhaps a djinn is trying to steal your soul. Let's hope it is a kind spirit, this one with whom you banter."

In her tone, M'nalo recognized a familiar response as to recently reported adventures. Still, back in his sling and headed home, his mind dwelt on the marvel of the tiny, outspoken elder.

Came time M'nalo outgrew his mother's back-sling, and many a day while she gathered he was left safeguarded by the casual eye of village authority. Elder men taking the shade. Women at home with daily humdrum. Layabouts. Commonplace adults.

Like the other youngsters, M'nalo roamed and wandered, explored the settlement and surroundings, learned the ways of his world naturally by testing himself. Stronger than his age, able and fearless, he was always welcome to hunts and games, and could join the activities of the older boys whenever he wished. Sometimes though, he preferred to be alone trapping olose, the flavorful hairless rats, or squirrels, or land crabs, or lizards. A choice companion and favorite, he was.

Not so his brother Izi Onamuli by first wife Tebika. Frail and sickly, compelled to wear a cap against colds and ear infections, and snobbish by his mother's instruction, Izi knew only mischief and disdain from the other boys. Shunned like a sickness, only his shadow as company, most often he disappeared into solitary pursuits.

For some time the brothers went different ways. The will of Eshu, however, decreed that whenever they came to sleep in their father's house, they shared a room and often, a single new-straw mattress. Sleep seldom came quickly to Izi Onamuli. He would lie beside his brother talking his daydreams into slumber substitutes.

Most often M'nalo would close his ears to the chatter, enter his own dozy world. But there were those dim hours when he, too, was wakeful, and let himself enter his brother's dream worlds. Through these bedtime journeys, M'nalo drew closer to Izi. Understood him past wary tolerance, even to comradeship.

One hot dry afternoon, the village drowsy, the restless brothers managed to stray unnoticed to a distant edge of the settlement. They squatted near the tall, brown and gold millet fields ripening in the sun and gazed intently among the drying stalks. A heady aroma of honey melons sweetened the air as they searched between the rows of millet. Three rows deep into the patch, in the shadows of the golden grain, they could see them. Dark green and big as a man's head, the tempting melons lay.

"We must not," M'nalo repeated, even as thirsty desire drowned the dry duty in his throat.

"If we go far enough into the patch and find one, or two, who would know?" Izi argued. His thin yellow-brown face was a mask of set intention.

"We didn't plant it, so we ought not to reap it," protested Sikivu M'nalo, his last words almost swallowed by a gush of anticipation. And anyhow Izi, hand firmly on cap, was already skulking off through the tall millet. So, with a look around to make sure they were unobserved, M'nalo crouched down and followed.

No hindrances. No watchful gardeners. So putting caution aside, the boys freed a pair of fat melons from their possessive vines. They broke them open and gobbled down the sweet, red succulence. They spat out the shiny black seeds and giggled with delight at their delicious larceny. Everything was fine.

At last, slaked and sated, they rustled out of the field and started home in a guilty haste. Not ten steps on the way, as M'nalo cast a final look back for betraying traces of their passage, *Bwupp!* he ran flat into Izi Onamuli, who had stopped short in front of him.

There before them was an elder. A skin and bones man in a ragged reddish boubou standing on one leg, gripping a sturdy staff planted like another. His hair was dirty grey, matted in spots, missing in others. In his long face the eyes were nearly hidden in wrinkly sockets blacker than his dark skin. His teeth were big, white with a smile that declared: "I know all!" His rank stench was itself a barrier.

M'nalo raised both hands palms upward, said, "Greetings, esteemed elder."

"Greetings, mud-child," said the elder then looked directly at Izi Onamuli. "And you, have you greetings for me?"

Izi raised his eyes to the elder, his golden gaze glittering defiance. "My hat is open to you. Respect enough from a son of Dan," he replied, naming his mother's royal lineage.

The elder's eyes crinkled even more and he let forth a private chuckle. "Yes, yes, yes. But come with me," he commanded then walked past them toward the millet fields.

M'nalo and Izi exchanged uneasy glances. Should they bolt? Suppose he was the owner? Still, the manner of this elder did not encourage challenge. So despite misgivings they turned and followed.

M'nalo averted guilty eyes as the elder led them directly to the looted melon vines, then perhaps ten paces past their feasting spot. There he paused and pointed a scrawny forefinger.

Looking where directed, M'nalo and Izi saw a full-grown lioness lying on her side as if dead. Her pink tongue hung helpless from yawning, yellow-fanged jaws. M'nalo sucked in breath sharply, caught a whiff of her furry stink. Beside him Izi was silent as a rock.

The elder hooked his pointing finger toward the animal and beckoned. Very slowly, something like a bee wiggled out of the lion's ear, buzzed straight into the elder's matted hair and disappeared. Except for the slightest twitch of the ear the bee-thing had occupied, the lioness remained still as death.

Alarm and terror jolted through M'nalo, forced him to his knees. He blurted the first words that came to his mind, "Please, most powerful sorcerer! Don't let my mother know!"

The exact words from Izi, spoken from the same pose, chorused in his ears.

The elder's frown at them was fierce. At last he said gruffly, "On your feet. Thanks to my protection, your careless greed is safe."

Izi Onamuli was first to scramble up. He cast a sidelong glance at the elder, his smooth brown face closed. M'nalo, still bewildered by the elder's magic, was slower to rise.

Cockiness quickly regained, Izi walked around the lioness, examining her closely. "Is she dead?"

"No, just dreaming of discouragement she learned from my *lobir*. From now on she will fear humans rather than hunt them in melon patches," replied the elder. "Come."

He turned and strode off through the field. Setting a sprightly pace, he led the boys to within sight of the village walls. There he stopped. "Do not speak of this," he commanded. "And remember, little thieves are always in danger from bigger thieves. Go home, now."

Manner penitent, they took a few steps, then unable to resist, both looked back. Their stink savior had disappeared.

From that adventure forward, the brothers were inseparable for whole days in a row.

Khufu's face was a fine-hewn mask of confidence as befitting an upright leader. He maintained a dignified pose on the headman's stool and watched the council members assemble. He nodded gravely to this or that person. Even so, M'nalo knew that his father's mind was jumpy, questing and measuring. Last night, at family dinner in second wife Ammaa's zangala, Khufu had spoken of the growing disagreements between certain council members and the sorcerer, Lathso, who was also Khufu's babawalo. First wife Tebika's every response to Khufu's arguments seemed to fluster and annoy his father, which caused an odd disquiet to overcome M'nalo.

Now in the meeting hall, as he discerned a slight trembling of Khufu's hand, a word for last night's feeling came to him: disappointment. Chagrin at his father's weakness. And he found himself at a loss for how to cope with this embarrassing turn.

M'nalo started out of his reverie as the assembly burst into a gaggle of agreement and supportive grunts about whatever they had been discussing. Khufu quelled the babble, suggesting that the debate address the main question.

Codjo Talla and Enekwe Ngidi both reached for the speaker's staff, Talla graciously giving way.

"Whatever else, we are all together against that old deceiver," charged Ngidi. "He has poisoned my authority in my own household. My two sons, big boys that they are. All of a sudden they are rude to their mothers. They won't help in the field. They won't tote water. What are they doing instead? I will tell you what they are doing. They are down by the river. Down by the sorcerer's shack. They are experimenting with bush potions. Potions that that poisoner, Lathso, with his own hand, is teaching them to make. Something must be done!" Ngidi glared vexation at the audience and passed the staff to Talla.

Before Talla could speak, Khufu objected, his voice tinged sarcastic, "Why should my uncle be blamed for this? Must I point out that every adult in our settlement knows how make up potions?"

Right away Codjo Talla was up smiling. His oily voice observed, "With all respect, highborn headman, this is not a family matter. Our complaint against the sorcerer is specific. The facts of it cannot be denied. Many witnessed the ugly spectacle last full moon. Yaaa! At the southern end of the thoroughfare, everyone with eyes saw it happen in the bright moonlight. They watched as the children discovered Fon Xamara's lapdog with its skin turning green and its belly swollen. They all saw it rolling about on the ground frothing and choking to death. And who was it that inflicted such horrors on this poor creature? I dare not say, although I'll tell you there is a stench to this whole matter. A stink of one who knows the secrets and poisons associated with dread! It might take a blind man to explain the breeze, but everyone knows where this stench is coming from!"

A robust buzz of agreement followed and Talla passed the staff to Khufu.

Voice pitched indignant, Khufu responded, "My brothers and fathers, listen to me. I remind you that anyone can kill a dog. It is common enough and many familiar poisons are available. Why direct these petty angers against the elder? Should we shave a man's head in his absence? Yes, Lathso is my uncle. But that's not why I speak for him. By the dictate and guidance of his guild, he is a recluse. But by many measures he's useful to our compounds. He is no threat. I vote patience. I say let us abandon this disrespectful stance and if only in consideration of his age, let's leave the old man alone."

But Khufu's defense could not withstand the tide of opinion and the meeting concluded with a decision to completely banish the sorcerer from the community.

So decided, so it would be done.

All the way back to their home compound, trailing at a distance like a reluctant dog, M'nalo slouched in the shadow of his father's public humiliation.

Tebika, from an inner room, heard a slight rapping on her back window. She went close and without opening the window, answered quietly, "Yes."

A steady murmur of information replied.

Tebika clapped her hands in warm satisfaction when her spy was finished and gone. Matters were progressing just as she wanted.

Big and round as a golden calabash, the cool moon rose early, and smooth as that, everyone forgot how blistering hot the hard day had been. Just the occasion for storytelling, decided some elders, and they settled themselves within the buttresses of the great baobab. In minutes word passed around and, ready with sitting stools and nibblings, several families abandoned their after-dinner routines to make eager audience. M'nalo and Izi sat near Koita's low stool. Khufu and Ammaa reclined against a buttress root, their daughters at their feet. Tebika, as usual, had refused to join the gathering.

His face wrinkled as rough water, ancient Bembe Oswali would be the storyteller. Grandfather to mature men, the elder sat in a cranny's shadow nodding his scarred baldhead to a private rhythm, sucking on his pipe's stem. Perhaps he chose his story because he saw his audience as homesick settlers from a port city. Perhaps it was to pleasure the quiet children who sat in breathless anticipation. Or perhaps it was simply for his joy of telling.

"Yes! Exclusively," Bembe Oswali began in a vibrant voice, "we are speaking of the aged man with the beard. That vagrant man with the wonderful scraggly beard. Exclusively where did he come from? We hear that he came from nowhere and that no one knew him. He set up harmlessly beneath the public tree bothering nobody. A tree like this exclusively wise baobab that blesses us right now. The oldest tree in the village, under which all had passed or played.

"Now this vagrant, he laid himself down and stray animals, the dog, the goat, rooster and hen, they gathered near him and laid themselves down, too. Soon the youngsters joined them. Then some women came for their children, and they, too, joined the exclusive peacefulness under the tree. Same way for fathers who came for their wives. Soon everyone of the village was crowded around that big old tree whose exclusive shadows had blessed them all their lives.

"A hush fell. An exclusive quiet, mysterious, and everyone looked at each other with wondering eyes. Then, softly as a breeze just born, the old vagrant spoke. A spirit-sigh more than a sound, and everyone deeply felt the *cool* message of this gentle whisper. The old stranger stood up. Exclusively he pulled out a strand of his scraggly white beard and gave it to Ma Hnugi, whose baby was ailing. Straightaway knowing what to do, she fetched the child and passed the hair over its eyes and nose and ears. Then she wound the wisp of hair around the child's frail wrist, and there and then, exclusively! the child became well. Sparkle in the eye, bounce in the step, happy toothless grin of old. The vagrant then sat down and settled himself for sleep, and the minute he closed his eyes the exclusive spell was broken, and the village folk felt free to go home.

"Evening come, amazed villagers recounted the happening. In the warmth of their houses, in the privacy of their beds, some felt amazement, and some knew promise, and in Ma Hnugi's heart there glowed an exclusively special gratitude.

"There were others who felt differently—the village babawalo was one such. An opportunist, and a practical man, he saw the importance of the strange elder's beard hair. What if the stranger decided to wander on along his mysterious vagrant way? So, the babawalo reasoned, it would be for the people's good if he ensured an exclusive supply of the ancient's white, potent hair.

"Deep in the night, dark as the shadows under the enormous baobab, a tree just like this exclusive shelter above us, on his belly like a great black viper, the baba crept among the tree's twisted buttress roots. Carefully he went, little bit by little bit, until he was crouched right beside the vagrant. Chin raised to the moon, the elder slept, his scraggly beard trembling from gusts of wheezing breath. The sly babawalo drew his sharp knife, gently snipped off a few strands, and, stealthily as he had come, he went.

"Next day matters went evenly until a hunting party returned bearing Maalix upon a makeshift pallet. An angry boar had shaken him from a tree and the fall had broken his leg. His companions had managed to kill the beast and bury the carcass for safekeeping. But Maalix was the best hunter and, with how families had grown that year and everybody needing more, his skill would be sorely missed, an exclusively unfortunate turn indeed.

"Mindful of recent events, the hopeful villagers bore Maalix exclusively toward the cool shadows beneath the baobab tree. As they passed his hut on the edge of the village, the wily babawalo came forward. 'Come in from the hot sun and take your ease a moment. Maybe I can save you the rest of your trip," he offered.

"They accepted, and he gave each as he chose—cool water, pepper soup, palm wine, sweet mangoes. And while the hunting party was slaking thirsts, the baba went aside, took one hoary strand from his cache, and passed it over Maalix's eyes, ears, mouth, and crotch, then laid it on the broken leg. And even as the baba's eyes blinked clear, the leg began to heal—its cruel angle straightening, the grisly broken bones knitting perfectly beneath the bleeding flesh. Then the skin itself sealed up smooth and black, even grew a light sprouting of hair: Maalix was an exclusively hirsute man. All of it faster than even the wily baba could disguise his astonishment. So imagine the drinkers' surprise when Maalix rose to prance before them demanding what was left of the wine, and that they quick-quick return to bring in the boar-hog for a celebration to the most gracious gods.

"Well, I need not say who remade his exclusive name and enriched his fame from that miraculous healing! Sham babawalo now felt like a baba-and-a-half, and in his tricky mind, he figured how to ensure even more exclusive prestige. Three straight nights he crept along and shaved the old vagrant's scraggly beard. So much so that it hardly resembled a beard anymore.

"And three straight days, the villagers noticed that the strange elder was losing his dignity and essential *coolness* as fast as his beard. By the fourth day, nearly bare-chinned, the vagrant was dancing about, and climbing trees searching for birds' nests and ripe fruits, and running down to the river to frolic with the young fellows. Fifth day found him even friskier. Within a week it seemed that the young village women could not get enough of the old fellow's exclusive company. They threw words and nasty eyes at each other, and every man who had a lusty wife or a daughter, every man who had a sister or a youthful aunt, all of these men were speaking exclusively serious threats and warnings to their female folk.

"Which might or might not have worked. The following week, the bole of the baobab was bare of company, particularly that of the not-so-elder vagrant. He had moved exclusively into the house of the babawalo down by the river's edge. And soon they became like brothers, close as ears on a narrow head.

"A few weeks later an exclusive oddness became obvious. Many village girls had become pregnant, and within a mere four full moons began dropping some exclusively marvelous babies: girls with precociously seductive eyes, skinny boys with white and scraggly beards.

"Surprise at these developments quickly turned to an exclusive consternation. As one, the young men turned against the strange vagrant and his too-close companion, their own babawalo. These two remained holed up in their zangala by the river, now expanded to a twelve-room palace to accommodate their young women and exclusive babies.

"Only out of respect for the scoundrels' healing powers did older villagers tolerate them. When the headman's wife was bitten by a venomous snake, the local babawalo, though at first hesitant under the aloof gaze of the elder vagrant, brought out a stolen hair, and the headman's wife was saved.

"Meanwhile, the exclusively strange and ever friskier elder appeared to have forgotten his life as a healer, trusting that function to the babawalo. As under cover of darkness, yet not so secretly, both of them continued misusing the village's young women, and producing the same results—pregnancies of about four months, delivering bone-thin boys with white beards and spindly girls with bold eyes, until there were thirty-two such children about. Sixteen boys, sixteen girls.

"Enraged by these events, many abandoned the village for parts unknown. A few lovesick young fellows camped on the village outskirts and spent much time watching over their old compounds and murmuring exclusive strategies to destroy the babawalo and his elder accomplice.

"Then in a flash of clear thinking, one young man noticed how their enemies were held within a prison of sorts, its walls formed by the river on one side, and by their own semicircle guarding the other. Jubilant and renewed of determination, the young men made several attempts to crush their trapped foes. Once, the local babawalo was struck in the shoulder by an arrow. Another time, the elder's head was bloodied by a well-slung stone. But, to the young men's regret, as with every other damage inflicted, that was quickly cured with strands of the scraggly white beard.

"Then it was observed that the strange vagrant was changing again. Keen eyes reported less vigor, less carnal excess, and remarkably, his beard was growing in midnight black. His babawalo partner noted that he was becoming moody, falling into fits and spells, and prone to loud disputes and declarations. Worst of all for the fed-up baba was the elder fellow's defiance of those who kept them prisoner: From the open door, he'd scream combat challenges to the lurking jealous youths, resulting in further injuries and the employment of more miracle hairs.

"Meantime, the thirty-two exclusive babies were growing unnaturally fast, even as the village baba was realizing that he no longer enjoyed misusing the young women. Beset by the troupe of peculiar toddlers underfoot all over his living space, he became so exclusively tired of his former paradise that one night he attempted to break out. But his black-bearded fool of a partner betrayed him, shouting alert to the vigilant world beyond, and the young men chased him back to his sorry, bewitched cage.

"The sun patrolled the heavens, and nights straggled along while it rested, and the thirty-two children kept growing under their mothers' nurture. Then one morning, the Baba rose from his sleepless pallet and scrutinized the old black-beard as if a wonder. After a while he whispered, 'Come closer, my good friend. There's something…' and after a few Ouches! and Ows!, he pulled a fistful of strands from the elder's vigorous black beard. Then, almost in the same action, he snatched up a rock and broke the eccentric old fellow's skull.

"Quiet as that same rock, the ancient fell.

"The wicked babawalo checked the body: no signs of breath or heartbeat. Then, he passed two strands of fresh-plucked black hair this way and that, and even addressed them to the elder's scrotum before abandoning them atop his exclusively broken bleeding skull.

"Breath bated, sham-Baba crouched, waiting for reaction.

"Wasn't long before he decided these hairs were less than magical, and that maybe the exclusive vagrant would not revive. Then he began to worry for explanations of the old fellow's passing. He squeezed sweaty palms together and tried to compose a convincing lie until *miracle!* He saw that the elder's corpse was disappearing, slowly dissolving into the red clay floor without even a stain. With an exclusive vulture's grin, the Baba watched.

"When the room was clean as before, he raised a horrible cry. And when some young mothers came to see its cause, he said, 'That elder was a demon. He changed into an eagle and flew off!' The Baba grinned like a rat as he exclusively declared, 'We are safe once more.'

"Since the room was indeed empty, the women believed, and secretly they rejoiced, as they had always been ashamed of their own lewd enchantment.

"The babawalo commanded a young mother to fetch him some water to slake his thirst, and she departed. Quite some time passed before he realized that she would not be returning: First time in many moons, someone had left the exclusively enchanted compound. Swallowing pride like sandy salt, the Baba skulked out to the rainwater trough, got his drink, and returned to his room to plot a next move.

"Later that day, hearing a great commotion beyond his zangala's walls, the Baba peeped out. And, stunned at the sight, his exclusive eyes buldged red, and his jaw gaped.

"For down on the muddy riverbank, the exclusive children were holding hands and swaying strangely as if at a game. All of them who had grown so wonderfully fast were now terribly aging at many times that pace. Ever so swiftly, the girls' sassy eyes were widening bigger and bigger, from calabash size to split-apart gourds to broken barrels of ever-enlarging sadness. And the rapid flow of these vast, gloom-laden eyes began consuming the exclusively flimsy female bodies, enveloping them even as they melted to the ground as pools of sticky brown muck. Slow, murky swirls between and about what the little white-bearded boys had become, their scrawny arms and legs grown into slender reaching shoots and pale-green brambly branches and haphazard creepers spreading through the sadness-flooded compound. And same way these sister pools sucked in their brother brambles, just so they slurped down everything within their reach, the exclusively terrified babawalo, too, as he tried too late to run away. Down went his shameful feet, his wriggling waist, his aggressive arms and shoulders, his chin and snorting nose. Until, at last, the queer mire he helped spawn had swallowed away his vision of this life.

"And that, exclusively, is how the first mangrove swamp came to be," said grandfather Bembe Oswali, nodding with a sly, conclusive smile.

Naked and relaxed on soft mats, his eyes closed, Khufu let his mind wander philosophic while Ammaa massaged his neck muscles. Was this attack on his babawalo part of some new rivalry? Did the council want to replace his leadership? So what did they anticipate if they took over? Grandeur? Extra privilege?

His mouth quirked wryly. They had no idea that he'd gladly give it all up. That'd be so easy. But it would also mean disappointment to all those good people who had pledged their lives and bloodlines to his destiny. Folks like Arungonu, the carver. Zizi Ado, as another.

As palace bursar Zizi Ado had a secure position handling the king's gold. He could have become rich by simply collecting the dust that fell through the weighing table cracks. Yet six years ago, because he was loyal, Zizi Ado had left all that to come with Khufu to this hinterland. "I am your friend, Khufu!" he had explained.

Could he now abandon such good men?

"No," Khufu murmured to himself. "I can't turn my back on them. I will not repay that way."

Hot midmorning end of the dry season. Cessevi, an exceptional hunter, returned to the sultry village with the story of a green-striped chameleon he had encountered. The creature was on a log preening itself when it saw him. Immediately it raised up on its front legs and screamed a war cry. Sure sign that it was protecting a nearby nest of ripe honey.

Cessevi made this announcement in the public shade of the great baobab. The news quickly roused the lazing listeners. Abandoning their usual day-to-day, they gathered around him for details and directions.

M'nalo was sitting in the subdued cool of his mother's zangala, reflecting upon nothing in particular, when Cessevi's hearty tones pitched the find into his consciousness. Honey, sweet honey, a rare and valued treat for all. So starting up from the shadows of his hideout, M'nalo went in search of his mother. Then, remembering that she was out gathering, he made straight for Khufu.

Found pacing his zangala's meeting room, his father gave permission and waved him on his away. "Go on, son. Go make yourself useful. We always need honey."

M'nalo dashed off to join the rowdy throng of youngsters all clamoring for a chance to prove their agility and climbing skills. He kept his hands down while the older men made selections. Tall, nimble, and stalwart, he could climb well enough, but he wasn't built for honey picking. Natural honey pickers combined agility, strength, and most important, small bodies light enough to dangle at the end of thin branches. Or using skimpy makeshift ropes, swing across wide spaces.

Eventually all preparations made, a sprightly group set out after Cessevi toward the white-clay hills half an afternoon's trek through the scrublands.

M'nalo was striding along breathing easy, when he glanced back at the stragglers and noticed a familiar figure in the distant haze raising dust in the hurry to catch up. He stopped and waited for Izi Onamuli.

"How you could leave without telling me. Eh?" his panting brother accused first thing.

Izi spoke harshly, what part exasperation, M'nalo couldn't guess. He palmed sweat from his forehead and answered, "I just ran out and joined them, little brother. Didn't know you were about."

Izi shrugged indifferently. "I wasn't. I was up in the trees exploring the monkey trail," he admitted.

M'nalo roughly chucked Izi's shoulder, stumbling him backwards a pace. "And you blame me?"

"Just testing the big brother's patience," said Izi Onamuli, cracking his cheeky grin.

These bees had made it as difficult as they could. They constructed their hive about halfway up a cliff standing high as a hundred men, and without ledges close enough for approach by natural predators. Still, the hardworking swarm had not planned for human grit and ingenuity.

The men studied the situation and soon agreed on a strategy. They explained their plan for an aerial attack, and requested volunteers from the previously eager boys. Now though, with the task at hand and measurable, there were only two offers, both unsuitable—the boys too large and hesitant. After several moments of general consternation, there was a small stir as Izi stepped forward. He would do the job, he said. Then M'nalo, more by way of brotherly support than inclination, offered to assist.

The other boys, privately relieved, now vied to be helpers. The men realized that the smoke calabashes they'd brought were too small. So, from fresh-cut twigs and vines, they braided a broad, shallow smoke basket. Then they spliced together varied ropes—supple lianas, woven raffia, and braided palm strips—and made two very long, strong cords. At a point where a ledge overhung the bees' nest, they fixed two firm braces deep into a crevasse. These held a free-spinning roller made from a hollow joint of bamboo with a sturdy length of hardwood running through it. From this device, they would drop the rope.

Finally, the men formed a harness at one end of the rope and beckoned volunteer Izi Onamuli.

A borrowed long knife at his waist, the boy stepped up, slender against the emptiness beyond the edge. He was hitched into the harness by his foot and around his torso. As he descended, holding the lit smoke basket, he'd have one foot free to maneuver himself away from scraping the cliff-face.

M'nalo would direct his descent from a precarious perch aside the braces. He thought past the anticipated bee-sting assault to greater dangers. What if the wind fanned the smoky embers of Izi's basket into flames? What if the harness bindings failed? What if Izi overshot the nest?

As M'nalo readied himself at his post, the men lit the basket. They waited until it began to smoke, then handed it to Izi and to encouraging cheers from those below, hoisted him out over the cliff.

Grunting with effort, the men steadily released the rope. M'nalo watched Izi sweep smoothly down the cliff and through a rising cloud of bees. "Too far! Too far! Pull him back up about my length," M'nalo shouted as the topmost bees of the swarm approached. Then they were upon him, making him flinch away from his lookout. Two, three stings scored. Another over his left eye made him slap at the sudden narrow pain. Then he heard Izi shouting, "Down a little more! Good, good. I'm getting them. They're falling."

Loud hurrahs said the onlookers below had heard. M'nalo grinned, realized the bees about him had been replaced by peppery-smelling smoke. With a severe squinting, he dared to peer down the cliff again. Vague in a bluish haze, Izi was still smoking the hives. What of his brother's weak lungs? M'nalo remembered with alarm. How was he managing to breathe? Just then, Izi shouted warning and tossed away the smoke basket. He swung himself onto the cliff wall and clung there by toe-grips. "Send down the pans," he called.

Amid choruses of support from below, the men complied. They lowered a second rope to which were attached a variety of calabashes and cans and pails and pans, all their mouths yawning wide for honey.

The rest of it went routinely and well before dusk the gatherers were satisfied. They camouflaged their operations against other honey hunters and set off back to the settlement. Izi had taken several stings and his eyes were swollen almost shut. He walked all but blindly, led by a string tied to M'nalo's waist. Spared the chore of bearing home his hero's share of the bounty, he seemed happy with his wounds. He also had the envious distinction of being the honey picker.

Grin or grimace, the swelling over M'nalo's own left eye throbbed each time he used his face muscles. Yes, he mused contentedly, his brother had done them proud. And he had his own brave part to report to his mother.

Since it was announced, the intended five-day journey to the marketplace was all M'nalo and the other boys could talk about. Tools and fresh seeds were needed for the coming season's planting, so Khufu and several other councilmen were preparing for the trip. What a venture! What a chance for boasting upon return! Like every young fellow in the village, M'nalo pleaded with his father how proven strong and capable beyond his age he was. How he'd follow along quiet as a wagging tail. All to no avail. He had to remain home, Khufu ruled. Brother Izi Onamuli, though, because he needed to visit a certain babawalo for medicine, would go wheeled like baggage on an oxcart.

Face swollen in a sulk, M'nalo stalked into his mother's fragrant rooms. "My father says that I must stay," he blurted. "Says the yard animals need tending. The servants have to be…" He couldn't continue for the choke in his throat.

Koita handed him a cup of guava juice. "It's as Allah wills, son," she consoled. "Drink this."

M'nalo sipped the cool syrup, scowled frustration into his mother's eyes and said glumly, "She gets him everything he wants, Mother, every little thing. every privilege."

"She is a royal princess, my son," Koita replied softly. "You drink your juice now. After sunset we'll defy their advantage. Perhaps we'll visit a special place where Izi Onamuli would not deign to go. Perhaps you'll learn of matters that he will never know."

Twilight had fallen to a luminous darkness when Koita led him through the family compound toward the promised amusement. Approaching Ammaa's threshold, they heard the fat woman's throaty murmur punctuated by a grating, suggestive laugh. Drawn from his earlier sour mood, M'nalo noticed how his mother flinched at the sound. Still sensitive of being a bought wife, did she feel out of place? he wondered. So protective and alert, he watched as Koita folded arms across her chest, and in proper manner quietly entered the zangala which was warm with a scent of roasted peanuts.

First wife Tebika sat at ease on the big river-cane chair. Behind her stood Ammaa's first daughter, Mesphi, plaiting the princess's hair into a regal pattern. Ezene, her ten-year-old sister, lay open-mouthed, lightly snoring on a mat. Ammaa squatted on a thick rug beside Tebika, her left hand grasping a narrow-necked gourd.

The fingers of her right hand were spread wide on the smooth floor as a stable base for the dimpled elbow supporting her weight.

She pivoted toward Koita and M'nalo, waved the sloshing gourd. "Welcome to my home, sister," she said heartily. "You brought your fine boy, a pleasant surprise for my eyes. Make yourself comfortable, young Sikivu M'nalo. Mind your sister's feet. She kicks like a donkey when she sleeps. And you, Koita, take some ginger beer, take a stool, take a listen. I was telling…"

Mindful of respect and duty, Koita interrupted, "Greetings and honor to you, Ammaa, and to you, Lady Tebika."

M'nalo, in a murmur, echoed her.

All haughty impatience and without turning her head from Mesphi's fingers, Tebika returned, "You, too. And to you, the dutiful son. But as she says, sit down and listen."

Koita nodded, lowered her eyes. Although not before she sent a brief whole-hearted smile toward the grinning Mesphi, who paused from hair grooming and cast a welcome look at them.

M'nalo, too, smiled back at Mesphi. He moved a stool close to the wall and sat on it.

Ammaa continued, "The heart is not a knee and can be bent. I am made one way. My joy is to study and provide what he likes. Indulgences? Yes, I study them. They're not so strange after all. He likes to be adored is most of it. Like everybody else, he wishes to be seen as the big man he tries to be. The prince he would be wants to be praised by his clan. Listen to me. I truly wish to praise him. So as I say, I study him.

"Since he's always trying to change me and make me over, I let him. I do it gladly because it's how he shows affection. He is an orderly man. He finds it difficult to bend his back to false gestures. His mouth squirms at speaking easy flatteries. His major aim is to make us into one grand perfect family."

M'nalo caught a private glance his mother smirked his way at mention of family.

"I try explaining to my daughters the puzzles of men's minds," Ammaa went on. "They will meet great competition for husbands. So it is important that they learn the ways of men.

"All I know is women's wiles. I know of women who might want to rule the world. You can find one or two in any royal court. They want to run men's matters better. They want to make destiny. I admire such women from afar. But I do not care to be among them. At the same time, neither do I favor regular women's work—all that hot sun and the toil of ploughing and planting and weeding and reaping. Harvesting all that stink and pain and sweat is not for Ammaa. I prefer to work in the shade and plenty of my kitchens. Get fat for my man. Feed him well and make him happy in his home."

At this, M'nalo bulged mischievous eyes at Mesphi. From behind Tebika's head, she winked back.

"You want to know my mind?" continued Ammaa. "Well, I'm for men doing the sweaty work. Let them plant and reap. Yes, my sisters may sneer as they wish. That does not affect me. No flesh off my big bones. What my people know is that the best servant is the true master, the one with the power in a household. When a woman has the twin happinesses of comfort and security, what more can she need?

"Best be a better servant. Run the master with fine service. Let others run the world. I aim to happy every part of my husband's home. I have said it openly. I am not wise. But hear me well. Neither am I so foolish as not to realize how I am happy."

Tebika, as she had been all along, was looking down at Ammaa with a tight, amused smile and a measuring gaze. "Your passions remain this strong?" she asked.

Ammaa met her eyes steadily. "He'll always be my prince," she declared grandly then undermined her fervor with a sarcastic laugh before slurping from her gourd.

She swiveled on her sprawl of floor-mats to face Koita. "Well, Thin and Silent, what have you brought to entertain us?"

"Pardon me, mistress..." Koita stopped, darted an embarrassed glance at M'nalo.

"Why don't you tell us a desert dervish story?" Tebika cut in snidely, not even turning her face toward his shy mother.

Koita shook her head as if about to say she knew no such stories. Then the light of memory broke through the fluster in her face. "Of my own experience I cannot speak," she answered. "I lack the words and the true knowledge. Still there is a story I know. Among my people, grandmothers tell it to granddaughters. About the subtleties of manliness, it was first related by Rumi, a desert mystic."

M'nalo had heard this story several times and pride surged warm through him as he caught Mesphi's glance. He nodded confidently at her.

Koita continued in formal tale-teller's tones, "The poet says, 'If we have drunk of the wine, how can we scorn the drunkard?' He tells this tale to elaborate his point.

"Ramosuli was a great lord, a mature man of wealth and power. At his palace, a passing trader said to him, 'Oman has a concubine too beautiful for words. She looks like this.'

"The trader wielded coal on parchment and made a likeness of her. Ramosuli looked at it and his mind whirled like a sandstorm of lust. Without pausing to think, he called his bravest captain, suited him with an army of hundreds and charged him to return with the concubine.

"Maybe there is truth in what my sister Ammaa says. There might be ways in which the master and the slave are the same. A master, alone, can be less than his feeblest servant. A servant alone, masterful. It depends on the situation of the moment.

"Such a moment as when Ramosuli sent his trusted captain to set siege and suffering on Oman's city. Many innocents died before Oman sent an envoy. A blunt negotiator unafraid of death, he asked the ruthless captain, 'How can we see eye to eye?'

"'My master demands this concubine,' the captain replied, and showed him the likeness that had so bewitched his lord.

"The envoy reported to Oman who, eager to return sunshine on his domain, declared without hesitation, 'Take her and go in peace! With my blessings, take her!'

"Now, among my people," continued Koita, "women are taught to remember that nectar is sweet to every bee. That every male dog scents the bitch. As certainly, this captain took but one look at the concubine and he too was swept up in a delirium of passion.

"Tormented by his own disloyalty, and the all-too-real risk of losing his head, he confined himself to his tent. That night, though, he saw the girl in his dreams and made love to her. He awoke to find his seed spurted wasteful on his bedclothes. So foolish the captain felt, he became awkward about himself. When a man's mind and his body are not one, there is no leader. No satisfaction or control. In this imbalance, the captain swore, 'I will take this girl.'

"The captain's desire was like a phantom in the darkness down a well. It was powerful beyond commonsense. Mad with a yearning to have the woman, he diverted his return to his master and made secluded camp at a refuge with date palms and cool wells, and flowers blood red in tall, soft grass.

"Safe in this private place, he went to the woman's tent, tore her clothes from her body, and at the sight of her nakedness, his reason was lost in a drumming sound. His lord and master became a squeak within that noise, and he himself, thunder. He stripped and set himself between the woman's legs. His member was moving straight to the mark when, just on the brink of fluid embrace, from outside sounded a tumult and a rising cry from his soldiers.

"Bare-bottomed, the captain leapt up, grabbed his spear, and rushed out. A hungry lion had gotten among the frightened horses, his soldiers shouted. Chaos and panic had followed close.

"Without hesitation the captain charged the lion and killed it with one spear thrust through its heart. Threat dispatched, he returned to the woman's tent. Again in the presence of her naked beauty his member seemed even more erect. The girl was amazed by his virility and her energy reached for him like flesh around bone, and their spirits were as one.

"Red flowers dry and crumple. Green withers into brown. The sun shines on all.

"There came a day when the captain recalled his duty to his lord and master. He tamped his passion, commanded the woman, 'Speak not a word of this affair to the master.'

"When trained to obey, what option does a woman have?

"Resolute, the captain broke camp. He fulfilled his charge and delivered the concubine. Whereupon, as expected, Ramosuli was himself smitten. 'She's a thousand times more beautiful than my dreams!' he exclaimed.

"Happy as a suckling baby, he gazed at her and everything else—his kingdom, his duty—fled from his mind. Only driving desire remained. So he took her to bed, his manic need raising his maleness, making it tremble and strain with ardor.

"Then came a tiny sound, the rustling, scuttling sound a roving mouse might make. But the whisper reminded Ramosuli of a snake slithering among the fine silk mats on which they lay. At which his virility drooped. Desire slipped away.

"Seeing so sudden a change from firm promise to flaccid failure, the concubine was overcome by fits of titters. Helpless to their tickles, despite all her efforts, her mirth grew until in shame and fury, Ramosuli drew his sword. 'What is so amusing?' he demanded. 'Tell me all! This moment grants me clairvoyance. If you lie, I will know and behead you. But let me know the harshest truth, and you will live in freedom. This I swear by my ancestors.'

"Though her life was on the balance scales, even that did not completely still the woman's giggles. Eventually, though, she controlled herself enough and told of the secluded camp, and the lion, and the virile captain, and how the contrast between his and Ramosuli's reaction had overcome her.

Stunned and humbled, Ramosuli sat down to think and soon came to his senses. 'What sort of man am I?' he asked himself. 'My pride drove me to take this woman from another. This arrogance turned my loyal captain into a traitor. And here I nearly allowed a mouse to make fool of my manliness.'

"So Ramosuli turned to the woman and said, 'My captain was brave in getting you from Oman. He was bold in risking his life for your company. You are braver still entrusting your story to me. Such bravery deserves its like. My captain shall have you in marriage.'

"So said, so it was done. Although the fate of the captain and the beautiful concubine remains for another song!"

"Perfect, sister," Ammaa congratulated, raising her gourd. "You must tell us another of these desert stories when again we gather. Ah! Look how your son's eyes glow. You've made him proud."

True enough, M'nalo's pride in his mother's presentation was complete, but the reason for his flush was another matter. As Koita had told her story, it seemed to him that every time she made mention of lovemaking, first wife Tebika sought to catch his eyes with a complicated glance, a look that strangely stirred him.

Mind set to disbelieve, M'nalo put down his water gourds and listened. "Right after midday, I tell you. With sun stinging the air," Izi Onamuli said vehemently, "I was just roaming the shade, aiming for nowhere but coolness. Then I come to that place in the iroko woods where the river bellies out. Where the undergrowth is so spiny and dense you have to think 'no farther', eh."

M'nalo well knew the patch. Knew it for its trouble (thorn-bush and biting ants), and its spoils (exceptional groundnuts, fat squirrels, and burrowing dwarf pigs). Most hunters avoided the thicket, preferring to make rough trails around the formidable place.

"As I approaching it I notice an open pathway leading in. Open enough, I mean. The bushes and brambles were forced apart as if something heavy had shoved its way through and left a trail. A clear invitation like that, of course, it drew me in. Then, one step inside, a strange shadow of quiet surrounded everything. This shadow somehow absorbed the rustling of the bushes, and the birds' chirping, and even the squeaks of the insects. Then a peculiar scent filled the space. Harsh, like after a green forest is fired. Yet still, everything remain very peaceful, the close bushes like protecting walls beside my rough-made track. So I prowled on, eyes sharp like a monkey's. But after a short while, I mean heartbeats short, I find I'm tired. Trudging-for-days tired. So short-of-breath, can't-push-a-muscle tired, I lie down right there by the track in the thick grass and fell into a deep sleep..."

In response to M'nalo's skeptical grimace, Izi declared with a fierce scowl, "I swear by our noble ancestors! I wouldn't deceive you, big brother. And it went even stranger. For while I slept, my àshe slipped into that other place and an orisha spoke to my essence. It's the truth, M'nalo. I'm telling you. True as I stand here!"

M'nalo sucked spit around his teeth noisily. He hoisted the yoke balancing the gourds of water onto his shoulder and started again for the compound.

"But wait. M'nalo, wait," Izi called out, and hurrying to keep pace he continued, "The orisha came in the form of a mother panther, the blackest panther ever, with no blackness to compare. Somehow, without using words, the orisha put into my head where and how to trap an olose family. She demanded only that I take the smaller baby and mind it even after it grew fat..."

"And," M'nalo interrupted in a tone that could have fathered scoffing, "when you awoke, the task she'd set you was easy as clapping hands together, huh?" His lips twisted with wry amusement. "No doubt about it, little brother, you tell a great story."

"You don't believe, eh?"

"No, but the story is worthy even so."

"Then how will you explain what I am about to show you, eh?" Izi snapped his fingers and skipped ahead, as M'nalo mindful of his burden, quelled an urge to quicken his pace.

"Show what?" M'nalo grunted as they entered their family compound. No answer but a tug on his awo as he carried the water to his mother's zangala. That done, he followed his brother.

Izi led him behind Tebika's zangala and his back to M'nalo craning neck, crouched down in the corner where Tebika's wall met the compound's. After a moment of gentle reaching, Izi got up, turned around and showed M'nalo what he held. White, furry and curled up sleepy, a baby olose was in the careful cup of his hands.

An awed sigh escaped M'nalo's lips. His doubt swept away on a flood of unreserved admiration and not a little envy. How was it that no such luck ever visited him?

"Didn't I tell you?" his satisfied brother gloated.

In the weeks that followed, Izi tenderly nursed the baby olose. Daily M'nalo stopped by the hutch hoping his brother would allow him to stroke the small creature's water-smooth fur. Only in his best moods—once or twice a week—did Izi grant M'nalo the special privilege of cradling its warmth in the nook of his shoulder and neck. Wasn't long before pride and frustration outweighed such meager reward, and M'nalo left off visiting.

Next he saw of the olose was maybe a moon later one morning when it slid out from Izi's awo as they ate at their father's. The sudden appearance of the fluid-moving female caused M'nalo a start—just as his brother intended—at which both of them broke into laughter. Impressed by the animal's largeness, M'nalo couldn't dodge the obvious: The olose was pot perfect for a feast. Still, another side of him craved to hold and heft the supple graceful creature. So humbling earlier resolve, he asked.

To his surprise, Izi was willing. Although the animal would not allow itself be taken, flowing back to hide in its master's clothes. So M'nalo had to content himself only with his brother's generous intentions. Later on, outside their compound when Izi showed off the exceptional olose, M'nalo readily became a strong protective arm against the jealous and the chop-lickers.

Not long after, M'nalo's circle of friends began questioning why his brother was not naming a pot day. Their admiration of Izi's hunting prowess had been always sincere, they argued. In the recent past weeks surely he had noticed that they had granted him unmeasured respect. They had invited him into their games and teams. So now they expected the appropriate gesture from the master olose hunter, namely, an invitation to the feast.

Canvassed for his support, M'nalo expressed indifference. So the group confronted Izi.

"How long?" the boys challenged.

"The animal is prime," they observed.

"Keeping it for magic?" suggested a sly critic.

"It's a good pet, loyal and affectionate," Izi pleaded. "Surely I can hunt you another, eh?"

As from one hungry throat, a guffaw erupted. "We, too, love the olose. When that fat and well-roasted, we love it so much more," they countered.

When Izi turned to him, M'nalo shrugged defenselessness.

Cornered by consensus and subtle betrayal, Izi gulped his bitterness and submitted. He invited each and all to the cooking fire that same afternoon.

When the young men had assembled, Izi firmly bound, with raffia string, the still living fat rat to a flat piece of bark. Then, with a quick wrist motion, he slipped a sharp blade down her belly and commenced to gut and skin the mewling, writhing animal.

Horrified, the fellows begged Izi to end the butchery.

Instead, venom in his every word, Izi replied, "Why the haste and gagging? Since your decision, hasn't it already been dead for roasting? So why not study it alive some?"

Disgusted and despising Izi's cruelty, nobody—M'nalo included—wanted a share of his sacrificed pet. The fellows fled the roasting fire. Teary eyed Izi Onamuli ate his fat favored olose all by himself.

Because he was keeping foot-dragging Izi Onamuli company rear of the party, M'nalo was last to hear the news. He did only when Councilman Dassa's son, Lamisi, had fallen back to report that they would see the big city marketplace from top of the next rise! Then, frisky as a kid goat, Lamisi raced ahead and caught up with his companions.

The promise seemed to provide Izi with new legs and a better disposition. "Let's get in front of them, eh?" he suggested and the brothers quickened their steps.

They won their race maybe a hundred paces from the top and, right away, like many of the other boys, were casting puzzled looks about. A strange sound was growing out of nowhere. A new sort of sound, something of a vibration, it thrilled and raised hair bumps on the skin.

One of the elders leading the party then stopped and called everyone to gather around. First he addressed the bearer slaves— two for each of the seven adult men. "Your primary duty in the marketplace is to watch out for the youngsters. In their hearts as well as their muscles, they're traveling an amazing adventure." He chuckled. "We must protect them from themselves."

Some of the men clucked tongues at remembered misadventures. Not a peep from the boys, though. Right then only deepest respect kept them in place as the elder spoke. They listened but hardly heard what he said. All they wanted to do was rush to the top. Their earlier tiredness had fallen away like loose khangas. The trials of their sweaty five-day journey were already a fading memory.

As the elder finished his talk, the eyes of every boy focused on him excitedly. He smiled and nodded permission and the boys were off charging up the hill.

Arrived up there on the plateau, they stopped and stared with wonder. First realization from their new vantage was the source of the strange noise. As they ran uphill, what had been an imperceptibly rising murmur quickly grew to the subdued roar, like from a fierce wind, or perhaps a waterfall.

On the plateau, though, they saw the source of the mystery. For down on the other side of the mountain was assembled more people than the boys could imagine existed. It was this mass of a marketplace that roared so thunderously. It was a chattering mix of thousands of calls and cries and bustling, a hullabaloo over which the boys had to shout their astonishment.

They looked big-eyed at the hurly-burly of business and screamed amazement. For beneath . them, less than an afternoon's walk into the distance, was a vast multicolored city of tents and shelters that extended from the base of the mountain to the banks of the great river Ugun.

"Look at this! Look," M'nalo marveled to his brother.

Izi nodded dumbly, his eloquent gaze exulting.

As if the magnificence were of their own making, the adult men chuffed up with dampened eyes and superior chuckles. Then one cleared his throat and set them moving downhill into the scene.

The boys quiet and keeping close, the party became absorbed into the marketplace. M'nalo tried to count the many vendors they passed but soon lost track. He was distracted by their enormous variety of offerings. Wondrous displays of fabrics. Dwarf coconuts. Heaps of purple mangoes. Giant guavas in red, yellow and green. Outsize dates. Other fruits with unfamiliar but tantalizing aromas. Salt-white okra. Barrels of lumpy brown sugar. Calabashes of molasses. Platters and pots of sweetmeats, too many of them inviting. Strange contraptions: One solely for squeezing juices out of fresh oranges and limes; another of a bent and twisted metal frame balanced on two wheels with a small seat and foot stands, which rode a man forward. Fantastic puppets and their players. A mirror so large a grown man could behold his whole self in it—and before which Lamisi refused to walk. Yellow-skinned narrow-eyed magicians and bizarre cripples. Tiny, perfectly-formed people.

In their wanderings, they came upon a cluster of twenty or so shackled youths squatting, mindless as meat, eyes cast inward. Over their circle of listlessness rose an air of misfortune. Generally about M'nalo's age, they were guarded by five tall warriors, lean-muscled men with unflinching eyes. M'nalo studied the elaborate tattoos on their broad chests, the emblems they wore around their arms, the designs on their weapons and armor. He decided the guards must be Lufembe, a nomadic people who rented out their second-best fighters as mercenaries.

Grown solemn at the sight, the party was about to amble on when the master of the pathetic captives appeared. M'nalo looked him over with incredulity: Under a wide-brimmed hat with several plumes, one longer and brilliant-green, this exceedingly strange pale-skinned fellow sopped at the blood-red splotches in his cheeks with a crumpled indigo cloth. Everything about him was pallid and narrow—his eyes, the flute-thin nose, the monkey's lips, his hair yellow as millet silk. This chief did not use the courtesy of a smile or the guile of hand movements. Flamboyant in flabby yellow leggings, purple khanga, and a broad white sash sheathing two black pistols, he strode among his men dispensing harsh words.

"A pretty butterfly," observed Izi Onamuli, amused.

"He brings to mind a colorful viper I once escaped," said M'nalo, the jolt of memory unsettling him.

The man was a factor, explained an elder of M'nalo's party, a 'Portugee' who traded with local chieftains. He bought captives at small markets and sold them downriver to holding forts and slave ships bound for misery. These unscrupulous fellows were always ready to snatch up a strayed boy and sell him into slavery, the elder warned as they walked away.

For some time afterwards, like a clutch of new cheepers, they all—even Izi—hurried close in the shadows of the elders; stumble-stones to the men's serious business dealings.

Khufu had given M'nalo and Izi each twenty-five beads to spend, a whole cowry's worth. Warned about thieves, the brothers carried their money—copper, glass, and natural—in belly pouches. The food and fruits offered sweet temptation, but M'nalo swallowed his mouth-water and kept his wealth in the thrifty goatskin where, despite the beckoning vendors, he intended to let it lie as they strolled through the excitement in the bright sunshine.

Meanwhile, amazements strove to top one another. Acrobats contorting their bodies into impossible positions. Muscular men, certainly crazed, wrestling chimpanzees for coppers. Parrots squawking poetry in strange languages. From one to the other, M'nalo could scarcely focus. Then he felt something slip into his hand. "Spend these for me," Izi whispered and disappeared back into the throng. M'nalo looked down and found six copper beads in his palm. With Izi so quickly gone, he couldn't even say thanks. The extraordinary outing improved immediately. Now with the unexpected largesse, he could sample several tasty bits of the appetizing scene and still guard his trove.

Izi Onamuli, as always, still managed to stir up trouble. While others gawked and gasped at the rare spectacles, he kept bothering the men with his dissatisfactions. He found it difficult to approach some fruit-sellers' sprawling heaps, he quarreled. He insisted that he had come up with a more efficient plan for them to display their goods. Sensibly, everyone ignored his shrill assertions. Then, eventually, he slumped into a mope and kept to himself the rest of the afternoon.

That night, though, lying on mats in their makeshift tent, Izi explained his solution to M'nalo.

"Think of how the vine climbs a tree," he began, "round and round, rising bit by bit. Never covering the same part of the tree-trunk. Eh? You following?"

"Yes," M'nalo answered drowsily. He was lost in his own picture of a strong vine up a certain custard-apple tree back home. He was remembering the delicious smoothness that rewarded a venturesome climber.

"Well, that's the point. Never cover the same ground. You see? If the fruit-sellers set up their heaps in the manner of a vine climbing, but flat on the ground, customers could look over every heap of goods as they came and left without blocking each other's way. You follow, eh?"

M'nalo grunted. Unlike his brother, who always needed to puzzle and plan, improve whatever he encountered, M'nalo had left the marketplace a happy glutton, sated by all the new fruits he had sampled. And the ingenious devices at which he had marveled. And all the different fowl, the strange beasts—

Memory suddenly stirring, he hoisted himself onto an elbow, turned to Izi. "Did you see that monster crocodile?"

"What crocodile?" Izi replied, sharp-toned, impatient at interruption. "What are you talking about? Eh? Are you too slow to follow my thoughts?"

Which instantly soured M'nalo's mood. "No, no. I follow," he growled. "But who cares about those ten thousand silly ideas stumbling around the calabash of your skull?"

Izi lay quiet in an offended air.

M'nalo curled up on his side, let drowsiness creep up once again. Soon dropped off, he dreamt of buying fruits heaped along his brother's spiral system while slavering, wide-jawed shopping crocodiles waddled past, parading themselves as if civilized. All the rest of that night, M'nalo never twisted variations of the ridiculous dream out of his mind's whirl.

As it had done for several days and nights, the Harmattan blew steadily, graying the northern face of everything in its way— stockades with their dusted animals, foliage and tree trunks, the village houses. Daylight was at its last hot gasp and the wind had softened when the jalis, Anandan, entered the meetinghouse, a cloth shielding his face from flying grit.

Arm's length from M'nalo, the jalis leaned his back against the doorpost and silently lit his pipe. The present boys had been waiting for him time enough. M'nalo's patient thighs had gone numb from squatting in the dimness. Izi Onamuli still had not arrived, his late habit a taunt to their father that nipped at M'nalo's composure.

This much-traveled jalis from Allada passed their backland way twice a year and stayed but a single moon's cycle. At these times, the councilmen's sons—M'nalo and Izi among them—would gather at dusk to listen and learn the stories of their endless land. Of strange philosophies and practices. Of peculiar foods, animals and weapons. Of new dances and diseases. And, sometimes, of notable family histories.

M'nalo started guiltily and straightened his shoulders as he noticed the jalis's eyes gleaming his direction. Half compensating for his brother, half driven by his station, M'nalo resolved to copy the teacher's dignity as they awaited latecomers. He would keep himself same way composed, part looking through the doorway as swift cool night consumed the burnt-out dusk, part looking on inside.

As usual, Adbo, the blacksmith Talla's son, was playing with the listless house fire. Barely ten years old, already familiar with the orishas that ruled his father's craft as toolmaker, he had roughed an arm-sized branch into the fire. The sputtering flames spangled into a rising spiral, reflecting off the boys' sweaty faces and glistening eyes. Their stares followed the yellow sparks upward, each hoping one might fire the roof's thatch, provoke some excitement.

"Fire is a weak servant," someone mumbled, got a giggle-chorus and the general wish for mischief was secret no more.

M'nalo closed his eyes, aloof. These boys might snicker and whisper, but they were not he—firstborn of Khufu, the headman, and a prince in his own right. Or maybe they had not promised their fathers to give full respect and attention to the jalis. M'nalo also saw there was little chance of a fire: The giddy sparks could hardly live all that rise up to the thatch's tough, cured veneer. The boys were being childish.

"Why are you grubs here? What do you want to know?" Anandan suddenly began, his voice whispery as the wind scraping the roof's thatch. "That nothing is of itself? That all proceeds from another, from before?

"Well, it is so! All of it from the ancestors. The fathers and mothers of myriad fathers and mothers. All messengered by ungungun and orishas who range between the spirit worlds and this other place. That's the all of it. Nothing is of itself. All comes from another. Do you want to understand this simple thing? Do you wish for this knowledge?"

Anticipation speeded M'nalo's breath. Anandan was speaking Twi, the tongue for storytelling, a language with *kuma* words specially saved for nighttime, for strong fables and myths. As one, the boys answered, "Yes, master. We wish for the knowledge."

The jalis swung a wine-gourd up from his hip and sipped. Then, with lips curled disdainful, he searched every eye of the group. He took another swallow, smacked thick lips. "Well, then, pups of men," he declared. "I will feed you stories of your ancestors. Secrets of our peopled land. Pup-milk for your black ashes. Blood's strength for the lives inside your masks."

M'nalo's hands were cool but sweating. A shiver threatened to spoil his proper attitude. This jalis was known for going too far with the sharing of certain secrets, although no one, as a teacher, had more right. But such information carried with it grave risks of offending the wealthy, the smug, and even some sorcerers.

"Like everything grand, our story flows out of the kingdom itself. Out of the flame, Dahomey, torch of the west. The fortress raised on the brazen belly of King Dan. The shining kingdom built by the all-powerful Ouegbadja.

"Our jewel Dahomey was made prosperous from the gold of Arabians and pale-fleshed foreigners given to gluttony for slaves. Yes, pups, this was the business that made our people wealthy. The practice of our culture for generations more than I have fingers…" Anandan thrust out his opened hands with extended fingers "…each one growing richer than the earlier as providers of slaves to the Arabs. And richer still when the markets across the sea opened…"

"I can make no meaning of these words 'across the sea'," a hesitant voice interrupted.

The jalis used the moment to sip from his wine gourd. "Why should you?" he replied gruffly. "To do this you must imagine a river so wide, it is farther than you can point. No matter how high you stand on this bank, you will never see to the other shore."

"It is very hard to imagine such a river," the voice answered. It was Odongo, son of a sorghum and millet farmer, who puzzled. "When it floods, where would all that water drain?"

"Be patient while the idea grows into your mind," the jalis said, his voice gentler. "No matter, I will tell you about the power that managed this trade in bondage. That power was the Leopard Guild. That fearful clan of sorcerers trained at combining the herbal knowledge of Osaynin with the mischief of Eshu-Elegbara…"

M'nalo lost thread as he realized that for some while now he had been hearing Izi's special signal—four sharply whistled notes same tone, an unharmonious combination no natural bird would make. What was Izi Onamuli up to, he wondered with some irritation. Was he on his way in? Or calling M'nalo to join in some escapade?

M'nalo refused to answer. Their father expected them to be at the feet of the jalis, and there he would remain. Disobedience would be Izi's alone to explain, easy for him with his mother as speaker. So M'nalo refocused on Anandan's story.

"...deception is the essential grease to a kingdom's politics. Advancement is reward and exile a wicked kind of death. Yet even advancement has dangers. For as more power comes to the powerful, that mightier power requires greater protection.

"King Ghezo had an army of eight thousand fierce wives to protect him but even that did not prevent his death by sorcerers. Neither did a multitude of warrior wives defend the throne of his successor, King Toffa. He, too, was destroy..."

Anandan stopped as a dark blur slipped through the door, headed toward the back of the room and faded into the dimness. Izi had come in so smoothly, M'nalo felt certain that had he blinked he might have missed the arrival altogether.

The room remained silent and M'nalo knew that Anandan was awaiting some manner of apology or explanation. Someone cleared his throat. M'nalo glanced where Izi had gone, caught only a fire glow reflection, perhaps eyes. He knew his brother would offer nothing.

Gaze hard on the back wall, the jalis slowly raised his gourd, took another long sip. Just as deliberately, he returned it to his hip. Then, in his soft, scraping voice, he said, "Exactly as I say, young gentlemen. Royal arrogance provoking the ire of the gods. The situation lives. It is all around!" His mouth curving into a malicious grin, he spread his arms wide.

Like subdued thunder, a snigger grumbled around the room. Snide giggling cracked out close to M'nalo when, all offended dignity, the jalis rose and departed the place.

Later that same night, asleep in his father's zangala, M'nalo woke to a black trilling night, his three souls flying away like startled birds. He reached across the reed pallet to awaken Izi.

But not even the slightest warmth marked where Izi should have lain. M'nalo sat up, drew himself full of breath and held it long. So when he released, his being had room enough for his àshe to return. He stood up now, and wearing only his sleeping shokono, slunk from the house.

Three steps beyond the threshold, a cold nose snuffled up on his bare haunches. An eager tail whisked the air. M'nalo made shushing sounds, pushed away the yard dog's energetic company. Crossing the cool dirt of the compound's yard, he stepped out of the deep shadow of the breeze-rustled baobab. He looked up at the gods' grand extravagance, the glitter of the close, curved black canopy.

From the top of a tall tree, with the reach of a long stick, it seemed he might almost touch the sparkle. Might dip a ladle into the enormous calabash of sky and pour out these streams of star-sheen that silvered the baobab's leaves to slyly outshine the absent moon.

"Aahh!" M'nalo sighed, his restless fit twisted melancholy. After a few moments he turned back towards the house. A cackle from Ammaa's house stopped him. The laugh was hearty from the throat and suggestive of private excitements. With a groin-ward surge of his curious blood, M'nalo recognized the voice behind the gaiety.

Ammaa's company was first wife Tebika.

Confident in the night's quiet, his movements hunter supple, he crept along the compound's wall. Careful around the bushy plant beds he himself had seeded, M'nalo trailed the tempting laughter through Tebika's herb garden. He sidled along the wall of Ammaa's zangala, got to an open kitchen window facing away from the yard.

He didn't look in, just squatted comfortably on the ground beneath, listening. He was discovered immediately, this time by a half-grown yard dog that crawled up to smother him with a tongue licking. He grabbed the puppy, muscled its vibrant affection down to tolerable and snuggled down with the panting bundle in his arms. His ears keened to Tebika's telling.

"...that young Tebika, aaiii," she was saying. "A sly, willful child who managed to get whatever she wished. That's the truth. Whim or craving, it didn't matter. That girl Tebika never would deny her precocious desires.

"Once, rambling through the city with her handmaids, she came to the quiet quarter where a royal carver lived and did his work. He was famous for his skill at fashioning fetishes and sacred objects. He was notorious, too, for his moral slackness. Although this no way daunted that little Tebika from entering his house all alone.

"Excited by the honor of her visit, the ageless braggart was soon describing how he had recently discovered a fine specimen of gray laterite: 'Pure yangii,' he gloated with black smile and beaming eye, 'this is the rock inside which Eshu-Elegbara conceals his spirit. Before I came upon this exceptional piece, I had firmly declared that the rock I held in hand was the best to be had. I am the expert. I had just said so. And then this perfection drew my attention to where it lay claiming otherwise. Smooth and symmetrical as an egg. Right away its spirit spoke to me of great wanderings. It recounted a lifetime within volcanoes. It recalled the weight of endless water oppressive upon the spark in its quick...'

"The carver's eloquence had fired her fancy, so that young girl Tebika decided she must possess this rare and marvelous rock. Perhaps she would learn a magic, become privy to the fetish-maker's passion, she thought. Perhaps she'd break it open and discover Eshu's resting spirit.

"'This rock,' continued the shrewd carver, 'spoke of the eons it had rolled hither and thither without purpose, wearing itself smooth as an ancient's palm, plain as experience. And then I came searching and touched it with my need. That's what the orisha inside it sang to me. 'Thank you, thank you for setting free my spirit. Your warm touch has quickened my spark beyond the push and weight of winds and water and forgetful Time.

"Well! On hearing this, that young Tebika wanted the special rock beyond mere craving. She moved closer to the royal carver. 'Maybe you would like to know another perfect smoothness?' she asked and bared her chest with its budding breasts.

"The carver sidled away like a crab from a sticky net. He searched a clutter of half-finished pieces absently. 'Let me see,' he mumbled. 'I might've hidden it here under this mask.'

"Then, standing behind the old artisan, that little Tebika unwrapped and dropped her khanga, and stood bold. 'You like perfect smoothness?' she asked again.

"Perhaps the calmness of her challenge persuaded the fearful stone-carver to turn around and behold her posed there, naked and nubile. With eyes fastened on this vision, he stammered 'Yes, I...I...like per-r-r-fect.'

"In a voice slow as lava, the young princess said, 'For the soulful stone, you can...'

"His hard hands tremulous, the palace carver pleaded, 'But your slaves, Your Highness...'

"All that child Tebika replied was, 'For the stone I will allow just one kiss...'

"Which was enough for the old ram-goat. And in the time one might take to swallow a cool calabashful, that sly Tebika had departed the lecher's house, the coveted stone smooth in her grasp."

Tebika's voice ceased. Ammaa belched, murmured a comment and a throaty chuckle. M'nalo barely heard. His mind was bubbling with perverse imaginings, all coursing towards his groin. He shoved the drowsy dog off him, skulked back to his sleeping mat.

Still no Izi, so with the pallet to himself, he seized the chance to be forceful with the tumult in his crotch. Hard at the job, M'nalo realized for the first time that, unlike many women in the village, the royal Tebika never bared her breasts. A riddle in this notion speared down his backbone and into the font of his excitement. He imagined her breasts—their heft and warmth, their yield and mystery—while he pressed and squeezed his unruly oko. Until a thrill in it ruptured and spurted the liquid fire, gave peace to his strained àshe.

But, oh! What he would do for an actual peek.

Surely it was cava in the sipping-pouch that hung from Lathso's waist. Everyone knew how to pulp pepper-plant roots and soak the mash overnight to yield the mildly bitter beverage that lightened heads. Respectable folks, though, indulged only in private. So Lathso's cavorting was somewhat an embarrassment to the steadily assembling audience. Even so, no one dared interfere. This was Leopard guild ceremony, and stumbling though he might seem, the old sorcerer was in full charge of the proceedings.

The musicians, from their grins and shouts, liked Lathso's behavior well enough. Drink and food were fine for celebration. But it was the vigor of dance that brought orishas to life. So as they worked festive rhythms out of kora and konting, and twangas and chac-chacs and drums, the musicians welcomed any bold soul who would shape their music human on the space.

Wasn't long before Lathso met with his personal spirit, and each became possessed of the other. Balanced on one flexed leg, the other raised behind, foot swinging limp like a pendulous tail, the sorcerer hopped about, showing his dance, chanting a driving praise-song.

Named as Lathso, I am.
Outcast from the Leopard Clan.
Sorcerer and diviner,
Lord Eshu is my master.
Hermit in the rat-runs,
Conjurer and subtle poisoner,
Magician and schemer,
For Eshu, the mischief-maker,

I befriend the darkness,
champion for the morning sun.
Eshu at the crossroads, facing back-back,
Looking farther on...

The audience could not hold off: Embarrassment runs not quite so deep as bloodline. One voice caught up, then another. And soon each and every soul was joined with the sorcerer's fervent chant praising Eshu-Elegbara, all-powerful god of àshe, singing the blackness of ancestry into the ready night.

Spellbound, M'nalo too followed the sorcerer into his enchantment. Pulled by the simple rhythm of Lathso's refrain, he fell into its sway, his shoulders shaking like a rattle, bouncing off a beat. Unaware of how deeply he had been hauled within the thrall, abruptly, without effort, he was prancing about the center of the arena. With impossible power, he was leaping so high that grown men at the innermost circle sprang to their feet to look up at him, their baffled eyes glistening.

And at that moment, the ivory dancing in his bones, a flash of insight told M'nalo he was helplessly bound to the ostracized sorcerer. In mid-flight, he caught Lathso's eyes as something baleful leapt from their stare, and pounced upon M'nalo's tender hesitation, pulled him further in. "*Dance with me,*" came the gruff unspoken challenge echoing in his head. "*Help me show these fall-shorts the magic of defiance. Help me dance my orisha.*"

For a flash M'nalo could see what Lathso saw. He thrilled to a vision of the enraptured assemblage. Their eyes closed, hands clapping, voices chanting, bodies moving brilliantly, all happy in the music's spell.

But just as suddenly, M'nalo could smell his own sweat, a frightened funk that stifled magical insight. Feet grounded once more, he retreated into the shuffling audience. There was his brother, Izi, smirking, and beyond him their father, eyeing about, apprehensive. Behind as ever, Koita meek-mothered the edge of the family group, disowning and disowned. A commonplace scene save for his sisters, Ezene and Mesphi, who were still caught in the romping chant of the praise-song. Both swaying in rhythm as if one person.

The ordinariness rooted M'nalo, steadied his blood. Sympathy now withdrawn, he could think straight again. Lathso and his ridiculous leaps into the night were no longer spectacular. Yet even as M'nalo marshaled his mind to stern logic, Lathso danced before him and, eyes aglow like fired coals, laughed in his face. A laugh that said: "*I know you want to prance. Join me if you dare.*"

Then with a chortle, the diviner sprang into a wild spin and floated away, his dried-out muscles moving with such fluid abandon that a choke of admiration moistened M'nalo's eyes. Oh! That he might master Lathso's grace so at one with the tug of his àshe. Oh! To learn the song to a spell so audacious!

Then by some mysterious flex of mind, M'nalo understood how he would come to know the magical charm. He realized that the only answer to the sorcerer's challenge was entering his dance. Only in such a trance could M'nalo's àshe reveal meaning.

But now Lathso had ceased his spry dancing and joined the musicians grouped just beyond the crackling fire. Spirits well in groove, they seemed in private conversations with their instruments. Flames reflecting umber from sweaty skin, their capped heads bobbing, barebacked bodies were swinging to a unifying beat. And to this syncopation of color and movement, Lathso lent the rhythms of his djembe bass drum, that singing voice of the gods.

Again M'nalo caught the sorcerer's eye held long and specially on him. A wily grin cracked the slick face, a smirk that goaded M'nalo's hesitancy.

Be strong for the dance! Be bold! Venture from your hiding place among the bashful. Resist the doubts that ground you to so longingly look on. Come forth and honor our generous gods. Come dance etutu to the spirit within you.

All of this and more challenged the divining gleam in the sorcerer's eyes. All of it taunting and persuasive.

Without quite realizing how the reluctance had fled, M'nalo found himself again in circle with the others. Lithe of leg as they, hopping in synchrony, he sought out Lathso's Leopard spirit. Caught and taught by the sentient drum, once more he was slipping in with the flow and lilt of the chanters. The rhythmic reap of the ringing twangas. Anticipating their staccato beat, he was timing sharp to execute the proper quaver and jump. The tremble and hop while the chanters and clappers and chac-chac players clipped the mood along, and blended the dance more deeply with the black, ecstatic night.

M'nalo felt the music pulling him humble to somewhere strange where his dependable will made no difference. Anchored by this new fear, at the last moment before he lost all, M'nalo jerked away and out of the ring of dancing initiates.

At that, a sour-faced Lathso glared up from his driving drum-spell, his hands on their own continuing to wreak percussive havoc. He briefly regarded M'nalo before looking past, toward the rhythmic frenzy of the dancers beyond. To their fleet feet fancy-flying and jiggy-jig-jigging. Stomp-stamping and slapping the ground with a sound like laughter. As if some primeval jubilation had transported them into a realm one flight above natural. Where it was a frolic to dance on fire and not be burnt. To leap far higher than the flames' flirting reach, and for a moment, steal the sky and float.

A calculating look gleamed in Lathso's eye as his long-necked head dropped back to his handiwork. His drumming now slipped the music into a melodic eddy. A gentler whip of a mood. A stickier, more intricate web. And Lathso's voice was suddenly sibilant in M'nalo's mind: "*Each note from my drum is a stream. Each stream is a vessel, traveler.*"

M'nalo then became one with the spectacle around the sparkling fire. The sheen from the dancers' skins. The gleam of their happy eyes. Their voices trilling ululations and groans to enrich the stomping, sweating, laughing music. All of the pure primal language of scent and warmth and closeness born of a good time spent in praise of ancestral spirits.

So with new courage, M'nalo chanted, "Hu hu hu hu hunh!" and knew a tremendous dignity in his surrender. He could feel his *coolness* heightening. He could disappear into this night's rhythmic tapestry and become one with the common trance.

Appeased by their rushing young blood, the orishas of the dance god goaded the novices to a faster, fancier clapping, to a warmer chant. It carried a message that wriggled through M'nalo's sinews and made his will as water. It tapped an ancient drive deep in his marrow that melded him with his initiating brothers as they all joined in manhood's dance.

Lathso long had disappeared behind a knife-wielder's mask when, later on, dazed dreamy by the potions they had swallowed, M'nalo and a group of selected initiates—eye sockets chalked white to enable sight into the spirit world—followed masked elders far into the bush. There, in the damp of a surprising dawn, the boys heard somber pronouncements of their destinies.

Afterwards, hushed by the glimpse of his enormous lifeline, each youth trod the forest pathway silently, burdened with awe and contemplation. Each knew that he would soon receive a personal mark of honor. An imprint into his flesh that declared to which guild—secret or not—he belonged. This was a statement of responsibility to the community. These scars on face or arms were in no way unkindly cut. The knife's touch was not of pain, but of love and significance. It transformed mature boys into men and husbands.

Thus entranced and ignorant of when his turn to the cutting had come, M'nalo, new apprentice sorcerer, followed the footsteps ahead of him to squat and hang his freshly circumcised oko over the bleeding pit.

Close minding the sorcerer's directions, M'nalo used the beehive cliff as reference point and directly found the bare uphill track he sought. Better test of his tracking skills came as he followed the winding trail across countless gullies and clefts. Around hillocks and humbugs and backtracking turns that gradually snaked up the mountainside. M'nalo concentrated, watching each careful footstep, glancing ahead—not too far—to locate the vague path. One foot then the other on the track before its brother, he climbed up the pale brown mountain to Lathso's home.

The trail flattened and narrowed, some spots skirting sheer, alarming drops. Nervous back to the cliff's cool face, M'nalo sidled around an overhang and the trail suddenly opened into a half-moon shelf of flat land that commanded his surprise.

A ramshackle dwelling was jammed against the cliff's farthest end. Excepting a broad path directly to its entrance, the entire enclave was covered by a wind-rustled garden of fragrant, thriving green. Wading waist-deep through it, M'nalo identified peas and beans and pepper plants, various yam vines, potato and groundnut beds. He didn't recognize several herbs nor the big-leafed greens nearer the cliff-wall. He excused his ignorance with an easy shrug. The exceptional garden in so barren a spot was knowledge exotic enough.

M'nalo stopped before the hovel's door, noticed its hide flap drawn aside. He called "Master!" and waited until the sorcerer's voice invited. Then he stepped into a dark space possessed by Lathso's harsh smell. Eyes slowly adjusting to the general dimness, it took time to see at all. Then a qualm in his belly, M'nalo realized he was sharing room with numerous fetishes and effigies and stones and animal teeth. They were hung from the thatch. Fixed to the wall with spines. Tied to odd extrusions of the shack's wattle frame. Set on the floor against the wall.

Each bit in its particular place, M'nalo knew, represented someone's spirit and destiny. So his three souls shrank at being witness to the spiritual life of whole families. Which group was his? Which piece he? M'nalo dragged his gaze away and his look smashed into Lathso's inscrutable regard.

"In the corner over there," Lathso directed with a casual jerk of his craggy head, "you make your bed."

"Thank you, master," said M'nalo and tossed his matting down. He was all too aware that on the other side of his bedside wall of wattled saplings and mud there was nothing but a lengthy drop of empty mountain breeze.

That first night, after a simple silent dinner that Lathso prepared from his garden's produce, M'nalo curled up tight under his rough raffia cover. Chilled more by consternation than the mountainside cool, he wondered and puzzled over his father's flat command that he spend three moons with the ancient sorcerer. Of what purpose would this stay be?

The noises of night granted no ease to his unsettled mind. Constant were the rattles and shuffles and shifting in the thatch. Then a chorus of plaintive bird calls. Then the winds began a rowdy debate about the shack. Some shrill, some gruff, they opined: How dare this skimpy shelter impede our way and clutter our prepared pathways?

Eventually more agreeable airs breezed through the dark room telling fables in whispers and laughing at his anxieties.

When sleep finally made rescue, he never knew.

"Make your water in the hole, in the middle of the pepper patch!" Lathso had instructed when he showed M'nalo around his garden and explained that his apprenticeship had begun. For the full cycle of three moons, he would study with the sorcerer. So every morning thereafter when he awoke, and every evening before he went to sleep, M'nalo showered the pepper patch with his first and last.

The peppers themselves remained delicious.

"Take a good look at your day's dung and judge. The darker is the healthier. Then throw a handful of fresh dirt over it," Lathso had also instructed. For containing such muck, he had dug a narrow pit back of his garden against the face of the cliff. Then he laid a piece of a stout branch across the hole as a seat. Simple more than comfortable, first time using it, M'nalo noted a robust stand of boc-boc banana risen up out of a previous filled-up latrine.

A reluctant trickle down a fissure of the mountainside supplied Lathso's house water. A large gourd jammed into the crevasse caught the drops into clear, quenching calabashfuls.

Cleaning his teeth with a fresh-cut length of twig, M'nalo stood beside Lathso's rude, falling-apart dwelling and marveled at the sorcerer's nonchalance. How nothing about it bothered the ancient. Not the gapped and broken walls needing patches where morning sunshine peeked through. Not the thatch thickening black with termite nests. Not even the worn-out animal skin serving as a hanging door. Still, dilapidated and transient as it was, the place seemed perfectly suited to the outcast babawalo.

Smiling admiration, M'nalo looked beyond the hut to its cramped location: a bare-dirt cleft in the mountainside. A near-flat patch of clay smaller than the dancing arena in which his village celebrated festivals. He swung his gaze more distant. Fifty paces away to his left at higher elevation the sheer mountain was pocked with holes, burrows from which countless rats' heads bobbed. Some casually directed their attention toward him. Most rats focused on the action a bit further up the incline where their food supply cheeped and sang about territory while keeping vigilant guard over family nests.

The cliff's face instantly became clean of rats' heads as, with its haughty neck directing its yellow eyes this way and that, a large black-faced hawk floated overhead. Wistful all at once, M'nalo followed its meandering drift over the plateau. That he might possess such solitary majesty, M'nalo dreamed. His eyes ranged ahead of the hawk and took imagination's flight across the continuous sweep of treetops. Over forested swells broken by basins of lowland swamps and grassland. Down a gentle incline toward the horizon where the vast green distance faded into dusky purple and blended indistinguishably with the sky.

M'nalo quivered to a sense of the land's largeness. What went on at that far-off meeting-place of land and purple sky? Over there were the storied peoples and practices of which the jalis, Anandan spoke. Elsewhere in the distance was his father's great home city with its royal palaces and intrigues. M'nalo wished for eagle's wings so that he might skim high above them all, find out what went on, who was who. Not to interfere—just to ease his deep longing to know.

A faint plume of smoke drifting upwards drew M'nalo's eyes across the distance he had trekked to get here. A sparkling streak at the edge of the great woods snagged his attention. It was a glimpse of sunshine reflecting on the faraway river a few curves above the slow basins where he loved to swim.

On the updraft of the daydream, M'nalo plunged into his river memories of liquid cool surrounding him, touching all over, holding him so loosely that he remained free. As he recalled the special blessings of the river-rain goddess Yemoja that he enjoyed, a rash of bumps chilled up his arms and shoulders. All at once overcome by an urge to compound his àshe and keep it close, M'nalo drew himself up straighter. He flattened suddenly damp palms against his thighs and concentrated toward stillness.

Just then, the hut's mangy animal-skin drape scraped open and Lathso emerged. He greeted, "Bring your souls back into their home, young leopard. New morning air is best for dreaming, but let me join you since we have much magic to share."

One look at him, M'nalo grew ill at ease. The usual flies buzzed about his head as Lathso stood before the doorway with his left hand raised shoulder high, the palm forward as if barring closer approach. A waist-tall drum leaned against his hip. An edge in the elder's voice reminded of Izi Onamuli and his vexing mind games.

M'nalo saluted with open palms. He bowed and answered carefully, "Long life, esteemed uncle. According to my father's wish, I am at your beck and bid."

Lathso leaned his bare buttocks against the hut's rough outer wall, tucked the drum between his legs. He flexed his shoulders several times, extended his arms overhead, then straight out chest high and then hard up once again before jerking them down to his sides.

"Listen to my fingers as they lead your thoughts into the riddles of my teaching drum," he commanded. Then, as the ready fingers flew to their work with a blat-a-tat flurry, M'nalo's mind underwent a fluid blurring and the sorcerer began, "*An open mind is a field for games...an arena where vengeance can seek satisfaction...a sorcerer's playground where 'bruise for bruise' is standard...a complicated terrain where a sorcerer sets his traps, drums his dances, potent and venomous...plants possibilities more numerous than the canopy of clouds...as vital as the raindrops and vines and the leaves and hardwood branches bringing sap to flower, sweet to fruit...a mind is simple as the insects and birds drawing sustenance from waste...*"

Ideas flowed within the notes thumped from Lathso's teaching drum. Bearing many-leveled messages, by tone and texture they pounded themselves into the three souls of M'nalo's being. They joined in the racing rhythm of his heartbeat. *Brram!* conjured up the tremble of a crystal tear along a pregnant belly, black and smooth as night. *Bidaph!* A scarlet flowering as his keen knife slid into an enemy's heart. *Bldup!* The predatory gaze of a hungry vagrant. *Bridipt!* promised to wound who wounded you, never forgive.

Such were myriad intricate messages blowing into M'nalo's àshe. Yielding to the drum-speech, he was lost to himself and before he could consider, a vast storm of sorcerer knowledge swirled into his souls.

"*...in this place where Lord Eshu commands and chooses to play, all of them and us are bits of a bigness strung together...all of them,*" *and us, are knotted close in a great net floating on the waters...all fishing the currents for Eshu's favor..."*

The sorcerer's drum commanded, *"...study these rats on the red-dirt hill, they teach our destiny...as sorcerers for Lord Eshu's cause, we must learn from these formidable competitors...look at how they eat men at hunger's chance while men hardly notice them...copy these clever adversaries with so many races, so many shades, brown and black and white and grey, mixing for survival...know more of these wanderer rats, and house rats, and scrabbling dirt-rats, cliff-burrowing rats, storeroom rats, refuse rats which are not latrine rats, and water rats which are not river rats, or wharf, or ferry rats..."*

Beyond the drummed messages, there came a snag in Lathso's tone as he crooned, *"...the day of sorcerer is nearly done...barbarians hardy as their pink-skinned rats now challenge our destiny...like big bullying rats, they are strivers with blunt noses and coarse grey hair... too true, my drum, too true...only if we are cunning and defiant as these extraordinary rats, only then can we protect our Lord Eshu's traditions..."*

Even within his trance, M'nalo could hear old sorcerer's singsong sadden. Yet the percussion never wavered as he continued, *"...adepts at survival, these creatures can wriggle through escape holes only wide as their skulls...so must a sorcerer use his head...driven by need, these creatures will eat dirt, grain, wood, cured hides, their own newborn...as if trained by our guild, these trap-shy animals recognize the subtlest poisons...they live in winding burrows with nervous exits ready...they trust no one, these scrappy fellows, they live long, they are fertile as sour flies..."*

On and on went Lathso and his drum, sounding lessons of rats and sorcerer secrets into M'nalo's bewitched, accepting mind.

M'nalo roused to sunshine hot on his shoulders. The drum had stopped. The mountain breeze was empty. He blinked his eyes open to a dark blue sky and moved into the hut's shade still squinting at the swimmy world.

"Hnnnn. Your mind is a cage strong beyond your age," came Lathso's approving tones. "Remember that a drum is silent until forced to speak. Time will teach how to recall the magic you now know." Then he coughed and turned his gaze to the violet sky.

M'nalo tentatively shook his head and determined it was clear. He remained squatting where he was, awaiting for more certainty that he had been dismissed. Then no sign to the contrary from his master, he quietly rose, bowed respects to Lathso's loose-skinned back and was out of there duty free for the rest of that day.

Four times the moon filled and emptied itself before M'nalo returned under his father's charge, and got back in the swing of the village routines. Today, grey clouds had seeped from the damp of the air to the gloom in his head. Beyond the doorway of this leaf-and-wattle shelter, all M'nalo saw was rain pelting craters into the soaked forest floor. On the palm-leaf thatch covering his head, all he heard was the monotonous lashing of the drenching, dulling, incessant rain, this season's last. In all the skies above, the mama gods were weeping pain.

M'nalo poked his head out through the door-space of the hideaway and searched the stormy dusk. He squinted this way and that trying to pierce the grayness between the close tree trunks. Like fierce rivulets flung from the sullen sky, the stinging rain came down. No sign of Izi Onamuli in the dim wetness, though. So he waited while the rain streamed and cut a swath for its companion wind, waited while shrieking wind drove mist across the landscape, blanketing all in cloud.

The brothers had planned to meet here in the clearing where the old forest met high country not far from a meandering tributary of the great river. Izi had insisted on this spot. Twice before he'd secretly trailed these fetish-thieves this far. Or so he claimed, M'nalo mused with familiar annoyance.

He crouched on his heels waiting, shaking his doubtful head occasionally. This was partly from disappointment at his very need to wait. Partly too, because the action squashed the tickle of droplets sliding down his neck. For even though he figured the tremendous downpour had canceled whatever were his and Izi's intentions, M'nalo, as was his nature, waited. Absently using his forefinger to crush a trail of numberless, tiny, reddish ants moving up and down the shelter's main post, he waited. Only because he had said he would, he remained.

With more stink than sting, the ants dutifully returned to their trail regardless of casualties and M'nalo soon lost interest in brutalizing them. Their smell slid his thoughts to the one place he would rather be: his master's hovel up in the hills beyond the scrub-bush and forests. From the sorcerer's teachings he had learned that enough of these ants crushed alive in a gourd with a certain prickly-leafed herb would form a solid scab on the most persistent runny sore. Drowned in sour fruit juice, these same ants made a blue stain that glowed in the darkness. So bad-tasting that few birds or insects preyed on them, they themselves were meat eaters. They scavenged graves, carrion, and offal, raided birds' nests, fat worms in their holes, even baby rats in their dens. These ants, though they would float, were confined only by moving water, being too slight to maintain direction, and...

A splash of running feet through puddles. A shadow blinking through the door and Izi Onamuli was beneath the shelter stomping and shaking and sending splatters all over. "Bbrrr! The rain's grown cold," he grumbled, "and yet you had me coming here."

M'nalo's daydream fled but still reflective, he made no response. Tone of voice alone revealed his brother's contrariness. The rain complaint was just a starter. Predictable as wet in water, Izi continued after a moment, "Though with your ox-like hide and fortitude, such doesn't matter. Eh? You realized the thieves would not be venturing out in this storm. Didn't you? Eh?"

Expected as it was, his tone pricked a familiar puzzle in M'nalo's mind. Why was it that ever since they could recognize each other, Izi had appointed himself as M'nalo's scold? What kept M'nalo bound to this abuse? He did acknowledge that part of him—as if by a spell—was held to the situation. M'nalo's main defense was always the pretense of a grim and stoic pose. As if his heart might suffer but not his àshe. Still, the mask he wore was fragile.

Neck alone moving, he slowly turned cold eyes to Izi's scrawny figure.

Wet and shivering despite his sharp-edged brain, with false smile and calculating glance, Izi offered, "Just teasing, my brother big and strong. You know how I envy your hard hands and hunter's strength."

With same deliberation, M'nalo returned his stare to the post and its crawling ant columns. His brother's barbs were like wasps disturbed in darkness. M'nalo was certain only of their sting. It might be the nipping impatience in Izi's voice, the bright amusement in his eye, the private smile as he talked through one of his notions of how things should work, matters to which M'nalo was indifferent. Yet always it seemed that while the gods had given both brothers breath, Izi Onamuli was granted all the Tortoise wits and curiosity.

True, M'nalo was a full head taller and broad-shouldered. He had the muscles to outrun and out-swim any youth in the settlement. Yet it wasn't until they were grown striplings that M'nalo even tried his superior strength and size against his brother's mischief. Often as not, though, this defense forced Izi to subtler maneuvers. So much so, sometimes M'nalo wasn't certain he had been challenged at all. As time went on, it seemed Izi had been blessed indeed with keener mind and insight. And that these gifts were mainly used for caging M'nalo's intelligence like a trained monkey. A strong and nimble monkey, true, but one always vaguely aware that his scrawny brother used him for purposes shrewder than he could discern...

Izi Onamuli interrupted his thoughts, "I've been hiding near the door of Banalo's compound since before the last clouds rolled over. He didn't appear although I never expected him to."

M'nalo kept his stare on the ant trail.

"He's the ringleader. He didn't have to send messages. The others looked at the rain and they knew not to come. But I knew you'd still be here," Izi continued. "Only reason I had to risk this drenching was to verify that single fact. That by the ancestors, like beans in a marketplace, you would be here. "

As if uncertain that his point was sufficiently made, Izi kept on, "Let me put it plain, my stubborn ox of a brother. Didn't the heaviness of the rain shout into your head that I would not be coming? Eh? Yet here you wait as if…"

M'nalo concentrated past his brother's railing and kept his muscles ready. With peripheral vision he measured the varying distance Izi maintained as he plied the abuse.

"Now tell me you're making a point of your patience. Tell me you're displaying how well you keep your word." Izi tossed his hands upward and a sprinkle of his wetness hit M'nalo's forehead. "Oh, clever Lord Eshu, show this fool some better way to use his noble bloodline."

He grabbed at his own head in a mockery of pleading. "M'nalo, my brother, don't remain a slave. True, 'dutiful' is the demand of your birth name. But 'Sikivu' can mean much more. Dutiful soldier that you may seem, my noble ancestors also dance within your àshe. You are not completely common. My father's royal blood is in you. Not as much as I, but you have inherited defiance to this slavish duty. You can rise above the grubbiness and hard-hands of your mother's kind to…"

As the one-way argument caught him up in his own spite, Izi Onamuli strayed from safe distance, closer and closer. Until at last, gesturing disdain for M'nalo's servile compliance, he lurched forward off balance.

And in one smooth swift motion M'nalo sprang from his haunches, grabbed and brought down his unready brother.

Izi, though, despite his scrawny stature, had grown tight-muscled as a wild dog. Clawing and writhing, wriggling like wet fish, he didn't stay held for long. M'nalo had to content himself with whatever punches and bruises he managed to inflict on Izi's bony body before he'd wrestled himself away.

Breathing hard, eyeing each other, the two brothers crouched at a wary distance, Izi nearer the doorway well out of M'nalo's reach.

M'nalo grumbled slyly, "Praise brother Tortoise as you wish, but remember that big brother Lion always has teeth strong enough to crack your skinny shell."

Izi Onamuli grunted under his breath, vigorously rubbing his sore parts. Then he straightened, and retying his boubou, sidled to the threshold and stood there irresolute, neither in nor out. "We'll see how brother Lion roars when I tell my mother how I got these bruises," he snarled and shot off into the rain showers.

Unimpressed by his brother's threat, M'nalo relaxed back into his melancholy. So what if Tebika became angry? Was one more whipping worth brooding upon? What gnawed more at M'nalo's peace of mind was why Izi Onamuli was so never satisfied. What compelled him to this permanent discontent?

Still, his pestering gone, M'nalo had to allow a most humbling conclusion: Izi Onamuli, a doubly royal son, came to the subtleties of nobility far more naturally than he, and always had.

When M'nalo arrived for this one moon visit, he found the sorcerer even more abstracted than usual. For days upon days that passed into worrisome nights, Lathso acknowledged no greeting or request by word or gesture. He just sat inside the gloomy hut and influenced by imperceptible matters, sighed and groaned, sniggered with gleeful malice, screamed curses to the unseen, and generally was more ancient and crazy than M'nalo had ever seen him. The moon was in its third phase before the sorcerer's behavior changed. Then his souls turned youthful and for many hours Lathso would carry on about his princely boyhood. Of foot-racing and marble-pitching contests at the Oba's royal court.

Of techniques he'd developed for making and spinning snail-shell tops.

M'nalo listened, fascinated by the notion of Lathso as a young boy. Then, as if these memories had triggered it, the sorcerer went off on a rant about the guild that had expelled him.

"Merciless abusers, every one of them. Tyrannical gatekeepers! They all became tails to their dog, Greed. All of us followers of Eshu-Elegbara had mastered the secrets of leading-from-behind. To all of us whom the teaching drum gave knowledge of Osaynin, the Healer. With these two gifts we had more power than any ruler. For by poison or magic we could decide which one lived, which one did not. That's what we did and we of the sorcerer guild became most feared in the land. Until some allowed greed to flatter their souls blind and steal their convictions. Such as these engaged in the commerce of slavery with pale-skinned foreigners. Which made all of us sorcerers wealthy and most despised. We well earned our guild the dread in its reputation. Using subtle poisons, we foiled opponents and fair opportunity. Selfish and efficient, we ran the country's slaving systems. Supply never outpaced demand. Sent inland, our idle armies culled remote villages, stole our simple folks and marched them back for sale to the hairy foreigners. In exchange, the sorcerers accepted gold and weapons and musket balls, fine cloth and valued metals and exotic liquors.

"Haii! This is the guild I departed vengeful. For this had become the extreme road the Leopard Society skulked along. From this business in bondage, the guild of sorcerers enriched kingdom Dahomey. Those of royal lineage were made richest of all. The coffers of every royal palace could well afford its intrigues. Corruption became the truest leveler. Every prince wanted to be king, every princess, queen mother. Avarice was each royal's sovereign and his àshe glittered golden. Crazed by personal quests, they embraced foreign creeds and no more practiced ritual *etutu* to assuage our natural gods.

"Haii! Certain sorcerers, royal and other, forgot that àshe is a privilege of righteous living. But the gods were sharp to notice and at their own speed went into action. Heavy trouble fell upon these traitors of Elegbara's path. The rich of these renegade poisoners afforded escape, while those with lesser purses lost their skulls to pointed poles."

Lathso stopped, turned suddenly sensible eyes to M'nalo and said, "Still, this is a private matter. A peeve that's only mine and should so remain. Though I will say, young M'nalo, that I will prevail. Already I have the weapon of my revenge. A tight, new drum as my apprentice. You."

M'nalo, already surprised by Lathso's abrupt mood change, was further unsettled by this declaration. Grave concern for the mind of his wrinkled master flooded forward.

But over the next day or two Lathso's normal spirits seemed to return. And when, at the evening's meal he commented that M'nalo was studying him like strange food, M'nalo grinned with relief and tried to make his caring more covert.

Sunny midmorning. In the hut's shade, they sat quiet in their own thoughts until Lathso snorted and flea spry, sprang up and entered the hut. Quickly out again, he held up a supple black animal-hide cape.

"Look at this," he said and flared open the cloak revealing its inner lining fashioned with numerous pockets and tie-strings. Each held a bottle, a small cloth, or a leaf packet bound by vine strings.

"Look at it!" Lathso repeated, as if the marvelous cloak hadn't already seized M'nalo's attention.

"These potions are gifts from the god, Osaynin. This one," the old sorcerer pointed at a light green bottle with dark liquid, "a single drop guards against the river-worm. This black dust here holds the spider's deadly venom. A death painless or hideous, swift or a whole life long. I will teach you how to mix and stir from these cups, my young Leopard. With the help of my drum, I will teach you how to employ their contents toward ends menial or mighty. After you've followed this hidden trail, you'll discover the sweet justice of Eshu's mischief." Lathso's rheumy eyes sparkled as he smiled.

Grown uncomfortable and awed by the diviner's grand designs, M'nalo averted his eyes from Lathso's gaze and studied the wondrous carrying-cloak. Age and use had darkened its hardy leather. Along its length and breadth, every cranny and fold and pouch was occupied. Animal bones were hooked in crevasses, feathers pinned into creases. Each nook contained its own potion or salve, poison or cure. All were pockets of some person's àshe.

How could he possibly fulfill the old man's expectations? Heart slipping into his guts, M'nalo turned to Lathso and quavered, "But, Master, how am I to learn so much?"

Lathso's passionate manner retreated and he laughed, *snif-snif-snif*, through his nose. "You only have to open your head," he said. "The balance is a trick I know. So, not to worry." He went to the door, flipped back an edge of the hide curtain and tossed the coat behind it.

Momuri had lost three cattle. A rogue lion was suspected. A score or so worried herdsmen gathered in a close semicircle around a brisk fire by the pens behind Momuri's zangala. Time and again his sons brightened the flames with dry tinder that they and companions—M'nalo among them—had toted earlier from the scrublands. Other youngsters settled near the family's softly gruntling piggery to listen to the men talk. The smells there being too strong for his nose, M'nalo perched on the top stile of the cow pen. Now and again, he reached over to nip one of the near-to-bursting ticks from a cow's dusty hide and, with a crispy squish, crunch it between his thumbnails. Above, empty of stars, the black sky somehow had startled a discussion among the night birds. Concerned coos and caws were echoing in the close darkness when Momuri called on Ajanaku, his chief herder, to shed light on this recent crisis.

Ajanaku was a small, bony man with seven or eight runny-nosed children. Custard apples and fat red cashews grew plentiful in Ajanaku's compound. But the fruit fell to the ground and remained there wasted to the indifferent pecks of his yard fowl. For fear of Ajanaku's wife, a skinny, scowling woman, no boys dared venture in to claim them.

Now, well fortified from the palm-wine and cava gourds that had been passing around, Ajanaku began his story: "Day started badly with a cloudy dawn stopping the sun from smiling upon me. Pink, spiteful, smoke-thin clouds all that morning and all the rest of that terrible day." He paused to shake his head and grimace despair.

Several of the men nodded in sympathy.

"Not a good sign!" someone grunted.

An excited voice claimed, "A man must have the blessings of the sun!"

"We all wish for it," agreed Ajanaku, "but all this day Papa Sun didn't watch over me. And after He closed his eyes so Night could thrive, darkness fell most threatening, with no wind to blow away the heat and cool a man's sweat. And then in the menacing night I heard the stalking lions showing off outside the compound walls! I could hear them coughing and calling out bold and loud. Proud at not having to crawl for concealment, proclaiming their confidence among the night grass and drying corn. Perhaps their grunting and growling was only for practice, or habit. Maybe they were teaching their young how to rule the dark."

Ajanaku paused and took a swig, providing his listeners time to murmur condolences and comments on the malicious provocations of wild beasts.

"Ahhnnn! That very night my beautiful bull fought off this savage creature. Truth is, I never threw eyes on the rogue animal itself. All I saw of the battle was my bull's wounds, his deep-ripped stomach, his blooded horns. All I knew was that he had won a valiant fight, and suffered great loss of blood. With hot tears and a heart heavy as iron, I tended that fine and noble bull, I tended him as the family he was. A big breed bull, resistant to tick sickness and malaise. But with these festering wounds, his nose went scaly dry, his eyes sunk. He would never raise the energy to jump a cow again. In three months he'd be so withered we had no choice but slaughter."

Ajanaku stopped and blew his nose. He swigged from the gourd to help compose himself. But tears had choked him up too much to continue.

Momuri went and squatted next to him, put an arm around Ajanaku's shaking shoulders. "Your loss has been ours," he said. "Our homes and stock animals have been yours to use. But what is the point of starting over unless we destroy this rogue? The piles of dung and other signs say it lurks like a coward and attacks the fattest cows. This is surely the method of a crippled lion, a male. That means we, too, must set traps, but clever ones baited with one more sacrifice. For this part we need a volunteer. The trap itself, I have already constructed."

The mention of traps diverted M'nalo, reminded that his master, Lathso, had promised him instruction about unseen traps and spirit fences and sound marks during next moon's visit. All at once unable merely to sit and listen, M'nalo jumped down from his perch and started for his compound.

"Say her mouth is a wound, flesh split open, bloodied and pulsing. Tell her you want to burst the fat tight lips of her obo…"

"Izi!" M'nalo shouted, equally embarrassed, amused, and annoyed. "You're a one-minded monkey."

"It's what you should say. Who do you think she is? Eh? A delicate flower awaiting your long black stinger? Listen to me, foolish brother. Probably she's already thrilled to a sting! And the one would be Fonshoi who has her in grasp every evening in the guava patch. What! You don't know? Well, love-struck one, you may well be the last to learn. Even the tree-trunks know it. Village eyes have seen them everywhere. In the cool shade of the banana stool. Among the bamboo groves by the river. Late in the evenings…"

M'nalo found his big hands all of a sudden forcing themselves about Izi's throat, trying to stifle it quiet. Izi grappled and wriggled and scratched and tugged and kicked at whatever he could of M'nalo. He struck out at the strangling fingers, the bone-hard thighs, the privates soft in his chokoto.

Some part of his underhanded attack diverted M'nalo from aggression to protection, allowing him to scramble from their sleep pallets and stalk out into the brooding night.

Grateful for the forced solitude, M'nalo gentled and soothed his abused groin. He moped as well, on considering his bruised and hopeless heart.

Above the roof's thatched overhang, like a tiny far-off eye in the heavens, a slice of pallid moon slipped between the clouds over the mountains, black clouds even in the darkness distantly threatening. For the briefest instant M'nalo hesitated, but then he strode off on into the gloom toward the path to the communal gardens.

A glimmer of warmth entered his soul. For there, a mere three days ago just before dusk, he had raced her through the yam and cassava fields.

Swift as a dik-dik, Jureyi had sprinted off. For playful moments she disappeared among the tall terraced yam vines. And fast as he was, he couldn't catch her. Yet, he persisted. For, even as she sped away, her teasing smile would flash back, as if eager to close the distance between them. As if it went reluctantly with its bearer.

So he was simply running on, not even chasing anymore when he surprised up on her hiding among the roots of a large banyan. Were it not for her betraying giggle, he'd have jogged past. With a rush of breath, M'nalo thought, surely she had been waiting for me.

Instantly his blood was rushing hot, fattening his oko, emboldening his hands. He grabbed her by the wrists. She did not resist. He shoved her against the tree-trunk. He roughed his damp hands over her perfect breasts, their pert nipples. She did not flinch.

Instead, she pushed up her chest to meet his heated caresses. Eyes closed, she threw her head back, bared her neck. A bead of sweat paused at the pulse of her throat.

An instinct to taste, M'nalo bent and licked. The salt on his tongue peppering him, he plunged a bold hand past her navel, beneath the waistband of her camiza, down the front of her belly, over the fuzziness there. After a trembling moment, she parted her legs slightly, and allowed his probing fingertips a warm slick. A heady instant thick like honey. Then she tightened up, pulled away. With her lustrous eyes earnest on his, she said breathily, "I only run so far as you can catch me."

Then she twisted her wrists from his sweaty grasp and mischief in her laugh, fled. Given the stiffness beneath his boubou, M'nalo didn't so much as consider pursuit. Instead, he hid farther in among the shadows of the upright roots and handled his yearning for consolation.

Now, he sighed in the night, brooding on his sour-sweet quandary. Although he had no doubt that she favored him, one hopeless fact remained clear. Despite their flirtations and stolen touch-play in the fields, back at the settlement Jureyi never looked his way. She hardly acknowledged his existence. There in that public gaze, her eyes were solely for Fonshoi, her betrothed since birth by family arrangement.

The river slid down from the hills, rolled through the high forests, and like a great snake, emerged in a curve along the northern reaches of the settlement. Sometimes narrow and deep with swift currents. Sometimes slowed to shady sluggish basins, it watered—thanks to Khufu's well-engineered aqueducts—the dark rich soil of the village's cultivated lands.

Born but four years after his father settled his people here, M'nalo had grown up with the village. He often accompanied his father as he supervised channeling of the river to meet new settlement needs. M'nalo had natural affinity with the water and plainly enjoyed being in it. With his father's encouragement he was soon a superb swimmer. Thus, he was welcome to join the men when they fished the river.

He'd just finished a long splash across a languid basin—too hard a swim to cool away the first sweat of a sprinted shortcut through the village's yam beds. Now steadily trotting, he felt champion, light as a breeze. At this pace, in this state of mind, his legs pumping to their own rhythm, he would daydream away the distance to his master, Lathso.

Not that for a moment he forgot the importance of the message he bore, the reason Koita had roused him at daybreak and sent him off into the still shadowy savannah on this mission.

Three days previous, Izi Onamuli had taken ill with his familiar problem. Trying to clear his breathing passages, Tebika had anointed him with the usual oils. She had burnt incenses and particular plants in his room. Ladle by ladle, she had dribbled special brews through his slack lips. But her son's condition only worsened. Frightened past her reluctance, the haughty princess appealed to the settlement's older mothers.

They came and offered their best treatments. Still Izi grew worse. His narrow chest struggling to rise and fall, he wheezed in painful gasps of air. His rich brown color faded to dun. His yellow eyes glazed and wandered in their sockets.

The servants reported to Khufu and he visited his ailing child. One look at Izi, Khufu insisted that Tebika surrender her pride and take the advice of the old women. Among themselves they had been whispering that only Lathso's potions and salves would heal the sore-sick boy.

So naturally, strong and fleet apprentice Sikivu M'nalo was chosen to be messenger.

About him the bush remained lush and alive. With every stride he had to squash his curiosity. Latest temptation was the distress call of a dolee-bird. M'nalo knew that the male sounded so attractively pained only when its nest was in danger. His aim was to lure hungry aggressors from the clutch and his female who never deserted the nest. For knowledgeable hunters, animal or human, this practice made for a two-course reward after a careful search. The hunter would win not only the savory flesh of the plump female, but also the prized delicacies her half-hatched eggs. This time, urgent duty in mind, M'nalo kept on course, steadily loping towards the sorcerer and his medicines.

The babawalo listened close to M'nalo's report of Izi's illness, then was busy preparing appropriate remedies. M'nalo, meanwhile, rested in the shack's shade, sucking oranges, letting his breath catch up.

Before long, the sorcerer handed him a leaf-wrapped parcel and said, "This will keep our young prince from getting too soon to that other place."

M'nalo sprang up ready to depart, but Lathso commanded, "No, young Leopard. The track is not safe. This pleasant time of day best suits the careless and the plump and hunters who seek suchlike. I have better intentions for you. Take your ease while I send my charms on ahead."

M'nalo sat, biting his bottom lip in anxiety.

"Don't concern yourself with your brother's sickness. Much of it springs from his mother's dreams. She is one forgetful that dreaming itself has magic." Lathso smiled mysteriously. "Dream, young M'nalo, but dream simple. Dream for health and knowledge. Some dream only of accumulating wealth. Some tie their dreams to power. There are those who dare not dream at all.

Close your eyes and open your head. Let me teach you something about dreams."

His eyelids grew heavy. So heavy, they fell shut and M'nalo was under the sorcerer's spell. Then Lathso closed his own eyes, entrancing himself to release his seeking soul so that it might find a way into the boy's unsullied dream world...

...like twinned bubbles moving swiftly through a glistening mist, the souls of M'nalo and the sorcerer are in the center of a grove of anya trees, at the boundary of a magical fence. An impenetrable wall of gentle sound is kept up by the constant breezes. Safe within this enclosure are the objects comprising Tebika's fà.

...the spirits of she and Izi Onamuli crouch at the threshold of the only door into this private place. The pair of spying seeker souls hover while Tebika speaks the spells that persuade the guardian orishas from the door. And when these terrible ones are quieted, the spying souls follow the princess and her son to a private altar. They watch as Tebika opens a green calabash and show Izi Onamuli's navel cord within. It still seems fresh cut.

...then the ambitious princess places her son upon the altar. She chants diviner spells, reveals to him what is forbidden. Then in the aftermath she shares with Izi malicious plans to betray the settlement.

...but Tebika's guardian spirits are becoming unruly. So rather than risk discovery, the seeker souls of M'nalo and Lathso flee, glide smoothly away and return themselves to the sorcerer's secure shack.

M'nalo came out of the spell and gradually became aware of the midday heat. Like a fading dream right at the edge of his recall, an important piece of knowledge was dangling. He shook his head, trying to nudge it forefront. But the information remained elusive.

"Your passage back is now safe," he heard Lathso say and a squeeze of anxiety in his belly reminded him of his mission. He assumed right away that he had nodded off and slept longer than intended.

"Time you start back," Lathso went on. "Even fast-footed cheetah can't outrace the afternoon sun. Next visit we'll talk some secrets about little creatures. Bugs and ants, fleas and"—a sharp slap at his bare bony chest—"mosquitoes!"

"Fleas?" said M'nalo, still bewildered that the sun was past its peak, that Lathso had allowed him so long a rest.

"Yes, yes. And ants. But go now," Lathso murmured absently. "Next time."

Answering her summons, no sooner had M'nalo entered her zangala than Tebika confronted him: "Tell me, man-child *Sikivu*, what magic do you learn from the outcast sorcerer?" She lingered on his name with insolent inference to its Swahili meaning of 'dutiful'.

Ignoring the intent of her mockery, M'nalo squared himself to the princess's amused regard and, bolstered by what was common knowledge replied, "You know, Princess, that the ways of the sorcerers' guild may not be spoken."

Tebika rose from her stool, took up a bamboo fan. She unfolded it, snapped it shut. Again and yet again she repeated this. As usual, she wore a close-fitting khanga that covered from shoulder to ankles. This one was a brownish-gold and blended with a shaft of afternoon sunshine beaming through her window. She went and stood with her back to the window, and her face was lost to the brightness behind. "But, *Sikivu*, surely you can tell me, such close family as we are."

M'nalo looked away from her shadow against the sunbeam. He rested his eyes on her loom. He knew that in this matter, even Tebika, princess though she was, dared not press. Royal birthright made her, and her son, honorary members of every guild—every one but the sorcerers'. For this one was chosen by ancient and mysterious means. Confident of his position, pretending to study the tapestry being woven, he said, "Royal mother of my brother, why must you make play of my commitment? You know I am forbidden to tell of such matters."

"Not play, *bound* Sikivu. Admiration. For I cannot but notice your self-possession. It must spring from your association with my son. Certainly such a manner was not learned at your humble mother's side."

The cut at his mother scarcely bothered; he had been expecting it. Indeed, M'nalo felt oddly braced by Tebika's sniping. How her predictability reduced its threat to that of a toothless lion.

He turned back to the window, looked where the eyes would be in the shadow standing there. "Thank you, royal princess. Many are the matters learned since I left my mother's humble side. Still, I'm always proud of what I gathered there. Now, with your permission, I will go tend your herb garden as you have requested."

Without reply, she stepped from the window's glare. M'nalo watched her amble to the stool before her loom. Not even a glance at him, she sat down, said, "You may go."

And feeling winner of the interplay, M'nalo departed.

When M'nalo reached the storytelling site beneath the baobab, gaily dressed family groups were already settled in, trading news, laughing with one another. Some had been there so long their cooking-fire coals had grown furry with thick, white ash. All of the shady places facing the performance site were taken. So making do best he could, M'nalo chose a spot on the periphery—open to the setting sunshine but providing an unobstructed view—and started his family's fire.

The exuberant buzz of chuckles and chatter shared the air with the tantalizing aromas of roasting groundnuts and new yams, and boiling topi-tamboo. The younger children chased about in boisterous games. Or whined for more treats even as their round bellies suggested festive fullness. Or squealed and squirmed with squalling impatience for the show to begin. Versions of himself not long ago, they reminded M'nalo of pleasures he had now outgrown. Of how youth and occasions such as these had privileged his childhood and taught him his people's ways.

Looking over the colorful throng of head-wraps and hats, he saw his mother approaching in company with Ammaa and her girls. M'nalo strode to meet and guide them to the spot he'd chosen, where his fresh, brisk fire had settled down servile. Ezene and Mesphi immediately set to roasting tidbits. M'nalo waited long enough to filch a handful from the first done batch. He stuck the hot groundnuts in the pouch pocket of his indigo hip-long awo. Then he was off to rove.

Not entirely by accident, he came upon Mother Elder Jao, the midwife who had delivered him and who was grandmother to Jureyi whose beauty made his three souls ache and his senseless oko rude. M'nalo gave the old lady some of his sisters' fresh-roasted savories and crouched on his heels for a chat. All the while his heart pumped with a fervent hope that Jureyi would arrive. So as long as was decent and then some more, M'nalo lingered. Probably sitting with Fonshoi and his family, she never showed up. So his dream withering from matters of fact, he wandered away to nurse disappointment.

He ambled through still-gathering villagers and paused to watch sweaty volunteers finish constructing a wattled palisade between the baobab's bole and Khufu's compound wall creating a space that would serve as a dressing area. Children competing for peepholes, and whoops of delight from within, baited the audience's anticipation. All the signs promised that the contestants were close to ready.

The dipping sun a golden signal, M'nalo returned to his family's circle. On his way, he stifled surprise as he noticed his brother's cap near the staging area. Izi Onamuli hardly attended community gatherings of any sort. Yet there he was, comfortable on a stool, looking on. Suppressing his curiosity, M'nalo squatted on a stool Koita had placed beside her own.

High torches were lit, and the contest began with young Evejo Pamba singing the story "How Tortoise got his back cracked." Partway through the call and response, he sang the wrong call. A smart-mouth noted the mistake with a pointed sally. That set off rounds of laughter and disturbed the aplomb of the story-singer. He promptly broke into tears and ranting at his unforgiving heckler. Family members had to help the disconsolate boy from the platform.

It took a bit for the amusement to quiet. Then it was time for the next contestant.

A murmur rose from the audience when a graceful figure emerged from behind the wattle palisade. A woman wrapped from neck to ankle in glossy white fabric, and with a stool perched like a crown up on her head. Her face was hidden by a terrific red, green, yellow, and black mask she held before it. Her carriage itself commanding attention, the figure slowly glided to the far end of the stage area. There she stretched an arm high as a palm tree, removed the stool, and placed it on the ground. Then she sat down.

From the figure—a special curve at her breasts—M'nalo recognized first wife Tebika and his quick exhalation did nothing to ease the sudden thrill that tensed him, and fattened the fill of his chokoto. Lost to lust, he stared at her until the audience's burst of applause rallied his attention back to the scene.

This story would be not told but mimed. His brother, Izi Onamuli—so the skinny bandy-legs indicated—wore the mask of Ogun, the thunder prince-god. Held with both hands, he wielded a steadily smoking outsize 'hammer' fashioned from a long staff and a reed-basket filled with live embers and slow-burning material.

As Ogun, Izi danced homage *etutu* and bowed to the glistening white Great-God figure before him. He then swung his hammer at a drum M'nalo hadn't noticed till that moment. Hammer struck drum with a loud bang and the hammer-head exploded, showering smoking leaves and embers into the alarmed audience, exciting screams and commotion. Those closest scattered to safety while those farthest back pressed forward to be part of the action.

But there was no real danger and soon the approving crowd quieted itself and resettled for more entertainment. Only to find that Izi Onamuli had vanished in the tumult, leaving the steadfast white figure to hold the stage alone.

By now most had recognized the performance to be the fable of how the king of the sixteen gods came to give Eshu-Elegbara the gift of àshe: the power to make things be. And like M'nalo, most were curious to know how Izi would next appear.

He satisfied them all right then.

With left leg tied up behind his thigh, right arm strapped along his side, he hopped out before them. A brief pause, then claps and whistles said that Izi had managed a convincing depiction of Osaynin, the crippled god of plants and medicine. But Izi Onamuli couldn't keep his one-foot balance and fell to the ground. He remained there writhing a groveling performance of *etutu* to the silent seated Great-God figure. The wiggles of an earthworm could not have been more ridiculous. The amused audience cheered approval when Izi once again disappeared behind the wattle wall.

Still seated, Tebika's masked figure eerily reflected both the reddish yellows of the audience's roasting fires and the scarlet of the setting sun. M'nalo wondered if she, too, was laughing behind her impressive mask.

For a third time, Izi Onamuli returned to the stage. Except for a simple white boubou and a scarlet feather stuck upright on his forehead, nothing covered his bony frame. He went directly to the Great-God figure and bowed deeply. Then he danced his *etutu*, open palms facing upwards. He pointed to the feather on his forehead in suggestion that Eshu-Elegbara had brought no gifts but Dignity and Loyalty. Izi performed with confidence and conviction and when the glowing Great-God figure arose to embrace him as the favorite Prince-God, the crowd shouted its delight.

Still holding one another, and at Tebika's stately pace, the two stepped from the stage, just as the sun finally set.

Two-thirds of the way there, in the last stretch of carowood forest before the hillside track up to Lathso's hut, M'nalo first heard the terrific tumult. An animal fight, he assumed, as from behind a thick stand of underbrush came fierce grunting and growling and ragged snorts and crashes. Hackles risen to the excitement so close at hand, he crouched low and hurried toward the commotion. He shoved aside the brush casually, confident that the racket he tracked covered his own noise.

Then he was stopped sharp by a closer sound, a whimper quite aside from the furious din ahead. The soft mewling drew him off his original trail. But a few steps on, he heard behind him a brief gasping cough that sent a tingle of fear over his skin. Danger! such a cough warned. He must flee, or die!

This time mischievous Eshu was his partner and had provided the carowood grove with numerous old trees with limber low-slung branches. Ten sprinting strides and a leap, he seized one such branch and clambered out of harm's slavering reach. More quick scrambling, and he was high up and away from the main trunk on a branch positioned for a good view over the gory battle.

In a roughly oval clearing some twenty paces across, a scruffy pack of wild dogs was at its deadly work, their constant yelps and birdlike cries at odds with the menace of attack. Some twenty of the mud-brown animals called to each other as they moved in on their prey. Yip! Yip! they coughed, their shifty, oversize bats' ears sampling subtle messages carried on the turbulent air.

Lean as bones, with an ugly cold-eyed ferocity all their own, they had surrounded a group of water boars. Despite a massive, tusked male among them, the squalling wild-pig family was overmatched and outnumbered. Half-growns, several sows, and the great powerful male bunched and milled in a tightening circle under the sidling dogs' continuous snapping raids.

From his swaying carowood perch, M'nalo followed their strategy. Most of the dogs harried the grouped boars with persistent attacks while others worked at distracting the dangerous male. Then a few larger dogs rushed a young pig, snatched it up and quickly dragged the squealer away.

Time and again, the boar lowered tusks and with a roar charged the pesky dogs. Often as not, he missed his scampering hounders. Each time he left his clan to fight, the wild-dogs moved in to nip unprotected young and females on their exposed flanks and soft underbellies, bloodying wherever their fangs bit. Then the dogs would hang on and tear open entrails to the victim's furious squealing. The frazzled boar would rush back to protect his gutted family, only to be baited away once more.

Campfire nights past, chilling to the terrific tales, M'nalo had heard the best hunters in the village sing stories of wild-dogs on the kill. How the packs were fearless like fire, the dogs' muscles tireless like water, and as invincible. How the fierce animals harried prey for days on end and wore it down until it dropped from plain exhaustion. Then they set upon and devoured it still alive. How like a blight of meat-eating locusts, they would consume any creature that walked the earth, sometimes even their own young. Still, despised and savage as they were, now witnessing their brutal efficiency, M'nalo could not restrain his admiration.

Sometimes the boar changed direction and charged. Once it caught and tossed a small dog high in the air. But as he succeeded there, farthest away from him, the pack charged a mature female, two dogs at her neck and several tugging at each leg. Quickly dragging down her resistance, they hustled her wretched bawling off into the underbrush.

As if it were a signal, the rest of the pack at once abandoned their distraction tactics and homed in to share the kills. As if ceding the sacrifice, the remaining female, the boar, and two youngsters fled the terrible scene.

Rare treat ended, M'nalo found himself panting and spent. Although he hadn't once thought of sex, he was rigid beneath his bulging shokono. He felt strangely peaceful. The immense thrill seemed more a private homage to his black àshe. So he whispered gratitude to his orisha that now he, too, had a story to brighten the campfire.

After a generous safety period, M'nalo eased himself down to the end of his branch until its downward arch hung him close to the ground. From there he dropped the short distance, landed on all fours. His keen nose now tickled to the iron scent of fresh blood and the cloying taint of new-turned dirt and rotting leaves. Awed feet gentle, he wandered the sacred ground until a sound of labored panting compelled his attention. He stopped still, listened. The sound didn't shift. So after a moment he followed it, and came upon a whimpering wild-dog. Small, not so long adult, it had mottled yellow flecks on a dirty brown coat. Just above the paw right front leg was broken, the blood streaked bone showing plain. On the right side of the chest, a shattered rib stuck through a bleeding gash. Quivering from pain, white-rimmed eyes steadily absorbing M'nalo, the dog lay there, defiant in appeal, vigorously alert, and dangerous.

Struck by admiration, M'nalo at once decided to carry it to Lathso, certainly a healer enough to save it. First, though, he needed to bind and disable the wounded creature from hurting him. He scouted around to find suitable saplings, pulled off strips of pliable bark—down only one side of the trunk so it would grow back. He broke dry branches, made a fork-stick to yoke the snarling animal while he bound it up. Then, balancing its tense, vibrating weight on a long pole over his shoulder, he bore it up to Lathso's shack.

The moon being right for planting, mornings found M'nalo, Izi, and all their friends contributing their effort to the village's food supply. Under the supervision of the older women, they swung hoes and forks and shovels at the hard soil, tilled peanut beds, added manure to pepper trees, and terraced bean vines. They rerouted irrigation drains, pulled weeds, dug holes for taro plants, prepared raised rows for seeds of millet and chickpeas and beans. They transplanted greens, buried cassava sticks and yam buds for the coming season. True, in these communal gardens, the watchful women did the actual planting but the boys and young men provided essential muscle.

M'nalo hadn't noticed his brother behind him until Izi said, "Do you consider it fair, my brother, how we never get to set seed in the ground?"

Hands tight on the handle of the straight-hoe paused at the top of his swing, M'nalo glanced at his brother.

With a broken cutlass, Izi was stabbing at the clumps of dirt M'nalo had upturned, crumbling them smaller. Just like his surly manner, Izi's cutlass swing was awkward, a waste of his effort.

"Planting's women's work!" replied M'nalo in one brusque exhalation, making it part of his downward swing. In the found rhythm of raising and plunging the heavy, iron-bladed hoe, he was loath to disturb his own contented mix of intimate thoughts and vigorous exercise with his brother's typical disgruntlement.

"Why? Why should work be named as man's or woman's?"

"Take it to the elders," said M'nalo in curt dismissal.

When he next looked around, Izi seemed to have taken the message and disappeared with his grumblings.

Private again, M'nalo worked to the heartbeat of pleasant anticipation. With the following day to himself, he was off to the deep river basins upstream where the ablest swimmers along with the elder women and young girls went to fish. He hoped tomorrow would dawn sunny and hot and, biggest wish of all, that Jureyi would keep her almost a promise.

Now, at the slow crescent-shaped basin with a long gravelly bank, the fishing had come to an end. All day the men—and

M'nalo, too—had dammed eddies and pools along the river. Then they pulled nets, trapped the flashing, excited bounty of four large baskets of slick fish and scrabbling prawns. The men returned to their other business, but M'nalo lazed in the shallows, watching as the women gutted the fish, and the girls spoke among themselves, deciding who would tell a story.

His mother sat near the older women, her hands busy cleaning fish. Most of the catch was silvery river carp, pure slipperiness in action. M'nalo had seen Koita at this chore many a time. Her movements were expert and efficient as she stuck her thumb through red gills into the gaping fine-toothed mouth and held the fish belly up. She then slipped a short blade into the fish's vent-hole and sliced upward, exposing the glistening insides. Another deft cut or two ridded the gills, and the gutted fish was tossed into a carrying basket.

Noticing that the girls had decided on their storyteller, M'nalo rose from the shallows and strode up the riverbank to squat on his heels, back against a tree trunk. To his extreme pleasure, it was Jureyi who started clapping hands, rocking her shoulders, snaking her head. When she felt her chosen rhythm, she began in singsong:

"There was a melancholy water-bird that sang…"

"No, no. Start with the girl," interrupted chubby Tanana.

Her sweet tones changed by annoyance, Jureyi said harshly, "Who's telling this story?"

"You, but you still have to start right."

"Well, I'll start it my way or I don't have to say anything at all," reminded Jureyi, anger pulling a quiver out of her.

With the authority that age allowed her, grandmother Abufemi cut in, "Hold off, Tanana. Give practice to keeping your mouth out of others' business. You forget how crocodile got its snout. You go on with the story, daughter."

Grandmother waggled a hand as if fanning a faltering fire, while Jureyi snorted satisfaction, cast a triumphant wink, and continued, "Well, as I was saying, there was a girl who loved nothing more than to go by the riverbank in the coolness of the sinking sun. There she would collect dry reeds.

"Now, an honorable one was this girl, and she was skilled at weaving, and she listened well to the elders, and was diligent at learning the secrets of her family line…"

"So she was perfect," interrupted Tanana. "Hurry up with the rest of the tale."

"…her intention," Jureyi went on as if she'd heard nothing, "was to design a new pattern that would render her heritage as far back as she knew it. So she was quite particular about the reeds she collected. That time of day, the riverside is always beautiful, and more so with the warm sun setting. But even on dripping rainy days the gloom can be beautiful, much as a sad story can…"

"Keep going on and on like this," Tanana broke in impatiently, "and they'll run out of fish to clean long before you run out of story to tell."

Narrowing fierce eyes at her heckler, Jureyi continued with deliberate slowness, "I was about to relate how on that evening, a strange energy…"

"What you talking about? What energy?"

Someone tittered high-pitched skepticism at this new turn of the oft-told tale.

"Well," Jureyi said quickly, "it was as if spirits were crawling under the skin of her arms and back and belly. And yet she felt calm, prepared for something she didn't know what. And right then, a bird called out teeooaaw-wwnnng! and the girl was amazed and moved at how precisely the notes of the water-bird's song matched the mood of the place. So marvelous was this that the young girl's soul was filled. And choking from feeling, she had to sit on the bank to reclaim her àshe from…"

"Okay, Jureyi," one of the elders called. "We'll hear the rest over the fire tonight. It's time to go."

"Ohhh." said Jureyi, flushing.

"Told you we'd run out of fish," Tanana sniped, earning a warning eye from the grandmother, Abufemi.

Motionless on his rump, mood sultry as the approaching dusk, M'nalo watched them ready themselves for the walk back to the village. The squabbling girls scrambled about the older women like chickens around their mother hens. Although, as they gathered up baskets and scarves and knives, more than once M'nalo's careful gaze caught Jureyi. Each time she held his glance for an extra moment, giving perfect lift to his heart. Then, with a fleet final glance, she was gone with the chattering, laughing others. Sunk in longing where he sat, to help contain the missing, M'nalo could only hug his knees to his chest.

In the quiet following their departure, Jureyi's unfinished story returned to him—the memory of the sweet bell-like river-bird call she sang thrilling in his every fiber. As he looked over the calm water, now shadowed in the setting sun, in his mind's eye he could see Jureyi's river-bird gliding over the water. He could hear its clear melancholy call, teeooaaw-wnnng!

And he knew that, awakened by the beauty of Jureyi's telling, this spot would forever contain the orisha of the story's river-bird.

Testing his hunter skills, M'nalo slipped around the last corner to the sorcerer's shack with the stealth of a slithering snake. So far so good. He had yet to rouse a single head from the rat burrows on the hill. Yes! Just another few steps...

A low growl spoiled all his efforts, as a pack of rat heads shot out to investigate. Hackles raised stiff, the mended but still scrawny wild-dog slunk up, gave a cautious sniff. Then, recognition satisfied, it skulked off just as furtively. Same time, the hut's door-hide flapped open and the sorcerer himself stepped into the yard. Under his left arm, he was carrying the teaching drum.

M'nalo brought his hands up, palms open, and bowed his respect. "Wise and generous elder, greetings from my father, my family, and myself," he declared. "My father wishes you continued vigor, and that many fine seasons pass before you continue your journey to join our esteemed ancestors."

Beneath bright, red-rimmed eyes, Lathso grinned his big white teeth. Free hand shaking denial, he muttered gruffly, "Now, now, leopard pup, let us leave the ancestors out of this. And don't join your father at stiffening my tailbone. So tell me. Did you slip past my watchdog?"

"No, Master. He's too wild and suspicious, was right away sniffing my heels. Though I wonder if he's so crafty at catching those hill rats."

Lathso laughed aloud. Then, his mouth slowly closing in a pensive downturn, big teeth worrying his bottom lip, he regarded M'nalo with sly, sizing eyes. He put the teaching drum aside on the ground, said slowly, "Listen to me, young Leopard. Already I have thrummed a special dance into your essences. Eshu, lord of àshe, will protect your journeys. No need for you to understand more, except that you must follow close to this idea of harmony. You must work toward falling in with the harmony of this surprising place the sixteen gods made. Imagine it as a rushing river, a great flow comprising seasons, and winds, and hills and humps of living things, all of them together creating a vast, intricate current. A complicated rush in which grains of sand and drops of water are as valuable as the touch of Eshu-Elegbara when he measures the heat in sunshine, the work in each woman's day, or the distance a man's life will travel. Think how all this essential business proceeds unseen, though not always unnoticed. There are those who study as, from time to time, uncommon balances shift. Some simple thing occurs—perhaps a boy-child is birthed before his time—and this is enough to interfere, to send smoothly paddled purposes spinning as driftwood in the flood, floating into unfamiliar channels where they cannot perform their intended functions. Their natures changed, they fall from proper courses, become fatal to whatever they encounter."

Foundering in the flood of obscure statements, M'nalo gave up and muttered, "Uncle, I cannot follow."

"Close your eyes and open your head, young sorcerer," said Lathso. "I am suggesting of a princely threat was born unscheduled. Come, M'nalo Fanta Bembo. Close your eyes now, and open your mind. Let me help you dream a better understanding of such an event."

Readily M'nalo shut his eyes, relaxed, and at once his seeking souls were witnessing...

... the babawalo departing his former home beyond the river's bend, slipping like a shadow into Tebika's zangala, into her sleeping room where she sits on a stool beside a weaving loom. Her youthful face is set stern. Her bare arms are plump.

Dirty and naked, but for his ragged boubou and the mischief in his smile, Lathso presents himself. "Great lady, here I am, servant to the serpent who steals darkness. No god's poet, no man's beast, the fool unwelcome at funeral and feast, I am your Lathso."

"Save your prattle for commoners," Tebika replies, abrupt and haughty. "You belong to no one but Lord Eshu, who consumes the will of his servants. I summon you because I have a task that needs your unique skills, and none must know of it."

His smile still sly, Lathso shrugs as he says, "With whom would an outcast such as I share privacies? And what might this special task be?"

Tebika glares, says firmly, "Though cast out from the Society, I know that your discretion is bound only by your vow, and I demand such a promise that you will respect my condition for secrecy."

Without yielding her eyes, Lathso slightly bows his head. "Royal princess, you have my word I will tell no one."

"Well then, poisoner," Tebika says, raising herself from the stool and passing her hands over her swollen belly, "I want my baby born this day."

"I understand, my lady," answers Lathso. "Many moons ago, when little Koita first found her belly, I prepared for this request..."

"Of gold, or cowries, or favors," Tebika interrupts, flat-voiced, "what payment do you wish?"

Lathso rubs his forehead, stares for a moment at his crusty feet, then declares, "My reward is your trust in me, and the success of our mutual enterprise. But now I must consult the holdings of my medicine cloak. Prepare yourself."

The sorcerer spins, crouches over his cloak, withdraws potions, and passes them to Tebika. She swallows without hesitation, lies down upon her bed. The sorcerer slinks away as midwives arrive to a labor in last stages.

They remark about Khufu's good fortune that so soon after Koita's delivery, the royal first wife, Tebika, has also birthed a small, but perfectly formed baby.

Every detail remained clear in his mind when M'nalo opened his eyes. Before him Lathso was standing and stretching, the joints in his back crackling with every contortion. Then the sorcerer reached down, gripped M'nalo's shoulder with a bony hand.

"So now you know how your brother was born from his mother's dream? Ah-ha, my confused apprentice, listen well. There is a practice you yet must learn if you wish to be more than a simple drum," he declared.

"There is a tried and proven system to employ when thinking around a matter, when seeking its hidden knowledge. You must practice at this. Study a confusion, a disorderly issue. Throw cool eyes upon it from many angles. Then step away, apart, and look again. Seek to divine for it some natural purpose. Because problem it might not be. I tell you true, young leopard, more than the mystery of dream travel, within this practice lies all magic. It is the true source of our sorcery."

With that, and a queer, long look at M'nalo, Lathso turned and went inside his hut.

From which departed a boy whose thoughts were fixed on rats, his brother's too-early birth, and a complicated harmony of rushing rivers.

As expected, it had come to this: M'nalo standing defiant before her. While well to his right, Izi Onamuli squatted down expectant. Though M'nalo's focus on the wall of Tebika's room did not waver, he could feel his brother's triumphant smirk burning the air between them.

M'nalo maintained an impassive face, and behind this mask his spirit remained undaunted. He heard his punishment approach from behind and readied himself. Ten strokes of the flexible Anya rod was twice as much as any previous whipping. Yet M'nalo was determined not to flinch. Tebika would never crack his resolve that if ever again Izi dared slander Koita's ancestry, he would once more bruise his brother and bruise him well. However smart, however subtle Izi might be, M'nalo was faster and stronger and learning to enjoy the vengeful power of superior might.

Smack! the rod shocked a flame into his buttocks at the top of their curve, then all through the meat of him.

Smack! it striped its fire right at his waist, but tolerable.

Hardened and ready, M'nalo scarcely felt the next stroke and an odd notion teased at his mind: The Princess Tebika was not being so fierce as usual. Her strokes were more deliberate than painful. They almost clung to his skin before the rod glided off.

Once more the anya rod fell, catching his buttocks at the high of their hump. Again the lash was only hard enough to suggest she was holding back her strongest blows. Intrigued, some perverse part of M'nalo's mind grew curious.

As right then, the next strike smarted in, back near the first spot and failing to persuade one way or the other.

His challenged umpiring essence nearly welcomed the whip when Smack! it swiped down again.

M'nalo now heard Izi rise and leave the room and a spark of triumph thrilled through him. "Too tough for little brother's stomach," the hard shell enclosing him gloated. He took a harsh breath, clenched up expectant. Instead, he heard her threshold's curtain shifting closed on its bamboo rings. The room dimmed and flickering shadows rose up in the yellow light of the single oil lamp behind him.

Then while he was so distracted, Tebika swung the rod—smack!—yet again.

A complicated lash, it suggested promise. And to his absolute surprise, all of his hard-rock muscles relaxed like a sigh as some spirit of gross might stormed hotly within his souls. Through a haze of instant confusion, M'nalo heard Tebika's soft exhalation. A sound of satisfaction as she struck him once more, smack!

From his scalp to his toes, fire shot all up and down the back of his body. A flame of intense pleasure, of flaring celebration, it was. Humbled by his surging blood, M'nalo dropped his gaze to the mound under his chokoto and moaned.

The rod still in her hand, Tebika glided in front of him. She raised M'nalo's chin with cool fingers, met his eye. "You are a man already, M'nalo Fanta Bembe. Much too much for a frail boy like my son. Don't you think?"

Unable to hold her steady gaze, M'nalo looked to the matted floor.

"Aren't you too strong for my Izi?" she murmured.

His eyes downcast, M'nalo could feel her examining him, scrutinizing his pulsing oko, his sweat, searching out his every embarrassment.

She drew closer. The crown of her shorn head reached his chin. Her mouth, his chest. As if thinking aloud, she said, "So what are we to do with such a powerful young man? My son's big bullying brother."

Tebika lightly touched his sweating belly with the rod.

An eruption of intricate emotions made M'nalo cry out, "No!" and pull his hips back, fearing she intended to strike. Yet for the zing of an instant, another of his selves wondered how it would be. Could he withstand? In moments of private passions past, he had assaulted himself dearly and had absorbed the damage.

Tebika took the rod away, then in a strangled voice commanded, "Close your eyes!"

He did and heard a shuffle and shifting.

Her clothes?

S m a c k! The rod stroked his tense belly somewhere between gentle and firm. His eyes fluttered confusion.

"Don't look." She guided his reaching hand, "Feel!"

He knew the touch of coolest yielding flesh—had to be her breasts—then an instant surrender to the forbidden. A craving to again draw out her pleasured gasp.

They now lay naked on the rough floor mats, M'nalo's eyes closed. He knew the rod had been abandoned when as if under great strain, Tebika heaved up a sigh and passed both palms down his chest. The gust from her mouth carried a coarse complex scent, green with life. She covered his mouth with wet salacious lips, licked his gums.

Hardly able to breathe because of a clutch in his throat, M'nalo opened his mouth and instantly, in slid her tongue. Long and slippery with wrongness, tapping into an awful power that welled deep within him. At which M'nalo gave in to all of it—to the swimming in his head, to the provocative slick of her damp skin hot on his. To her warm tongue seeking along his neck, his armpits, his navel, the crease of his buttocks. Finally, her body straddling his and all his straining force slipping in somewhere that suckled and soothed. Someplace delicate and smooth that moved with its own elusive grip, that milked away his mind.

Then from his marrow burst a mighty rushing stream that seemed to squirt all vitality out of him and leave his àshe swooning.

Still, from this happy state of tingling, absolute lassitude, M'nalo measured his new condition as nothing but Eshu's just though bittersweet punishment.

The boy shoved out into the night, Tebika wrapped a cotton cloth about her nakedness: She felt vulnerable otherwise. Her mood still triumphant, she picked up the anya rod. With both hands, she flexed it until the ends met, then released her left grip. She smirked at the swishing sound and placed the whip crosswise under her sleeping mat. Then she took a thoughtful seat on her weaving stool.

Above her devious head in her zangala's thatch, house lizards hunted buzzing night insects. A curious red-eyed fruit bat flitted about purposefully.

When she had her plan sorted out, she rose and stole from her plotting stool, headed for the slave quarters. She needed a trusty messenger.

Not much later, waiting in the darkness, Tebika heard a special tapping at the closed window of her weaving room. In a breath she was there to whisper her message: "The harvest is ripe for the reaper."

So softly she spoke, only a lurking bat would have heard.

It seemed he had been buffeted all the long night, sleepless as he tossed between one horrible imagining and another. How extreme might Tebika react? How would the elders punish his act of taboo? The shame on his family. And Jureyi, the disdain she'd have for him. Round and round his brain, all these black anxieties flapped and blundered, made confusion, tormented and terrified him. Until at last his anguish exhausted his battered souls and he fell unconscious into sleep...

...and right away M'nalo heard the drumbeats of his master call...

Certain that the master sorcerer would know without telling, when M'nalo reached the shack early next day he offered no details of the dilemma that oppressed him, only that it had been sexual and reckless.

Lathso's manner was benign. "It was your own souls' anxiety that summoned you to me," he said.

M'nalo looked to the ground glumly and shook his head.

"Now you hang your thinking head," said Lathso. "Too late. Too late, is what I say. The head of an oko is mindless. Its eye knows only how to weep." His tone was light and he gave a self-appreciative chuckle as he continued, "When you eat hot pepper, recall the pleasant tang in your mouth and not the sting in your bottom-hole later."

In similar manner, the sorcerer offered more such foolish comfort, which gradually worked a shift in M'nalo's mood and lightened the enormity of his trespass. Over the following nights that saw the round moon grow thin to a blade, M'nalo's spirits gradually slipped back into his body, returned him to his normal nonchalance.

High in the dawn sky, a sliver of moon lingered to greet his rush to the pepper patch. "Moon runs, but Sun will catch her," he observed to himself, echoing Lathso self-consciously as he arched his hips forward and every muscle morning-slack, spewed forth his first. He was concentrating to direct his stream center of the hole amidst the dark green leaves when strangers surprised up out of the new-morn chill. Helpless to his business, M'nalo could only watch as the three lean men burst around the curve of the cliff and onto the track to Lathso's hut.

Assured, supple fellows who had M'nalo thinking of vipers, they showed amused smiles. But for long, thick, charcoal-colored braids hanging down the back of their necks, and flecked with entwined gold and silver threads, their shiny pates were shaved. A sheathed cutlass hung at each waist and in large competent hands, each man lightly bore a sturdy shoulder-high staff.

Out of nowhere, Ajo, the wild dog, all hackles and growls, charged up to challenge the men.

With a move so swift M'nalo didn't quite follow it, the leading man swung his staff and sent the dog high over the cliff's edge to fall yowling the long way down. Then, before M'nalo could even manage to stanch his stream, the strangers were upon him.

No other threat in hand, M'nalo pointed his fading flow at them, forcing the ruthless leader to leap away out of spray range.

His companions to burst into guffaws.

M'nalo hurriedly fitted himself back into his chokoto, raised his hands to a defensive fighting pose.

At which the lighter-colored of the three called out in words unknown to M'nalo, which somehow encouraged the leader to lower his threatening staff and shrug in seeming agreement.

Baring a file-toothed smile, the dirt-colored man warily approached M'nalo. Palm forward, fingers fanning the air, he stuck his free hand out, and in perfect Twi said, "My companions offer greetings, young traveler."

Confused by this sudden change in demeanor and distracted by the reference to himself as "traveler," M'nalo relaxed his aggressive stance, began a bow of formal obeisance. When without warning, the fellow swung his staff and thunked M'nalo just over his temple, spinning the world away in peals of the assassin's laughter...

...as a furious flapping suddenly whooshed down from the silvery sky...

...bright brown eyes just like Lathso's beamed amusement and a great shrieking night-black eagle with red wingtips sailed across M'nalo's soupy view...

...as with shouts of consternation, the tail-headed assassins rushed toward the ramshackle hut...

...but M'nalo could no longer keep his eyes open to this dizzy, whirlpool world...

Too late, his essences returned, bearing the full weight of an elephant's sore head. A load so heavy, it staggered M'nalo as he struggled to his feet and tottered towards the hut. There, he braced his back against the rough wall and soothed his painful head with clammy hands until it felt responsible enough to manage the jarring of his most careful footsteps.

Only then M'nalo groped at his master's door-flap and looked in.

The hut was empty. No signs of the sorcerer. No signs of assassins. M'nalo's heart sank when he saw Lathso's staff cast aside on the floor, the teaching drum broken open. But no sooner plummeted, his spirits soared again: The hook where the sorcerer hung his cloak was unoccupied. Never would Lathso's captors have allowed him his medicine cloak and all of the dangerous magic it hid. Never, if Lathso had any power whatsoever, would he have left it behind.

Clearly the old sorcerer remained in charge of his own welfare.

Heartened by this conclusion, M'nalo started for the trickle at the cliff's wall to bathe his sore head when all at once, he remembered last night. After dinner, Lathso's eyes had gone vague and distant, and he had begun speaking dire predictions—all about invasion and wildfire and spilled blood and heart pain. And now this morning.

Alarm spiked through him and stopping only to fill his water-pouch, grim and anxious, M'nalo set off for his father's settlement.

His nose was abused by the funk of urine-doused campfires in the bushes alongside the broad path. Then came faint explosions that could only be musket fire. Then he discerned a new tang to the smoke that hung faintly in the air, different from that of burning fields. His anxious belly grumbling with tremble and cramp and knowing that it was much too late for alerts, M'nalo hurried homeward at a steady trot.

At the edge of the settlement, near the guava patch and burial grounds, his hunter's instincts urged caution, bade him climb up the slower aerial route that he and Izi Onamuli used for trailing monkeys.

He clambered along up there and not until he had slunk down to a low enough perch in the great baobab that shaded his home did M'nalo, breath ragged with anticipated dread, look down. He didn't see much directly beneath: the back of his father's zangala, the thatched domes of his family compound bespotted with baobab fruit, a curved section of the village thoroughfare. No one in the yard, though. No parents, no servants or slaves, no Izi Onamuli.

M'nalo clung to the thick branch, his heart pounding with queries and complications, while from beneath him rose continuous sounds of turmoil. Beast-like screams and howling. Cracks of lashes. Hollow smacks of clubs on sweaty flesh. Hoarsely shouted commands. The noises of a slave raid in progress.

Hanging there helpless above the scene, from time to time M'nalo cried out. In desperation, he punched the gnarled tree trunk with tight fists that welcomed the thuds of pain.

Moving about, shifting his perch, for moments at a time he could watch the slavers do their work. Dozens of them were being busy. He recognized several Lufembe warriors, some keeping a coffle of men in line. Others of the gang were raiding compounds, tugging out their screaming spoils—older boys, young men and women.

He glimpsed "Dik-Dik" being hobbled, her bearing docile, her eyes wild like a trapped antelope of her nickname. A pang of sympathy seized him. He saw tag-along Enweke in a pointless struggle to pull himself away from his captors. Same as was Cece Ubaddo's robust second wife. Off to the right, herded against the walls of their compound, was a group that included two daughters and a son of Zizi Ado, his father's good friend. The two oldest boys of Talla, troublemaker of the council, were also there.

A straggle of villagers—toddlers too young, youngsters too gangly or crippled for the slave market—trailed the brutish confusion. Crowded close to each other, they followed as if stupefied. They stopped when and where the raiders did and looked on mindlessly. As if the violence about them had dulled everything quick in them. Each time the jackals emerged triumphant bearing another writhing relative or neighbor, the watchful group would whimper and huddle a little tighter.

Then, in a flicker, M'nalo's ranging eyes caught sight of a single black braid hanging down a familiar slope of neck. A queer pinch of hope stung within him. Then, as quick as it was sighted, the braid was lost in the tumult.

He squinted and shifted, adjusting his view through the leaves and branches. He saw a guard of jittery rifles keeping people in their places, but no one like his mother. He saw slavers busy attaching rope hobbles to captives. But no more of his mother or her braid.

Off to his right, some distance from the main party, a small raiding group was making personal claim to certain female prizes. Chubby Tanana was being dragged along, her scraped skin leaving a trail of blood.

Close behind, screaming that she'd rather kill herself, came her distraught mother. Slashing her knife futilely, she was beaten down by raiders, which set off a whole other commotion.

Then M'nalo saw the single black braid again!

Now he was sickened by the sight as an understanding denied but moments earlier was made again plain. Around the familiar slope of his mother's neck, a metal collar now shone!

The meanings of that shiny collar made his world twist into a dizzy sway. Caught in a fugue, he clung to the branch on which he crouched. The fact of his enslaved mother chastised his souls. Faint with despair, his stomach heaved up bile. He held tight to the branch, closed his eyes. All while the noises of the slave-raiders' grim business continued below. All while—this one fit, that one lucky—the roar and rage of selection continued through the village.

Like an ant in gum-seep, M'nalo hung stagnant on his perch. His only movement was the occasional pummeling of the hard bark. Rough penance for his fixedness while all that he knew was savaged. Lashed by swells of despair and shame, his three essences washed away into a strange stillness. He might have howled his agony to the all-seeing concealing leaves, but who'd have heard him above the riot? Blood might have flowed from his raw torn fists. But surely the bark would have absorbed the seep and not one red tear would have dropped on the violence below.

Vague time had passed into ominous quiet when M'nalo at last roused from his stupor, mind already set on following the marauders. First, he climbed toward the crown of the baobab for a view of the surrounding country. There, from the sun's brightness, he judged it was long after midday. Uncertain of how much lead he had allowed the raiders, he set off. He was mindful to rein in any hastiness, though, for at the height he traveled, mistakes were merciless. Back down on the forest track, he would make better time. Until then, steadily reaching with hands and feet, he moved across the treetop trail as did the silent, watchful monkeys.

Doggedly following their trail, M'nalo was halfway across the shallows before he saw the ravagers—several of them surprising up out of the brush on the far bank as if waiting for him. He looked back and saw a greater number behind him entering the river. No doubt! He had strayed into an ambush. Right away, with a heaving intake of breath, he dove under and away, pulled himself powerfully into deeper water.

Staying close to the bottom as he could, he stroked silently toward the overhanging bamboo stools abundant along the riverbank. In particular, he aimed for a recent discovery. This season's floods had carved an airspace among the bamboo's underwater roots. The bell-shaped hollow there with its pocket of musty air was a perfect hiding place.

Close enough to his goal, he ran out of air and rose cautiously to the surface. Slippery bamboo roots slid past as his face broke into air. He breathed in slowly, blinked his eyes clear and observed the pursuit.

The slavers' confusion floated over the deep water where they had faltered some thirty paces distant. M'nalo could scarcely stifle a giggle—part amusement, part anxiety—on seeing them. One spear wielder was in up to his shoulders. Others stood waist-deep sending baffled looks first towards the mass of roots where M'nalo hid then over to their left.

M'nalo followed their glances and his satisfied grin fell into an awed gasp. Silhouetted against the burning sky, a horseman gracefully spun his mount about and rode out of view. The rider was a mustached, golden-skinned fellow wearing a many-colored turban. A man poised straight-backed in loose tan and white robes that floated down to the glossy flanks of his impressive black horse. He was clearly the master of the ruthless marauders.

A rash of fright chilled M'nalo more than the water. With a deep breath, he dove quietly down to his safe spot under the bole of the bamboo stool. Unable to discern anything in the dim, clammy space, he closed his eyes. Waited for the human hyenas to give him up as drowned.

All the while, the image of the beautifully clothed horseman and his splendid mount remained ablaze in his mind.

After time long enough, then longer still, M'nalo slid out into open water. All was quiet; no sound or sign of the slavers. Head hardly breaking the rippled surface, he swam toward the bank like a tracking dog, crawled on hands and knees through the mud at the river's edge. He lay there on his belly, took a patient look around. Still no one. They must indeed have left him for dead or decided that lingering was a waste of their trouble. Still wary, he rose to a crouch, cautioned himself against losing concentration and resumed his chase at a slow trot.

Right into the trap. Some fifty strides along, one instant M'nalo heard a growing thunder behind him. Next, he looked back as fast as an eagle the robed man on his midnight horse swooped down on him, nearly knocking him over first try. Only an instinctive leap and rolling fall saved him from the hooves. Rising to his feet in the same motion, M'nalo sprinted back towards the river but the horse thundered past and cut him off.

All the while, the golden-skinned rider laughed. The horse, too, seemed to be playing. It pranced and snorted, danced this way and that, daring M'nalo—serval to a mouse—to dodge and escape its superior agility.

Dodge he did, feinting one way, rushing another. Back and forth horse and rider maneuvered, easily blocking M'nalo's every move. Then with a taunting peal of laughter, the horseman urged his mount in. With a swing of its sweaty, muscular neck, it struck M'nalo as he braced his arms before his chest, and knocked to the ground.

Helpless, he lay looking up at the quivering underbelly of the powerful animal. Great hooves that could crush his head pawed threat a pace away. M'nalo rolled himself up in the dust, a tight knot of defiance, his souls crazed and humiliated. Faster and faster, his passion drummed to the quick of his pride. And caging his rage, he vowed one day to strike against the beautiful black beast. Swore on his essences to make mite of his captors' high-necked mastery.

Chapter Two
SLAVERY and SAFETY

Roughed and hustled in among the other captives, who were paused not far beyond the river, M'nalo eyed about, tried to make sense of the scene. After conferring with the slavers, the lordly Arab rode away accompanied by two horsed soldiers leaving the caravan in the charge of a small, bossy fellow. This man issued curt orders in a language with sounds reminiscent of a certain Arab who'd traded with Khufu at the great Ugun river marketplace. The thought of his father knifed through M'nalo's souls: most likely the worst had befallen Khufu!

M'nalo cast a futile, searching glance around. Meanwhile, quick with whip, rough at rein, the lieutenant head-slaver turned his horse about, impatient with everything. His dozen or so donkey-mounted men were swift to his bidding, separating the female captives from the young men, loading them onto mule-drawn carts. Squint and peer as he might, though many of the stunned and sweat-streaked faces he glimpsed were familiar, M'nalo could not find among them the two that he most sought, his mother and Jureyi. This gave him relief and equally tormenting uncertainty as the carts swiftly rolled away.

M'nalo, perhaps because he stood tallest, was coffled last in a line of ten. He knew most of his fellow captives, though none were among his close-held friends or family. Each fellow was tethered two paces from the one before by a thin brass chain fastened to a loose metal collar around his neck. Each had his wrists tied close to his waist, but not tight, with a belt of new rope. Waiting while two other similar lines were assembled, M'nalo rope-burned his arms each time he reached to slap away the buzzing, biting flies and gnats feasting at his eyes and lips. His fellow prisoners squealed complaints into the humid air, sounding more like pigs than men. He wished they would bear their plight with better dignity and grant the raiders less satisfaction. At last, with shouting and threats and, here and there, the hiss of a convincing lash, the caravan moved on.

To cope with his own discomforts, M'nalo strove for a defiant mien. He narrowed stubborn eyes, focused on the feet shuffling the forest trail before him. He resisted even a glance at the stolid captors. Neither did he turn eyes to the red sun weeping over his left shoulder, nor watch it burn violet, then black as his dispirited àshe. As the solid mountains slipped into the vast night, he would not look back at a life disappearing with every hobbled stride.

Past the fact of the settlement being raided, there were so much he wanted to know. What had happened to his family? To second wife, Ammaa, and sisters Ezene and Mesphi? Did they have time to flee into the forest? And what of Izi Onamuli and his mother? Somehow M'nalo couldn't conceive of them being captured. Surely the Princess Tebika was too canny for that.

This line of thinking was so upsetting, M'nalo tried to empty his mind of anything responsible. He just trudged along, eyes fast on the feet before him, repeating their commonplace action, soothing his worries. Heel doing a smooth roll along to the flat sole, then toes spreading as they pushed the foot forward into another step. The spring off the thick pad beneath the big toe, right then left. Again right, and left. One ahead of the other in simple order, again and yet again. Roll and spring, heel to sole to toe, right, and left, pushing on, carrying their captive bodies step by step by further step away from all they called home.

"Aahhh! Stop this muddling, son of Khufu Bembo Dan, apprentice to the master sorcerer, Lathso. Use this plodding time to craft a plan!" a voice within him urged.

Yet it seemed the best strategy was to avoid special notice, hide passive amidst the others, be patient and alert. So M'nalo tamped down the nagging to act against his circumstances. He let his mind return to irrelevancies: How long would his footprints remain in the soft loam of the scrublands they now hustled over? And if they continued north, would they not be soon in desert sands? What then would be his footprints' fate?

With such distractions scattering through his mind like bats in an evening cave, M'nalo hobbled through the quick-settling dusk. But as real night stifled the broad trail in blackness, growing weariness undermined his brave resolve, and he yearned for a close campsite.

The captives' fatigue was no factor in the guards' plans, it seemed. Some strict rendezvous to keep, they roped their mounts to each of the three coffles and pulled the captives along at a punishing scurry. Then someone in the line next to M'nalo slipped into an unseen crater in the trail, causing several of the men and boys to trip and fall one over another. Which stopped the passel altogether, provoked the guards to try the rough persuasions of their nipping whips and thumping cudgels.

Then their quick-tempered leader decided it was too dark to continue. They halted, set up camp for that night.

The days trekked by, exhausting and monotonous. The landscape changed as gradually. Densely overgrown bush-lands gave way to a high-forested expanse of slow, punishing rises. Then came a tract of packed, dusty soil, bare but for an occasional stand of a thin-leafed prickly grass, clearly the threshold of deserts to the north.

One evening, shortly after their arrival at what seemed to be a rendezvous camp, two captors approached and separated M'nalo from his group. They led him past a crescent of six large tents pegged down by ropes into the hard sand, past three or more smaller low tents within the crescent's curve, and into the one most set apart, not far from a tether of horses. Oddly solicitous, they loosened M'nalo's coffle so his arms were freer, directed him to sit on a mat then left him to himself and the passing time growing dark. Wondering what was to happen, despite himself, he gradually relaxed, idly watched the wind tussle with the tent walls.

A sudden brightening of his consciousness, hairs risen all over his skin, aroused him. Had he dozed? His widened eyes were useless in the dark. There was no sound, or movement, or scent—just a feeling that the dark space was besieged by some menacing presence. He squeezed shut his eyes, carefully turned his head a slow semicircle, but could glean no further understanding.

To mislead the stealthy invader, M'nalo slackened his muscles, lay limp as if dead. Let himself crumple into the warp and weft of the carpet, cool and gritty under his bare body. Then, perfectly quiet, he waited. The threat, too, remained lurking, as if patient for his pose to falter.

Countering stealth with stealth, M'nalo burrowed deeper into himself. As his master had taught, he strove to separate his mind from the situation, shift his focus to other matters. To amusing puzzles. To natural mysteries like eggs and lodestones. To the low-pitched buzzing of a moonlit night.

A growing urge to scratch the tickle in his nose intruded. He concentrated on creating a countermanding itch in his big toe, and teased this against the floor. Then, trying to imagine how such an itch would sound, he came up with a chac-chac's scratch, which somehow returned him to the magical music the night he was given the doubled scars on his cheeks. The marks of his allegiance to the Leopard society of sorcerers...

...an imperceptible transition, and his spirit was traveling back there, back again in that special glowing darkness.

Beguiled by a breeze's seduction, once more his skin tingled with every cool thrill of the bushy trail's leaves.

Dazed by the notion that miracles were just out of reach, he walked his fellows' footsteps, a dreamer edging close to magic.

Blood rushing, heart thumping, he was again among the driving drums, the blazing fire gilding his sweaty skin, the conversations between the music in his mind and the music in the night.

Then he was with different spirit, a powerful friendly one taking him along to a certain Anya grove with a particular shrine. And his soul was returned to the scene of Tebika conspiring with Izi Onamuli to feed his navel string to the anthills...

M'nalo startled back to awareness, trembling with a sense of profound betrayal. Some hateful action was being practiced against him. Its details remained half-hidden in the dreamy spirit realm. Yet somehow he knew the challenge was contemptible and involved his brother's treachery.

The urge for vengeance tripped as there came from the dark a small fluttery sound, a gentle sigh surrendered. Or maybe the rasp of a tent flap against the dirt floor.

Another coil of time wound away. Clouds of wind lashed by. Then, without any obvious indication, M'nalo knew with certainty that the peril was past.

Still wary of traps he might relax into, M'nalo hefted the prospects of threat, worked at maintaining his stillness, and listened beyond the wind outside for some lethal rustle. He resisted the urge to flex his left arm, whose muscles now dreamt of being wood. His left thigh and buttock were tingling toward a similar state. Then of its own volition, his numb arm flopped to the ground.

M'nalo gasped apprehension and waited.

No response from the darkness. So he relaxed, began to rub feeling back into his muscles, wondered what had been his company. Until, the rising wind outside as lullaby, sleep crept up and claimed him.

First there came a soft scraping, then the tent flaps were drawn aside and as M'nalo blinked at the sudden brilliance, someone entered. He scrambled up from his mat, stood squinting while shadow stole shape from the light outside—a small figure in a black turban, the bossy, in-charge fellow, the one who'd driven them so hard for days past.

Shoulder-height to M'nalo, he wore a loose indigo khanga long to the ankles of slender bare feet. His leather vest, embroidered with silver patterns and clasps, hung open, revealing skimpy strands of hair on a smooth chest. His pale face was top-heavy with a single black eyebrow, a thick line above intense brown eyes and a small nose. He had a sparse moustache over narrow lips set in a taunting smirk revealing gleaming, pointy rodent's teeth. How strange it seemed to M'nalo. Big strong he being trussed up helpless by one so unimpressive.

A tremor in his heart, M'nalo lowered his head. Deference, he figured, might disarm the prettily garbed young rider.

In and out of M'nalo's vision, the serious fellow strutted back and forth, appraising him. Then with husky urgency, he broke the silence with a spate of words. A quick switch to Dioula startled M'nalo into an upward flick of his eyes.

Seeing it, the young man continued, a jerky rhythm to his delivery, "No need for you to pretend. Your companions from the village converse in this tongue as they do in Fon and several other dialects. So perhaps you choose your silence," the man cocked his head one-side like a lizard "Or maybe you are a stubborn one. Whichever djinn possesses you, thank her and humble yourself to her grace. How lucky you are. But for her, you might be out there, naked to unfriendly elements like the rest of them. Yet here you are, sheltered from the sandblast, significant in the mind of our sahib. Here you are, soon to be generously fed and freed from your tether."

Although he was still collared and tied, M'nalo realized, his arms were indeed hanging even more freely than the night before. His wrists tethered more loosely to his waist. He could raise his hands as far as his head. When had this happened? Had he slept that soundly?

The Arab eyed with amusement as M'nalo discovered his modified restraints. Smug authority edging every word, he continued, "Sahib Medeni, my master, has commanded me to study you thoroughly. Provide a full description of our captive's abilities. Report on his intellectual and physical…" his glance lingered meaningfully on M'nalo's chest and thighs, his oversize feet "…potential."

He drew a finger across his upper lip and its wisp of a moustache, offered a squirrel's smile. "My master estimates that you have enjoyed breath for perhaps seventeen, even nineteen years. He spoke of how ably you swam the river. That is a valuable prowess. A swimmer can have a good life in Tripoli, a splendid swimmer such as you are. Such a graceful body. 'Hardy sinews on a beautiful frame,' my master described you perfectly. Ahh! We nurture grand plans for you, the master and I.

"But he worries about the hatred he found in your gaze, your fury when taken. I would prefer to inform my master that you have adjusted. I would prefer to report that when I came to look into your eyes I met a silent, beautiful calm. A mystery I am pleased to encounter. I would prefer to say, 'A priceless soul, this village stalwart.'"

The young man stepped close and grasped M'nalo's chin, shifted his face side to side. "And what a mouth," he declared. "Lips full-fleshed without weightiness. An appealing bow of wide defiance. I will enjoy describing such a mouth." He cast a strange, intent glance that tangled M'nalo's essences in a knot of complicated concerns.

The fellow clapped his hands, a sting of sound. Instantly a guard was at the opened flap. With a grunt of acknowledgment, he deposited a basket in the tent and left.

Turban nodding, eyes glowing, the Arab indicated the basket. "See," he said, "decent, filling food. Wholesome milk for strength. After this storm we have far to travel and you will bring a poor profit if your body is worn down from our journey. So, open the basket. Eat hearty."

To M'nalo, caution blurred by hunger, such insistence was superfluous. Without hesitation or regard for his smiling observer, he snatched up a bowl that proved to contain foofoo mash mixed with milk of a tongue-twisting flavor. Quickly finished, he gobbled down some dried nuts, then a bowlful of dates plumped by their own sweet sauce.

Seemed only moments later that he crumpled to the pallet and was lost in the vastness of a most unnatural rest...

...he's been poised so long in this swirling dive, yet cannot recall leaping from the riverbank, or arcing through the air, or slipping into this warm and fluid glide...

...a glistening black wetness welcomes him down, down, without effort, downward to its slippery bottom...

...he's been so long at this daunting plunge, fish flutter up and slide intimate against his skin, exploring armpit, buttocks, every fleshy crease, tantalizing and reminding, as his oko rises, that this watery cavern is a bed...

...he's been so long down inside these private places, indignant river spirits use their long grass tresses to assault his chafing maleness...

...he's been in this whirl too long, too long, yet apathy holds him captive, and raspy hands reassure that he can survive one sultry moment more...

...then comes a howling instant and his àshe escapes into a hollow blankness...

Darkness again reigned over the rattle of fierce-blown sand when, his tongue feeling shrunken and furry, M'nalo awoke. Immediately he was aware that his oko was sensitive and sore. He reached for it with tender hand, adjusting to the tug of his restraints, and attempted to relieve his distressed member. He tried to recall the dream that Night had used to ravage him. But his memory offered only vague impressions involving demanding hands.

Although, even now, some perverse pleasure from these dream traces summoned a chafing thrill. This was shrunk instantly by a thought that these hands of his dreams were callused and familiar. Hands roughened, perhaps, from pulling reins and wielding whips. M'nalo's speculations flooded him with humiliating doubts. He shied from the question in his mind: Had the intense young Arab fellow misused him?

M'nalo reached a hand to his buttocks, passed tentative fingers over intimate areas. Found no soreness. Relaxing, he mulled over the substance of his original impressions, the shards of his recollected dreams, and finally persuaded himself that his misgivings had no cause. He returned to his soothing ministrations, marveling at how a dream could have so bruised his oko and the soreness notwithstanding, dared himself a return visit.

Next day the storm continued unabated and as dusk fell, another food-laden basket was brought and offered by the smiling Arab. This time, suspicious, M'nalo ate only what he recognized— the dates, the goat milk—and managed to crumble and conceal much of the rest here and there, under his mat, behind a pillow. Then drooping his lids almost closed, he let himself fall back on his mat in a pretense of deep sleep.

No sooner had M'nalo flopped down than, with a keening murmur, his young watcher attacked. Large eyes aglow, he knelt by M'nalo's feet, began licking and sucking between the crusty toes. Then, moving upward, he crouched over M'nalo's slack form, delicately unwrapped his chokoto.

Fury suffused M'nalo's head as he realized that his body recognized these caresses. That his suspicions had indeed been well-founded. He shivered revulsion but held himself stone-still—the Arab wasn't yet best positioned. Then last thing M'nalo expected, his oko began responding to the lascivious attention.

Different, yet provokingly similar, one other had done as this fellow was doing. Same way humbled herself and sucked and licked all over M'nalo's body. Same way persuaded his oko to rise unbidden and collapse his three essences into an unbearable tension at his crotch. A straining trapped there until a splendid surge of fluid flame escaped and cooled him to the sweetest submission.

The hard hands were caressing all the same way as that other un-nameable one. This man-boy now lapped a fluttering tongue up M'nalo's belly. Then onto a nipple, tingling both to hardness.

M'nalo raised his eyelids ever so slightly, peeking. Eyes glistening behind dark lashes, the Arab slavered up to M'nalo's smooth chin, snaked his tongue onto M'nalo's slack mouth. Just as M'nalo caught his narrow neck in a vengeful grip.

Powered by rage and disgust, his hunter's hands closed viciously and squeezed and shook. Held long and strong through desperate jerks and spasms and stifled gurgles as the small body wrenched itself about, its own hands snatching feebly, blunt nails scratching at the crushing fingers clasped round its throat.

But all the Arab's struggles might have been like feathers beating against M'nalo, the stone. He struggled the flailing body down, knelt over it with better force as his merciless hands increased their effort until the fellow's body lay slack. A passive weight with startled eyes that stared into that other place.

Only when he released his grip did M'nalo notice the hair. In all the violence the Arab's turban had fallen off, spilling a flood of long black tresses. A mass of perfumed waves filling the close, dim space with an unsubtly feminine cinnamon scent.

Breathing deep gulps through his mouth, M'nalo tied up his chokoto, listening for signs of threat from outside. For the moment, nothing but the whistling storm sounded.

The dead rider's dainty dagger was sharp enough to cut through all of M'nalo's bonds, all save the brass collar around his neck. As he freed himself, he scanned the tent for useful items, clothes, another weapon. Nothing but the food basket and the fellow's turban, loose on the ground. M'nalo snatched it up and draped it around his shoulders, glancing once more at the body. Curiosity prodding, he tugged open the embroidered vest to discover a bulged flatness of breasts with pronounced, female nipples.

M'nalo shook his head with true wonder. Too late to matter, he thought, and hastily wrapped the turban about his face in anticipation of the blowing sand. He unbound the tent's flap, reached a foot outside. A single step, though, told him that the blow was fierce enough to rasp away his exposed skin and that, but for the turban at his face, he was essentially naked.

Ducking back inside the tent, he decided the boy-girl's trousers would do and set to stripping the corpse. As he did so, with a quaver M'nalo saw that his victim was indeed female. As if concerned about further damage, he handled the body gently. Pulled off the loose trousers, gave them a shake and slipped them on. Next, he chose the thinnest sheet of his bedding, wrapped that about his shoulders.

Then he shifted the tent's flap, again poked his wary head out. Again he found only the gusting wind there, into which he cautiously stepped. Better shielded from the blast, but without a plan, he paused. A horse whinnied close by. All at once, M'nalo's heart began a mighty drumming. Vengeful messages rushed between his blood and mind. Demanded that the sorcerer's credo be his course: Bruise for bruise. Man and horse alike. Bruise them as they did him. Until that was done, there could be no other plan.

This way then that, battling the wind and swift-blown sand, he skulked about seeking. Then from his right came an animal's soft snuffling. A suppressed snort?

Wrapping a loose end of the turban around his left hand, M'nalo raised it as a shield against the stinging sand and crept toward the sound. Squinting through the cloth, he came upon an animal standing quiet, hindquarters to the wind. A horse, its color obscured by the sand-filled gloom, a heavy sack shielding its head.

Daunted by the size of the animal and still without precise strategy, M'nalo paused. But as if sensing wickedness close, the horse snorted and reared up on its hind legs. The startle focused M'nalo. He freed his left hand and wrapped the protecting cloth about his head, knotting it tight behind. Grasping the slight dagger in his right hand, he commenced a slow prowl close around the horse. Twice, three times he circled, yet no susceptible spot presented itself. All he sensed was the force waiting to erupt beneath the smooth hide.

Once more the horse reared up, stood there a moment, shuddering assurance, then came down and stood quiet.

As the horse raised up, though, M'nalo had glimpsed its maleness. This jolted a memory of how the black stallion had knocked him down and stood above him, exposing its barrel belly and slack balls. Now he edged closer, dared his hands to smooth along the animal's rough, vibrating hide. He reached tentatively underneath to the cleft of belly muscles where it joined the thighs. Then with his left hand, and ever so tenderly, M'nalo cupped the warm yield of the stallion's virility. He paused, and at the animal's momentary flinch, gave a reassuring grunt. He hefted the warm mass as his fingers located tissues holding them to the horse's underbelly. He positioned himself appropriately, then with a firm, swift strike slashed the dainty blade deep, and sprang back.

Just as a furious gust of wind caught and catapulted him away. Just as the animal's hideous screams summoned an immediate commotion from the storm-lashed camp.

He had not accounted for the force of the sandstorm, nor how quickly the gale would cast him stumbling along, blinded and helpless to its raging currents while fine grains sieved through the fabric wrapped about his face, and whiffed up into his nostrils, and seeped through his gasping mouth, and choked down into his throat so that he could not control the coughing spasms that provoked even more desperate gasps of gritty suffocating breaths. After an endless time, unable to endure the punishment of breathing a moment longer, he crumpled to the ground...

...his àshe was mellowing into glazed comfort when a parrot, char-black with a scarlet streak down its back, fluttered down, lighted beside him and commenced an elaborate folding and unfolding of its stubby wings. Job finally done to satisfaction, the fastidious bird cocked its head, gave M'nalo an imperious look. "Well," it squawked, "is this what has become of you? A convenience for vultures?"

...the tone, so true to his testy master, sparked defiance within the nearly insensible M'nalo. A perky part of him shrugged reply. "What option do I have?"

...the parrot slowly raised a foot, extended its crusty middle claw, and scratched its still-cocked topnotch. "Obvious to me," it said, adding after a moment, "If a body knows how." Then it gave a hoarse cackle that bore not a tinge of amusement.

...the cheeky spirit within M'nalo piped, "Ah! You are so generous, master flyer. Dare you make this body your student?"

...the scarlet-striped creature turned full circle once, then again. With each revolution it flared its tail feathers and bared its pink wrinkly bottom to M'nalo's face. Then it regarded him, chuckling like a fat-bellied man. "Your wit seems returned enough for you to attempt such shallow flattery. Maybe I again will teach a fool how to be a fowl."

...then the parrot began to speak, quick sharp words, percussive as drumbeats, blurring into M'nalo's mind: He must consider this. Give in to that. Abandon ordinary presumptions. Approach his situation *as a sorcerer would. All of the notions weaving into an undeniable harmony of purpose so clear he wondered how he'd never seen it before...*

...and as he surrendered to the knowledge, M'nalo found the blast to have lost its spite. The airborne sand no longer a tear and tumble, but bearing him up, buoyant as a bubble. So he slackened himself to the will of the wind. Curved his body just so. Cupped his hands to catch the slope of the now compliant gale. Rose up and slid through the storming night sky, the imperious black parrot with the scarlet stripe leading his aerial pathway...

Thoughts dwelling on the knavery of merchants, the foremost of the Tuareg salt-traders guided his camel over the hard-packed desert sand. Pace after pace he walked, a rolling gait giving rhythm to his brooding, until his pensive gaze was disturbed by an object swiftly sliding along the sands.

"Hey!" he called out, and his two companions followed the finger he pointed towards this mystery and just in time, they too caught sight of the object tumbling along the ground, rolling for a fair distance before it finally stopped. The curious Tuaregs turned their mounts and quick but cautious, approached it.

To their amazement, they found a naked whimpering young man, weak like a new-hatched bird. A scarf was wrapped about his head. A burnished collar gleamed on his neck. As if from a merciless scraping, much of the skin of his upper torso was abraded raw and seeping watery blood.

Demon or spirit, they couldn't agree, except that he was outcast and ailing. Their ancestral code was strict when it came to preserving life in this harsh habitat. So they wrapped the young man on the sand in soft cloths and bore him in a makeshift sling towards a cave they knew.

Therein lived an always-veiled woman and an old blind iron-maker who gave her refuge. With these kind people they'd leave young fellow to heal, and check on his progress on the way back from their salt trading venture.

...he was afloat in the sound of a memory, a gurgle of water singing praises to the river-rain goddess, Yemoja...

...he was afloat in a trickling sting of sand against blood, a flow of pain over his essences...

...all his fluids were boiling their way to his head. Steaming blood and marrow, all his seared inner core was streaming to his brain...

...his eyes rolled back, agonized yet curious about the catastrophe. Their effort so exhausted him he found it difficult to breathe. So he lay like a mournful dog run out of howls until he was swallowed by a nightmare of man-length river worms being pulled from his meddling eyeballs...

...a cool breeze flowed over his skin like thorns across a raw bruise and there was his mother, Koita, pushing her blurry face close to his...

...gently, she taunted that he was a lazy child trying to avoid his duty in the fields. Limbs slack as water, M'nalo tried rousing himself to her challenge, but the pain was so comfortable as it crawled through his bones, taking its good time, pausing to elaborate its wicked presence. He just couldn't raise himself from the pallet...

...and here was Izi Onamuli roughing his shoulders. So forcefully that M'nalo was near to losing his stomach. Then Koita was back, fussy with his face, touching cool hands that softened his inner edginess...

...we know you are unwell, they reassured. We are sorry our coolness makes you shiver. Soon you will be warm again...

...as he passed once more into nothingness, the sweet hands repeated, You are well cared for...

...now feeling only as sick as a wormy pup, with extreme effort M'nalo opened his eyes into a space that flickered swimmy-yellow. With an echo of a keening female voice, a sympathetic ululation that rolled around the hollow, soothing as familiar waters...

...then again, M'nalo returned to oblivion.

The wandering souls of M'nalo Sikivu Fanta Bembo and his tender body reunited to a trickling sound in a dim, liquid place. A warm sheath of water tightly encased him, held him upright. His memory returned as well—vivid about his ravaged village, his capture, destroying the mannish Arab woman, maiming the stallion. The workings of his escape in the sandstorm remained hazy. Somewhere, somehow, though, an incongruous parrot mattered.

He stretched full-length, much as a great snake would flex its pained muscles within a cocooning skin before sloughing it. The action roughed the enclosing liquid enough to make it swell past his neck, spill over the rim of whatever held him.

Quiet though the splash, it summoned quick footsteps, and soon the slow hands of his dreams were gently turning his liquid casement this way, that way, examining him side to side.

A veiled head swayed into his focus. "Ahhh!" came a soft female exclamation. Then spoke the healing voice of his dreams. "Welcome to our shelter, Man-of-the-Sandstorm." A tongue he understood. Soft as a warm bubble burst a memory of his mother's voice, telling stories as she scrounged the barren scrubland.

M'nalo tried, but the effort to speak was too painful. Instead, he sought the eyes deep within the folds of the veil and smiled gratitude.

A balm of emptiness then reclaimed his souls.

Slow as an egg maturing, time passed; hobbled by on invalid crutches of lessening misery. The dimness of M'nalo's recovery chamber—a cave of some sort with a sound of running water—remained constant. So did the visits of the veiled woman. Mostly she came to feed him, fingering an unfamiliar but sweetish mash into his mouth. Occasionally she brought goat milk, spooned it into him. She spoke little, except to tell necessities: warned when she needed to touch his painful skin; reassured him about voiding bodily wastes; reported the steady progress his body made. She explained about the soothing liquid: Rock water from an underground stream, it was not good for drinking, but her master had found it to have special healing properties. By a slow constant flow, it sucked and swallowed away his skin's damage.

Dim as the cave, more time passed, M'nalo asleep, or halfway there. Lying in the trickle, he dreamt of river basins back home. Of his family and friends. Of his master, Lathso. Aimlessly, his befuddled mind shuffled speculations: Would his master's potions have healed him better? What had become of his captured mother? Was the raid and rampage part of Tebika's plots? And this woman who cared for him, why was she veiled? What was that raw smell to her? That he couldn't see her eyes was bothersome. What did she think when she looked at him? She had called him Man-of-the-Sandstorm. Had his body succumbed to some sorcery? Or might she be some aspect of his mother's spirit come to tend him?

Dreams and memories interwoven, he dozed...*in Koita's back sling, safe and happy as a gurgle, soothed by the lilting cadence of her voice telling the story.*

"...*tired from the day's long journey, and after unpacking all of the regal finery, Rooli spilled her mistress's heated bathwater to waste upon the carpets. For punishment, that night she was sent to the stockade to keep watch over the camp's goats.*

"*A raised human voice scares away even the fiercest animal intruders. So, mournful at her watch, Rooli began a song against her bondage, against the injustice and distress that entrapped her life.*

"*Ahhh! poor Rooli, singing her heart out to the darkness, to the contemplative night birds, to the silent four-legged stalkers, to the creatures crawling through the dusty weeds. Entranced by her soul's outpouring, they all paused to listen.*

"*In the way of mysteries, it happened that a group of djinni were using that part of the world for passage to their business, preferring the quiet night to the day's tumult. Coming upon Rooli's song, these impetuous spirits murmured amongst themselves.*

"'Her song is soft dew sliding to warm earth,' said one spirit.

"'Her voice is cool as darkness, sweet as breeze,' said another.

"'A treasure we should keep,' the djinni all agreed, and taking human form, they approached and bade her to sing again. When they had heard enough, they asked if her song was true.

"'As true as I stand guard here,' swore Rooli, the slave.

"'If you wish, you shall have no more reason to sing so sadly,' offered the spirits.

"'Ah! My gratitude would be boundless as the skies,' said Rooli.

"'Go home, young Rooli,' said the djinni. 'Sleep in peace and comfort. That rich house in which you slaved is now your own. And so that you'll nevermore slave at this chore, henceforth no harm will come to any of your household's livestock.'

"And when Rooli went in, so it was. Who had been her fellow slaves now addressed her as 'mistress.' They led her to beautiful quarters, a warm jasmine-scented bed, and, filled with amazement at such wondrous luxury, she fell fast asleep.

"When she awoke next morning, Rooli went about testing whether her dream life would remain true. Matters seemed the same, though. Whatever she bade, slaves did. They dressed and fed her, made her comfortable, and it took many hours before she was satisfied that her world indeed had changed. As that reality filled her joyful heart, she looked to the sky and filled her chest to sing her thanks to the benevolent djinni.

"But only an ugly rasp came forth from Rooli's throat. The djinni had taken her music with them!"

More time crept by—M'nalo couldn't know how much—but the day came when the shrouded nurse helped him from his watery cocoon. With a small knife attached to her finger like a ring, she cut the tight strings of the casement around his neck, letting the body-warm liquid pour away. Collapsed to hands and knees, he crawled from it. His palms and knees were tender against the hard floor. The air wafted cool and pleasant on his nakedness as the woman wrapped a cloth about his hips. He stood straight then, his skin stiff, stretching not as painful as he expected. With no hurt, he reached his arms above his head. Cold around his neck, the collar chafed. And so frail had he become, simply this standing to full height exhausted him. The woman had to support much of his weary weight as she led their long shadows away from the echoing hollow where he had healed.

She guided him along gloomy meandering passages until at last they reached an upper cave smelling of smoke. A place brightened by indirect daylight that made him squint his dim-accustomed eyes. A tall dome of a cave twenty or so paces across, it contained urns and casks of different sizes ranged along the roughly circular walls. And middling the space, sitting on a small stool and staring at those pallid walls, was the woman's white-haired master.

"Make certain his hammock is soft and wet!" the elder greeted without turning. His speech rattled out haltingly. An ancient echo like a last effort scraped from his chest.

Reminded by the man's stooped, naked back, M'nalo took opportunity of the better light to examine his own bare skin. He took a look and shuddered: His rich mahogany shade was now a mottled rawness, swollen and striped pink in places. Though in a few areas—upper arms, lower thighs—his remembered healthy skin remained. But even to his eyes, he seemed a harrowing half-cooked demon from some nether world. Disconcerted to weakness, he collapsed onto the wet animal-fur hammock the shrouded woman had hung for him.

Frightened and tired, M'nalo lay there wrestling with his anxieties and watched as the woman went to the elder's shoulder, bent close and whispered privately.

The elder straightened and raised his fine head high. Turning towards M'nalo, he chuckled gently. "Bisui tells me you seem discouraged by your unsightly skin. Believe me when I say it is healing well. Patient Time, with morning sunshine, will return your color. Praise your gods for your vitality. It's the reason you thrive."

Flooded with gratitude, M'nalo attempted reply, managed only a ragged exhalation.

"Don't try! It will only worsen the damage to your throat," the elder cautioned. "Bisui says that you cannot find speech. This may be due to the sand you swallowed. Or perhaps your voice has been grated away just like your skin. But what's all this need for talk? Our esteemed friends, the salt traders, requested that we provide for you, restore your health. It is in their honor that we keep you.

"They said that you traveled here by a sandstorm. How can that be? They offered no explanation. Perhaps they thought it rude to suggest sorcery. Hmm?" He paused and snorted amusement. "What a story you cannot relate! Funny, hmmm?"

Alarmed by the guile in his manner, M'nalo sharp-eyed the chuckling elder. Again, Bisui bent her shrouded head close to his ear.

"Ah-ha!" said he. "Bisui reminds me. I am Kaariba Masood," his words slowed, his tone grew contemplative, "owner of many names and titles among the Mali. I ask you, at my age, what value are these? Still, my people say that even if a thing be as false as a goat's egg, if it eases the bowels, it is important. For this reason and no other, sometimes there's need for a name. So, for easiness sakes, I shall give you one of mine. This is a name I was granted when, not ten paces from my tent's door, a stone fell from the sky and showed me a magical spirit still steaming from its travels. My friends say maybe that you fell from a sandstorm. So with the hope that it is not your own true and secret name, I will pass this one, Mbingu, to you."

M'nalo grunted and eyes alert to Bisui's hand on the old man's shoulder, nodded.

Kaariba Masood nodded also, continued, "And my companion? She is Bisui Dafra, outcast from the Tuareg, my faithful and essential slave."

Taking his time, Bisui shuffling alongside, Kaariba pivoted on his stool and fully faced M'nalo. "She carries my eyes," he announced with a broad, brown-toothed smile.

Not quite understanding, M'nalo searched Kaariba's level gaze. He quickly noticed how absently it focused. How it held onto a spot in space, lingered unnecessarily. A color like old ivory paled where the black pupils should be. Disconcerted by the wrinkled sockets before him, M'nalo's thoughts collapsed as he grasped the fact: Kaariba Masood was blind.

The brown, monkey-wise gaze was useless!

An "Aahhh!" of understanding forced itself from his startled throat.

"I hear your spirit's sympathy, Mbingu. But my blindness was not like a bolt from above. Ten seasons it gave me to become familiar with its deepening shadow. Time enough to pass my craft to others. You should know that I am an iron-maker. A master of the craft. An iron-maker measures his smelts by brightness and colors. When his eyes fail him, so does his product's quality. His purpose for pride in his community. His privilege to contribute. All this being so, after those ten seasons, after I passed on whatever knowledge I possessed, I came to this isolated place to end my dimming days."

Kaariba's eyes sparkled wetly. His voice, though, betrayed no sadness. "Perhaps you wonder why here. Why we live like goats in these caverns." A wistful smile squeezed a tear down his wrinkled cheek. "In my vigorous rambling days long ago, I discovered these mysterious flows. Seasoned member of our iron-makers' guild, I was driven to bettering the blends of our smelts..."

The mention of smelts recalled the iron pits of M'nalo's youth—sites of mythic creativity, set up in hard-to-reach places out in the bush, near riverbanks that only initiates to the god Shango's clan knew how to find.

Realizing his weary mind was wandering, M'nalo pressed his focus back to the old man's ramblings...something about testing materials and underground flows...something else about wholesome waters and lethal salts...and him evaporating these salts...and burning them in sputtering flames, red, yellow, green, and blue...

A slip of a dream featuring rainbows and river-birds invaded M'nalo's stream of thought. For a moment it smoothed the old man's voice to a watery rush more tolerable...but too soon, back came his drone going on about soured milk and nauseating tastes...about blending salts with animal fats...making salves.

Then to M'nalo's relief, the old man said, "I don't want to tire you, Mbingu, my weakened friend..." although, instead of stopping, he went on about "...the numerous methods I devised, trying to tease out the secrets of these underground waters. Because there had grown within me a most desperate drive to understand the properties of these peculiar flows. And it was not for iron-making, I assure you! Oh! Not at all! My search had become a quest for a cure to the affliction of my wasting vision.

"Then the gods—Bisui swears it is Allah—provided me with new eyes. Hers. Yes, she, Bisui, outcast of her people..."

Kaariba stopped as Bisui stooped and whispered urgently into his ear.

Dismissively, the iron master murmured, "True! True!" ready to go on with his telling.

But the protest in her manner aroused M'nalo's attention. More sharply now, he listened as Kaariba continued. "Yes! My slave, my eyes, my Bisui, had lived through fourteen blighted seasons before she was put out in the desert. Plainly, not a punishment intended for her survival. But Fate bestows unexpectedly. Some call it Kismet. However you name it, in the end, I was the one who found her. Came upon her, hurt and helpless in these desert hills of my fading domain.

"Well? What else! I took her in. Here she is. That's how you know I returned her to this life. In exchange, she returned to me my vision. Reminded me of how much I know. Kept my souls useful. Every once and again the iron-makers come out here to my barren hills. They humbly seek my wisdom and I help them with their smelts. With Bisui at my side whispering the colors of the burn, I am as much the master as ever I was. I tell you plain, life for life, for this alone, I owe her."

Kaariba grinned, his eyes again welling, spilling quick tracks. He dismissed that with an elegant wave of long learned fingers. "Don't mind this water, it runs by its own will. My feelings are not in the flood. Not always. But I'm talking too much and not telling what you long to know. Amusing, hmmm?"

M'nalo smiled ruefully. Then, yielding to an innate demand to mask his àshe, immediately he tightened his mouth, erased the telling expression. He threw an assessing glance at Bisui. Her shrouded silence at the elder's side. Her hand lightly on his shoulder. M'nalo wondered could her master now know of his grimace that only she was seeing? Were there other messages she might be touching into him? And if so, what personal insights about him did they share?

"Well, I'll tell you now, Mbingu," announced Kaariba in a voice once more vigorous as a rattle. "First. Your youth, your strength will make you well. This I can assure. But for some time yet, you must hide yourself from daylight. From sunshine. Your renewing skin is fragile. You have to sleep on damp pallets. Your skin can only manage the forces of night air. The cool. The quiet. But now you must rest. We will talk again."

While he continued healing, many a day found M'nalo as prisoner to the iron-master's musings:

...iron belongs to Ugun, god of blood. It fell to this earth in a sprinkle of pebbles when the thorn tree and the fig tree returned to the sky places to battle out a disagreement. Three times the moon spun full cycle while they fought, and all that while the sprinkle of pebbles persisted, and wherever they fell, a kahiya tree grew up. Mankind, more curious than Brother Monkey, tested every this and that about these sudden-sprouting kahiya trees. Eventually, he discovered how firing the clay from around the bole of the tree in a special manner would produce lumps of Ugun's most useful metal.

Kaariba's voice droning the messages into his mind, M'nalo learned that, "...a life arrives in this place with three blessings: a little body, a little breath, and a spirit. The first two belong to duty and community. Only the last is true and properly one's own to develop and master. A condition, a gift requiring careful nurture, this spirit is like a skin. To thrive, a man must find his appropriate touch. It's always special. It might be the measure of sweetness in a stolen caress. The insult of a slap. The close wickedness in a mother's pinch. Each reality sharp as another, every true man still has to understand and feel the exact touch of his particular skin..."

Sleepy eyes following the sway of the hammock's shadow on the walls, M'nalo scarcely listened as the morose tool-maker mused on, "We humans are significant. But we not special. The tree, the rock, the pool. They're special. The sun smiles as these places interact. All together, they create a child named Dirt. Then they nourish the infant with sunlight and seeds. And roots and maggots and rain and such special places in which man becomes a dangerous pest..."

Although he could not stop listening, M'nalo never dismissed a quirky notion that Kaariba Masood's wisdoms were those of an old man with blinded ambitions. Ultimately, they were useless.

With Kaariba's salves and Bisui's solicitous care, M'nalo's flayed skin slowly healed. During daylight hours, he dozed and dreamed in the protection of the caves. At evening-time, he emerged to walk the hills for exercise. At first Bisui was his leading guide, but soon they were walking alongside each other, like companions.

Dusk falling, he would sit outside the cave and wait for her.

That time of day, the stark landscape always gave him a sense of solitude. Somehow the distant mountains spun off echoes of bat shrieks into recollections of his past and stung him with a hollow pain named missing. He would stare at a dying sun bleeding onto the mountain faces. Tense with feelings, he would see a darkness that reshaped the aloof ranges, their scarlet glow changing into hard black shadows. Reminding of enormous crouching beasts. Menacing by their very stillness.

Some evenings as they walked, Bisui would tell of her people. When they stopped to rest, she'd sit low on a stone, turn her shrouded face away from M'nalo, and talk. Once, in her peculiar nasal tone that gave her Bambaran dialect a curious lisp, she said, "My people's land is hard. Hot sun and fierce winds on bare rocks in sand. That's all. Still, my people scratch a living out of this forsaken place. Because nomads we are, and hard as our land, we are. Our harbor is any oasis where the date palms grow. For what food is more dependable to any with baskets, fiber ropes, and a pinch of hunger for courage? We leave one camp for another where, with a memory of palm-granite flowers, our home can make itself again."

She paused for a moment, complained, "You mind my words with less constancy than a wind-vane."

Not knowing the term, but guessing meaning from her tone, M'nalo marshaled his attention. She being his nurse and he unable to speak, they had developed a simple code. He shook his head sideways for "No," nodded for "Yes" and "Thank you." He snapped his fingers for attention.

So now he turned to her solemn-faced, nodded twice, then closed his eyes and bowed his head low.

He held that pose until her hand was gentle under his chin, raising his head. His eyes opened to her shrouded head so close to his own he could smell the sincerity on her breath as she said, "I forgive you. I must. Why would Mbingu from the sandstorm want to hear the dusty ways of desert people?"

M'nalo looked into the space in her veil where her eyes should be, a shoulder's length away, level with his own. He nodded earnestly, snapping fingers for emphasis.

Then Bisui stood and moved close behind him. He felt the cool of metal pressed against his skin as she handled the coffle's collar around his neck. She said, "But it could be that Mbingu already knows some ways of my people. With collars such as these, many masters mark their slaves. I wonder what might this copper's story be?"

That was her final utterance that evening.

A day or two later M'nalo was roused from a doze when Kaariba stopped droning a praise song to his gods. He blinked open his eyes and saw that Bisui had drifted into the chamber. She stood whispering into Kaariba's ear.

The blind man nodded and chuckled. "What harm can come of it!" he declared.

Bisui moved farther into the cave, stopping at a flat wooden chest against the wall. She raised its cover, searched for a moment. She made her selection, let the lid fall into place with a soft suck of air. Then she came over to M'nalo and said, "Mbingu, Kaariba says there is no harm if I remove your collar."

The idea a jolt by itself, M'nalo instantly swung off the hammock. Grinning eagerness, snapping his fingers, he looked at her shrouded face, searched her hands.

Rather than the file or hammer and chisel he expected, she held a hand's-length of thin, flexible metal, bent sharply near its end. Without a word, she turned the collar around so that she could work on it from behind his shoulder.

M'nalo held his breath, choking with anticipation. Since she planted the promise in his mind, he had been in anguish. The collar's clammy cool was now a torture. Just its clamp alone was a weight of horrid memories. Of ravaged house and home. Of lost identity. Of caring parents killed or captured. His poor sisters, who knows what? He thought of the mannish Arab woman he'd killed. He shuddered at his recent blunders. At his terrible revenges, achieved or intended.

All this history running through his mind, it took the utmost for him to hold still as Bisui handled his collar, delicately probing with her slip of metal and concentrating on careful insertions and confident twists. Then a deliberate push, a sharp click, and there! The collar swung open on its hinge. Bisui took it from M'nalo's neck and offered it to him, smiling. "Now you owe me a story," she whispered and turned away.

M'nalo snapped his fingers sharply.

Bisui paused, asked without turning, "You wish for something?"

Twice, M'nalo snapped his fingers.

"Tell me," she said and faced him.

M'nalo held out the collar and, with exaggerated eyes and gestures, queried how she had opened it.

"You wish to understand how to do this?"

M'nalo nodded eagerly.

A brief pause, she answered, "It is not difficult. I will teach you." And she beckoned him over to Kaariba's chest.

A hold of sharpness, it was. Numerous implements neatly arranged in small compartments: scissors and small tongs, pins and needles in many sizes, fine-pointed pincers, more thin lengths of flexible metal. One beauty of a warrior's knife with a gleaming blade a man's hand long, and a thick ebony handle. From first sight of it, a weapon for which M'nalo craved.

Bisui chose a pincer from the box then took the collar over to the better light near the cave's entrance. She sat on a stool and, using the unlocked collar for demonstration, instructed, "A lock is made of springs and levers. When a key is used, these springs and levers are made to shift, and the lock fastens. Those who value possessions favor locks. They are a false security, though. For one has only to reverse the movements of levers and springs to open a lock. Keys have special shapes that allow this release. Although anything that can perform the same will open the lock. So those who value freedom favor keys."

Good teacher, she illustrated her instructions with careful demonstrations. Avid student, M'nalo learned every lesson.

One night as Bisui walked with him, a drizzle began. With quiet surprise, M'nalo bore witness as a flare of obvious delight took hold of this somber woman who cared for him. Clapping her hands, she spun around and around, her veils and clothes winging out about her. As if roused from long slumber, M'nalo's own dancing spirits reached out to her soulful assertion, and he, too, began moving. Body bending to the rhythms of the rain's gentle splatter. Feet tapping a slower, cooler beat that fitted inside Bisui's whirling, he danced. Balancing her delirium just right, he coupled their emotions with the rare wet night.

Then, sudden as it came, the shower was done, leaving the pair to catch fled breaths, and M'nalo to suppress an exceptional longing beyond family and circumstance. A yearning for some bit of who he used to be, a water dancer under river god Yemoja's thrall. The sigh worked out of him as a deep breath and he firmly shifted his mind towards closer matters. Like how to widen this breech into Bisui's demeanor.

They sat arm's-length from each other on low boulders, the space between them charged with awkwardness. Her voice slurred into the quiet: "I thank your spirits, Mbingu. Tonight they have blessed me. I have not danced since I was a child." Bisui let forth a moan into the cloth covering her face. "I tell you true, the child I was danced for every occasion."

Surprised at the image, M'nalo looked at her, beamed encouragement.

"You want to know more," she affirmed.

M'nalo nodded.

"And since you cannot repeat it, to whom better should I tell my story? But I will not spoil this beautiful night with such a tale as mine. Some other time. Tonight true marvels are about. Because of this, the sweet rainfall, the hands-of-god will blossom, and for three magical hours some maiden will be seduced by the beautiful aroma of these white embroideries."

Bisui rose, took a fitful step away, her body slightly rocking.

M'nalo did not move. Just watched her tension.

Then into the impassive night, her words continued: "And if the girl is unlucky, as love is unlucky, she will be disgraced, disfigured, and put out in the desert. And if she is to survive, she must know the ways of water. So listen well, dancing Mbingu."

Bisui spun around to face him, spoke in a false, bright voice. "My words may someday save you. More than silver or salt, water is most precious, richer even than life. And the desert-traveler must learn to seek it in unexpected places if he would not feed the vultures. He must look at the rock faces for changes in color and texture. Attend to crumblings and puckerings among the stones we walk around. Study each oddness. Beside a rock, scrape a gouge in the sand, see if water seeps into such a kleelay. There are other signs. Look how the tamarisk provides. These dried secretions from the tamarisk tree look like crusty webs. But they are sweet and filling with more than plain surprise..."

And pausing only to sound her air-sucking whistles, such was the survival lore Bisui shared.

Another night, an object detached from the starlit sky in an instant of flying flame.

"Look! A wish," Bisui cried out, pointing, as the sky-spark seemed to fall into a nearby gorge.

M'nalo turned toward her and with many nods, shared appreciation.

The quiet moment of magic pervading, her low, slurry voice began: "There's a story from our caravan about how, at each and every holdover, a certain young woman used to roam the sparse gardens between the dunes to her heart's delight. She was of solitary disposition and, evening chores completed, she would leave the other women and go lean against a palm tree and solemnly contemplate the creeping sands.

"'Some household might have tried to settle here,' she would dream. 'Perhaps the mother put down a garden of pale-green beans and leafy watercress, or even a grapevine. Perhaps the grandfather taught the sons of his sons tricks of wine craft, and the daughters learned to sew with thin ivory needles. Found out how to braid and weave, and steam spiced millet wrapped in tender leaves. Perhaps they were preparing for marriages into wealthy families.'

"Such was the opulence of this lonely woman's dreams until a djinn, rambling aimless through the melancholy terrain, happened to rest eyes upon her and grew curious about her bemused manner. So one spare evening, as the sun cut the earth apart from heaven, this djinn presented itself in the guise of a beautiful horse which said to her, 'O delightful young maiden, would you mount and allow me to carry you about the myriad pathways?'

"The young woman felt a surge of strange power on hearing this. With a sense of authority and command, she replied boldly, 'How would you repay if I grant your mad request?'

"With a toss of his noble head, the horse answered, 'I would repay with wonder.'

'Would you do me no harm, and return me to my family?'

'If it be your wish,' said the horse.

"Satisfied and intrigued by this answer, the young woman mounted the exceptional animal, which at once was swiftly off, taking her by diverse ways unto the limits of excitement. All night they visited grand marvels and mysteries, and the young woman's amazement kept her breathless. Then, true to its word, the horse returned her to the very spot from which they had departed.

"'Do I receive my payment now?' asked the woman.

"'Did I not provide you wonder?' replied the horse.

"'Yes, noble creature. But I expected a wonder more practical, and of more practical value,' said the girl.

"This fair answer fully annoyed the djinn. 'Well, then,' he said. 'You shall have your wish. Take this monkey into your family'—at which a wise-eyed, white-faced sand monkey materialized before her—'and they shall find wealth.'

"'Thank you,' said the young woman, and ran through the dried garden toward her home and family.

"She found them frantic. All night, everywhere, they had searched for her. Angry, suspicious, they demanded, 'Where have you been?'

"She recounted her marvelous experiences and presented the sand monkey as proof of her honesty.

"But what they saw was not a monkey but a naked, sneering baby with goats' horns atop its head. Frightened and crying 'effrontery,' they accused the maiden of consorting with a demon. Picking a prickly staff, her father whipped her without mercy for such a grave transgression. But after delivering many blows, he noticed that each drop of her blood was congealing into a ruby that fell among the sand and pebbles around the public whipping post.

"A growing treasure was sparkling the sunrise.

"In sweet quandary, noting his daughter's distress, the father paused from his righteous discipline. Then his reason won through. She was only a female after all, and untrustworthy at that. An assessing look at the rubies, he figured he could risk another ten lashes.

"Of which he made best use. But by the time he released the unfortunate maiden, she had bled to death, and was immediately transformed into a glistening black rock, smooth except for some ragged gouges in its hump.

"The father gathered his rubies into his clothes. Then he turned attention to the demon baby, which lay there swaddled, mewling innocently. Braved by family and his curious watchful community, he dared to examine the infant more closely. But as soon as he put hands on it, the horrible child disappeared. And that is the whole of that story."

Bisui remained silent where she sat, her soft snuffles suggestive of distress. So to give her privacy, M'nalo rose and strode a small distance away. There he paced back and forth. Although in truth, her tale had not moved him specially. Notwithstanding that the hard rewarding life it mentioned did remind of his mother.

M'nalo had often wondered about the ropy meat Bisui regularly slow-roasted for them. So one day he gestured this question to her. She murmured that she'd show him as soon as Kaariba judged his skin able to withstand evening sun.

Evening sun? M'nalo pondered to himself but asked no further.

Not long after, late on a cloudy afternoon, Bisui led him from the special coolness of the cave. "A hunt" was all she'd answer his snapping fingers. The special equipment for this jaunt seemed to be a fair-sized, square, cloth-covered frame; some material carried in her leather pouch; and, in a sheath at her waist, the splendid hunting knife.

The daylight outing excitement by itself, M'nalo kept trying to match now-familiar nighttime trails with the paths over which she led him—here the bare face of Crouching Lion, there, Crescent Rift—but he soon lost his bearings and was content to follow her ascent. They stopped on a ledge overlooking a wide chasm. Up that high, a sturdy breeze fluttered Bisui's skirts and veils, and his own knee-length djellaba.

Within the partial shelter of a crevasse, she set down her frame and drew from her leather pouch a long, narrow strip of cloth. Many thread-thin, finger-length iron hooks were fitted along it. She attached the length of cloth to the frame, and at once M'nalo saw the assembly for what it was: a kite, like those of his youth, though much larger

He snapped his fingers *Click!*, and Bisui turned her head. "Yes," she said, a laughing lilt to her tone, "with this child's plaything I hunt. But now I must hurry and you must watch."

Out of her pouch she pulled a spool of yarn. Fat like a calabash, it was. One end of which she firmly tied to the kite's loose angled neck cord. Then, with the casual expertise, she set about launching the kite into the valley's wind currents.

First try she had it aloft, swooping and dangling like an airborne tadpole busy going nowhere beyond its tether. M'nalo wondered 'What now?' Asking information, he snapped fingers at her. She looked at him sharply, signaled patience.

Tinged purple with tiredness, the sun was sinking rapidly when M'nalo first noticed the flitting specks up in the sky. In swiftly growing numbers, from high mountain caves all around they were emerging and banding into a huge cloud.

Bats! M'nalo identified them at last.

And in startling abundance they were. As a great dark swarm of them flowed down the valley toward the forests of food south of where M'nalo and Bisui waited on the barren ledge of the mountain. They came swiftly swooping toward Bisui's kite with its many-barbed tail which was not-so-innocently riding their aerial passage.

The result was like fishing from a pail, and soon Bisui was drawing in her yarn. M'nalo helped by spooling the thread as the kite descended. Then it was on the ground and he could see its abundant catch.

Of the twenty or so hooks along the kite's tail, more than a dozen held bats struggling to free themselves, enlivening the strip of cloth into a writhing length that wriggled madly across the rocky ledge. Before Bisui could knock it unconscious with her knife's ebony handle, at least one victim succeeded in freeing its impaled wings and whisked away. The hunter in M'nalo was roused, and affronted at Bisui's casual manner of bagging the prey, he held out his hand.

Without hesitation, she passed over the knife.

As he had divined, it fit his hold perfectly. Then quick and deftly, he used the fine blade to sever every remaining bat's ugly, squealing head. He paused only once, losing concentration when he caught a sudden overwhelming earthy scent that might have come from Bisui. A disconcerting waft of remembrance that brought alive the fetid aroma of his family compound's old baobab after a soaking rain. A most out-of-place puzzle on this sterile plateau.

Arriving before dawn, the committee whistled its approach from a good distance away. Then, closer to the cave, the four men sat in a boulder's shadow and awaited the iron-master's reply.

Up in the cave, their coming had stirred up worry. Hardly the first summons from his former clansmen, and even though Kaariba considered it an exceptional honor, this time Bisui did not want him to go. Last visit as his eyes, she said, she'd felt threatened by the forge-men's manner. Too vigorous with their singing and dancing and pumping the bellows, their raw maleness.

She had not confessed these words to Kaariba. But M'nalo could see the story in the flinch of her shoulders, the distress her splayed fingers expressed. Testing with his seeker soul, he could feel the concern behind her masks. He understood, too, why she was unable to explain this to her master, why she insisted, instead, that she did not trust them with his care; that her reluctance was because last trip the committee's food had sickened her master for many days!

Then M'nalo saw a strategy by which to save both dignities. With patient signing until they noticed him, he volunteered himself to guide Kaariba. After brief reflection, Bisui relented and agreed. She would pack them food, though. As the occasion would be M'nalo's first exposure to full sunlight, she suggested he wear a light, hooded, full-length djellaba to cover his scars, shoulders to knees. All else agreed upon, M'nalo could resist no longer. Weak to his craving more than to any need for protection, M'nalo pointed to the splendid knife. With an indifferent shrug, Bisui handed it over. And to her request that he keep it sheathed beneath his djellaba, he quickly nodded.

Later that morning, to the delight of the patient committee waiting outside, Kaariba left the cave on a journey to share his expert knowledge with those who'd once been his students. Kinsmen whom, he admitted, he had missed.

Giving little consideration to the master's age, the committee walked many paces ahead, and kept up a sturdy tempo. Their appointed campsite was a kahiya tree by a red mud gully. Clearly they intended to get there before nightfall. Kaariba, though, was so enjoying the jaunt, he seemed unmindful of the brisk pace. Tethered a long stride behind M'nalo, firmly holding his walking staff, he hardly stopped his incoherent expounding.

They arrived at the site well before the sun sank, and M'nalo cast about curious eyes. A forge was already set up against the bank of the river basin. Formed of thick brown mud, it was a deep oven with eight bellows pipes entering its base to provide smelting heat. Necessary raw materials were gathered close and ready: Lumps of red clay from beneath the kahiya tree; special grass for layering it inside the forge; stacks of chopped hardwood for fuel.

The men who worked the bellows were assembled. Squatting in a loose circle in the slanting shade of the bushes, a rangy, hard-muscled dozen or more joked and passed around a gourd as they nursed a mood more companionable than festive. Together they had done this thing before. Well they knew the effort, and anticipated another routine try.

Watching them, all at once, as if his bones had turned to water, M'nalo quivered to a feeling too elusive to be named memory, except for its tinge of melancholy and his sense of isolation.

While that they waited in the tree's shade, M'nalo stood silent beside the seated Kaariba. Gradually it came to him that he might as well have been invisible. For although several fellows spoke to the iron-master, even took detailed instructions from him, not one, in any manner, ever addressed M'nalo or acknowledged his presence.

Breaking into M'nalo's thoughts, Kaariba grinned broadly and observed as if to himself, "Iron is like a baby made. The forge is the woman's place of entry. A place for stroking. A place from which the new thing emerges. The bowl inside, a womb. Not so?

"Listen to the songs for the dance of iron-making. Don't they teach the right rhythms, the right strength and stamina? And how we add heat to the bellows? How we stick the charge in? Funny, hmmm! New-made iron is a fresh-born child, I tell you. We make…"

"Master," interrupted an older fellow who tentatively approached them, "we are ready and the sun is about to leave."

"I know, Sewa Dangbo. I know," replied Kaariba. "You need not speak so loud. The ears in the folds of my garment might find out the sun's secret. Just as my skin was aware of the cool of evening come."

The fellow took a step back, bowed his head. "Indeed it is I, your servant, Sewa Dangbo. Forgive me, master. Of course you knew. I spoke without thinking."

"Enough, Dangbo. You worry too much," said Kaariba, pushing himself up with many creaks and pops of his old bones. "Begin the fires."

Cool though the night breezes, the heat from the forge grew fierce once the men started pumping the bellows, their fast-paced chanting giving tempo to their work. Timed to Kaariba's chants and calls, every response referred to some exaggerated sexual coupling. The scarlet fire was a female organ, the bellows' tips were male. An eight-man team it took to force this mighty entry, for iron was indeed a hard babying.

All through the long hot night, the bellows men—two teams of them—kept up that frenzied rhythm. The forge with its contents burned with searing pink heat. Twice it paled to almost white and both times, as Kaariba had instructed him, M'nalo squeezed the iron-master's shoulder to alert him. Each time, Kaariba took a small earthen jar from his garments, called over Sewa Dangbo, sent him to throw jar and contents into the forge upon which the matter inside hissed and flared from terrific transformations.

"Is it firing yellow and green?" Kaariba asked quietly.

M'nalo squeezed the elder's shoulder twice, yes. He wished he could speak of, really explain, the special greenness that was cheerful as morning sunshine through new bamboo leaves.

"Then all is good. Pump this iron hard," Kaariba called out, and with a cheer of renewed vigor, the men heightened their bruising barrage with the bellows, feeding the flame as they chanted.

"*Ogun, master of the world...*
Ogun, virile creator of newborns . .
Ogun, who wears a coronet of blood . .
Ogun, father of hoe and axe, and black cutlass...
Ogun, who terrifies the lazy . .
Ogun, who screams a sound of flames."

On and on, until finally, Kaariba called out to the fire-feeders, "Sufficient." And right away they set to breaking down the forge. Tired and joyful, they found at its womb-shaped base a lump of new iron, ready to be taken home and shaped to their useful purpose.

The great fire had smoldered into a wide heap of furry embers when M'nalo roused the dozing elder. They broke fast with a mouthful of water apiece, and morsels of dried meat taken from the pouch that Bisui had packed. Then into the cool dawn, M'nalo led them homeward.

Midmorning sunshine blazed down, toasting Kaariba's yesterday enthusiasm into today's crusty lament. "The sameness is the trouble," he grumbled. "In the desert, there are no especial signs. Not stones, nor risings for the feet. Not bird sounds, or scents. With no diversions to draw scenes, no clues to lead, the sightless here are truly blind.

"For many years, Mbingu, Bisui has held my eyes. Every day she opens a familiar world, accurate according to my memory. I could not have wished for more when I saved her. So long she has allowed me this easy world. But now you have arrived and changed the shape and smell of the place we make our home.

"These days when Bisui is near to you, the cave grows sultry with licentious vapors. I expect someone soon to slip into forbidden pools. So I must speak of what every fly should know before he dares the web.

"Our Bisui was cast out for opening herself to temptation, then accusing the man of the trespass. At which, for honor's sake, his life was taken. Then, sensing deceit, the wronged man's brother risked his own life and honor and challenged Bisui to put hands on the sacred book while holding to her charge.

"But the magic of the holy caused her to break wind instead. That rude display of guilt made her subject to a righteous vengeance. Her community deemed expulsion to die in the desert was insufficient punishment for so grave an injustice. So when I found her, her nose hung by a sliver of skin, butchered off. Her right cheek was sliced from ear to lip and formed a grotesque grin. This is the reason for her veils, for the lisp to her speech. This is the shame that has made her content to serve as an old man's eyes, as a guide and handmaid not needful of tether.

"Now Mbingu comes and reminds her that she is female. That she has passions. Now, forgetting the sin that sent her to me, she feels her life is a cage, that her shroud is a trap. Now, in longing for escape, she cares less about taking away my vision. And then what am I to do?"

This last was said so softly, M'nalo paused his stolid trudging, looked back at the elder. He found Kaariba's gaze blank as ever, and weepy.

"…and for this, we toolmakers will ever answer to our gods…"

Bisui interrupted for M'nalo's benefit, "Kaariba has always criticized weapon-making…"

"Mark you," Kaariba continued, speaking over her, "useful weapons I do not oppose. A sturdy blade is necessary protection. But to use such a blade against a weak unarmed man is clearly foul."

As if reminded, Bisui interposed again, "The master knows a way to make a stronger iron…"

"Truth is that I was taught this secret by a sorcerer from the mysterious lands south of us. A commonplace ingredient was all that…"

A trumpet's call sounded through the hot, dry air. Then another, and after a pause, a third short blast.

Bisui clapped her hands, cried out, "The salt traders!" She ran to the cave's mouth, peeked around its sunset lip. She skipped back to Kaariba's side. Excitement made her tumble of words slushy, as she said, "They have already raised a short tent. Our supplies must be waiting beneath it."

Kaariba raised his hands sharply, lowered them in a quieting gesture. "No need for hurry. They are going nowhere but back to that kleelay to refresh their water bags. We have time to manage our exchanges. Heat won't spoil raw millet."

"Even so, Master, shall I not gather our barter?"

"Yes, do. At least it will busy your zest."

Bisui hurried off and disappeared into an adjoining cave.

A few moments passed before Kaariba broke the silence grown in her absence. "And when they ask, my Mbingu, what shall we say about you?"

M'nalo shook his head, snapped his fingers once. Then realized he wasn't signing to Bisui.

"Does that mean no? Yes? You wish that I tell them nothing?"

Snap!

"Hmmmp!" snorted Kaariba. Then suddenly, in an unexpectedly sinister tone, he continued, "This is also what I might tell. What if I say that their sick stranger is a young sorcerer, who did indeed come out of a sandstorm? What if I say that this young sorcerer has imprisoned the spirit of his voice so that he cannot betray his malevolent intentions? What if I say that?"

M'nalo slid from the hammock, hustled over to the old man. Close, he snapped fingers once, grunted, "nnh-nnm." Again and again. He tried to speak but only exhaled a stifled wheezing. A small black rage began coiling around his backbone. A fugitive tension, it was in a fury to survive.

The blind old man continued, "When first you came to us and your souls were gone from you, as she described everything else, Bisui told me of the scars upon your face and chest. These scars reminded of my mysterious friend from the south. That sorcerer. I did not tell her of their meaning, though. She's yet ignorant of your identity, thinks you were a slave. Then, from my iron-making clansmen, I hear that a sorcerer wrapped in a mask of openness has visited Kaariba. I hear that if any man but Kaariba were to attend him, even to acknowledge his presence, that man would be in gravest danger.

"But hold. Now that I smell your fear of stories such as these," said Kaariba slyly. "Now I might simply say to the salt traders that your skin is yet too weak for you to emerge from our caves."

At this indication of danger loosening its grip, M'nalo grunted wary approval, "Mnn-hmmn! Mnn-hmmn!"

"Then so shall it be," said Kaariba grandly. With a chuckle, he added, "Such a story also benefits by being reasonable and close enough to truth's threshold. Funny, hmmm?"

M'nalo regarded the sightless elder with no humor at all. He walked a restless relief back to his hammock. Though he reclined again, an edge now needled his ease. It was a disquiet he sensed would not soon depart. As he studied Kaariba he had a thought. Would the time come when he'd need to do away with the canny iron-maker? He nodded slowly, absentminded, but confident. If at all necessary, he could.

A kid had strayed to the inner caverns, its piteous echoing bleats shattering the peace of the cool cave. When Bisui set out to find it, M'nalo snapped fingers for attention, and offered to accompany. With vigor to spare, these days he took every chance to explore.

"Follow if you can, Mbingu," she said and, agile as a goat herself, slipped through a large opening into dimness.

M'nalo swiftly followed. It took a moment for his eyes to adjust to the darkness, another to discern her crouching shape as she climbed a ledge leading to another narrow passage. He hurried after, thought he'd lost her, then found her waiting in a large hollow.

"Sight is not of much use here, Mbingu. Trust your hands and ears."

Easy advice to accept as M'nalo could scarcely see two paces away.

The kid's needy, nasal bleats grated again.

"He's lower down still. Come." Bisui set off again.

M'nalo closed his eyes, aimed his footsteps close after the quiet slap of hers, the darkness having stolen all other dimension.

Hands against cool cave walls, they'd traversed several spaces when Bisui said, "We will wait here for it to call again," and M'nalo, in a tentative forward step, bumped into her.

A sharp intake of breath, she said, "You should sit. The ground is smooth. Can you not see even a little?"

M'nalo crouched, closed his eyes tight then opened them. No difference in vision, he grunted, "Uhn-uhn."

Bisui sniggered, from her a surprising sound. "I can," she bragged. "Down here, sight is different. It's free of clothes and covers. In these caves, one must learn afresh how to see, how to mix touch and sound and even taste with memory."

From the source of her voice, M'nalo realized she had remained standing nearby. Her scent became abruptly stronger. Right away he recalled Kaariba's words on the way back from the iron-making. Instantly, his blood stirred into his loins, nudged his oko as if from an invalid sleep. Suddenly craving contact with her, M'nalo snapped his fingers.

From close by, she answered, "Yes, Mbingu, I am here. And while we wait for the kid to call us to his hiding place, I will keep my promise. Do you want to hear a story, Mbingu who dances in beauty?"

M'nalo reached out at the sound of her voice again, but the reach could not find her. He snapped his fingers twice.

Then his hand was grasped and gently guided to warm naked skin. Firm, smooth, maybe her belly. He scrambled forward, attempting to clasp her damp flesh. But she quickly moved away, and his pleasure was lost back in the dark.

Came her rushing lisp: "Mine, Mbingu, is a song of dishonor. No legends are made of the strength of a sinful woman. Outcast is her only history. But with my hair cropped close, my face a fright, must I be always weighted by my shame? Must my self be consumed by a hateful happy moment when life was too sweet for the tasting, and I was too free?

"Yes, it was a man that made my downfall. I went exuberant to the plunge though. Now half my life has withered in these caves. Because of one vengeful brute, ten thousand nights I have missed the sunshine of a young man's smile. To ten thousand longings I have been closed as a stone. And then you came, Mbingu."

On his knees, both hands tentatively reaching into black space, M'nalo crept toward her ragged voice. He smelled her pungent flavor, like wet clay, viscous and salty.

"My love is a sharp whip," she continued, her voice giving him direction, "genuine and pure as a spine through skin. Eager again is my love to the plunge. I am a daughter of sand and rock. Of sultry zephyrs too warm to soothe. In love I am like all women. A vessel of fire. A mix of dust and breath and blood." Her voice dropped to an urgent, slippery whisper. "Use my body, Mbingu, as only a man can. Make it live and burn. Use me."

M'nalo clutched through the dark toward her voice, finally met her grasping hand pulling his own towards flesh that though it trembled, did not flinched away. She was presenting her backsides, M'nalo realized, as his other hand slid down the knobby bones of her spine, and joined at her waist to hold her. His oko straining, he lunged forward, thrusting hips blindly, aiming for entry. Blind to all but appeasing the powerful lust that drove him.

They never did find that hapless kid-goat.

Craving the honey between her thighs and the welcome slip with which she pleasured his obsession, M'nalo made cave explorations his new pastime, Bisui as his ardent guide. With practice, he even mastered the trick of etching her image unto the blank dimness. If Kaariba was aware of the greater intimacy between Bisui and M'nalo—healthy now but for his destroyed voice—the elder never indicated. Rather, as if forcing the mantle of student upon M'nalo, Kaariba intensified his instructions about matters of iron smelting and melding and sculpting.

One technique he described in particular detail required the sculptor to fashion his object out of beeswax, then layer it thick and thorough with soft clay and set it to dry. This mold was then slowly fired until the wax inside melted and drained out a small opening bored in one end of the mold. That done, the sculptor poured in molten metal—iron, silver, whatever he chose—which slowly congealed into the original wax shape.

"I myself created a double mold that allowed second-metal inlays during the same pouring," Kaariba boasted to a trickle of his indifferent tears. "Yes, Mbingu. I made knives and swords with silver and bronze skin covering a sharp black iron blade. So beautiful they were, and deadly, from what I later heard."

M'nalo attended to the blind man's nostalgia with half a mind. His larger part, the heart and soul of him, remained a-loll in the erotic indolence of his times in the caves with Bisui.

Lust as license, they had sated themselves. In the afterglow, M'nalo had fallen into a fleet dream...

...he is strolling on a pleasant road lined by trees laden with ripe mangoes when a vudun with a rotund, hungry belly and a tiny-holed cone for a mouth appears beside him...

...its function, the vudun somehow makes him understand, is to terrorize sleepers with warnings against frivolous attachments, and it has decided to favor M'nalo...

...it begins its persuasion by pounding a clamorous drum decorated with death's heads along its silver spines. The strokes enlivened a group of tiny human skeletons to begin wild dances predicting terrible destinies for forgetful acolytes...

M'nalo started awake, dry-mouthed. Bisui was urgently prodding his shoulder, saying, "Mbingu, you were speaking in your sleep!"

M'nalo grunted, cleared his throat, tried to summon voice. He managed only the usual flabby sound, more breath than timbre.

"Not so strong," said Bisui. "In a whisper! I don't know the tongue, but I heard words. I was frightened. I thought that we had been discovered by a demon spirit. But it was only you whispering..."

Hope brightening his mind like a sunrise, M'nalo turned his head away and, soft to himself, tried a whisper in Twi. His ears alone caught the hissed results from the high reaches of his throat. Every fiber of his essences thrummed joy at the discovery. But turning to Bisui, he only grunted as if with failure, and heaved a doleful sigh.

Her excitement subsiding, Bisui consoled, "Maybe it happens only when you sleep. I am certain Kaariba will agree it bodes well for your healing."

On one of their ventures into darkness, Bisui led M'nalo to a vast black space. A wadi, she said it was. An enormous cavern of water where, when he let go of her skirt and threw a rock upward with all his might, it didn't strike a ceiling. No echo returned from its splash.

Bisui held his arm tight. "I discovered this cave by following the tether of a sick, old she-goat," she explained. "Even though I'm so familiar with this gloom, I would not have risked the turnings and twists to get here. That stiff-kneed mother had a wise plan. All the while, she was only looking for a place to die. She found it here by walking into that wadi. Is why I fear this hollow space, Mbingu. There is a sound to it, a fat whisper that suggests endlessness.

"Dared by curiosity, I came back here, once. I brought a bowl of tallow with a wick. I lit it and pushed the flame out to float this black wetness before us. On and on it went. I watched that small light glide away, smooth as a wing on air. I watched it grow ever smaller, until it became a weak red twinkle and disappeared." Bisui's hand gripped his arm almost painfully. "That took away my courage. I have not since returned to this mysterious, whispering wadi."

Halfway attentive to her story, M'nalo sounded a sympathetic grunt. Then grasping her arm for balance, he ventured with his left foot's toes into the edge of water. It was cool and thrilling and encouraged him to kneel, reach a hand in. Lick his fingers. Sweet to the tip of his tongue, it lanced a recollection of the comfortable pools of his river-rain goddess, Yemoja. And despite the sanction of his practical mind, he could barely restrain himself from plunging straight in.

The tease of memory also stirred a restlessness within, a boredom with his enclosed life. All at once his growing knowledge of the underground chambers seemed tedious. Useless. All those paths merely leading up and down to black nowhere. All those echoing damp caverns, large and small, sultry hideaways. All of those dripping walls and trickling flows that patiently pooled. All of them without promise.

Except now! From this endless water slowly flowing elsewhere. So pushed by such zesty possibilities of this grand wadi, he was eager to adventure.

What he needed, though, was a boat or a raft to explore the wadi. Had he a craft, he would reach a bit farther with each outing, always learning something useful. Lack of light would not dissuade him. With Bisui's help, he had grown accustomed to darkness. Saw it differently, felt comfortable and safe within it.

First essential, though, he had to construct a vessel. But where in a desert where even firewood was scarce, would he find material enough to make himself a water craft?

A niggling question at the back of his mind.

Half-asleep in the rocking hammock, M'nalo lay daydreaming of the river basins of his boyhood. He was dream-riding the cool water alongside the calabash floats of the fishnets, when his mind hooked on a notion and stayed put. He blinked smartly awake.

Floating. Bisui and her bat skins. Both ideas came together to show how they might suit his dreams.

Over the years, she had become a skilled skinner. She deftly used a crescent-shaped blade hooked onto her knuckles—a tool Kaariba had made for her—to remove the loose bat pelts without a nick. Lately, though, she'd changed her technique to accommodate M'nalo's swift beheadings. Just as one would slip a stone from a ripe date, Bisui perfected a method of cutting the whole bat carcasses out of their furry skins. She left the tiny winged hands and feet intact. And turned inside out for curing in the abundant sunshine, the pelts remained supple. She stored these fur pouches in the cool dry caves and cleverly sewed them together into warm beddings and mats.

Now, M'nalo slid from the hammock, threw on his djellaba and started for the shady, afternoon hills where Bisui might be tending her flock. Eventually, he found her in a small front cave milking a goat. Patient as the red rocks, he waited until she was done. Then he took her arm familiarly, drew her to the light of the cave's door.

"No, Mbingu. It is still bright," she protested, misunderstanding his intentions.

M'nalo shook his head and gestured same with his free hand while he forced her to sit. He then knelt on the ground and using a short stick, began sketching his idea in the dirt, shaping first the water, then his craft for exploring it.

Bisui caught on right away. Kneeling shoulder to shoulder with him, she gave words to the diagrams.

"You want me to sew their neck-holes tightly closed so that they might float on the air within them. Right?"

"And you want many and more."

"And you want one great pouch, like the one we used to treat your damaged skin. So you could put all these little air-pouches into the large one, which I'd sew up same way airtight as possible."

"And you want all of this by first light of yesterday," Bisui concluded with a little happy laugh with which, whenever they were alone, M'nalo was becoming familiar.

He turned toward her, grabbed her hand in both of his large ones while he beamed gratitude into her veiled face. Privately, his heart soared on the notion that he might yet find a way from her and Kaariba's caves.

Bisui lisped, "For Mbingu, my love, I will ply thin waxed needles, and tighten fine yarn even if my fingers bleed. Still I will construct your floating pillow." Then in her quick shy way she slipped her hand from his, firmly returned her attention to goat minding.

Midmorning one moon later found M'nalo taking careful time, bearing a cumbersome bat-skin raft on his head, sidling through the dim caverns, aiming for the edge of the great underground wadi. Once there, he unstrung a tallow lamp from around his neck, blew on the fire-stick until it flamed the lamp's wick. He planted the fluttery light on the ground to mark his launching spot. Then, in whispered Twi he hoped was audible enough, he gave praise to Eshu, Lord of Crossroads. He lay on his belly in his pillow raft and pushed off into the black water. The faint breeze of his own motions cooling his anxious sweat, slowly as he could manage, his hands paddled him into the unknown.

All went smoothly. With an appropriate wriggle, he adjusted his body's balance in the bat-skin raft. No water slopped in. Instead, the craft folded around his body, properly supportive whether he spread his legs wide, or kept them close together like a tail.

After a while of testing the raft, he turned himself around on the water and returned to his flickering beacon.

Over the next few days M'nalo made several short excursions. Each venture, more for reassurance than anything else, he strapped the splendid knife to his thigh. During one traverse extending two hundred or so paces along the left shoreline, he encountered a rocky outcropping. Just beyond it, at the limit of his straining vision, he thought he could see vaulted, seeping walls covered with pale luminescent moss. A sight that made him shiver.

From all his investigations, it seemed the wadi might indeed go on endlessly. The further into it he dared, the more he grew aware of a distant, muffled sound, a roar reminiscent of waterfalls. Made him wonder if the wadi was on a slow flow through the mountain. On such a passage M'nalo dared hope that he might float along and take his àshe to some place else. So this dream of a scheme became basis of each test he gave the cobbled raft. Each time he returned to his flickering yellow tallow beacon, the risky notion seemed more reasonable.

Raft, as usual, left secured at the wadi's edge, M'nalo was meandering back to the main cave when he heard the voices. At least two strangers were talking with Kaariba. M'nalo slowed, quieted his approach and detoured to a high ledge where he could hide and see.

The voices became distinct as he reached his vantage: "... know all about you, elder Kaariba. Your contributions and your punishments. Your great knowledge and generosity. Your hideous guide with her veil."

M'nalo edged forward and cautiously peered down at the fellows standing close over Kaariba. He couldn't make out facial features in the cave's scant light, but sight of their mostly shaved pates with thick glint-threaded braids down their necks tightened his belly into a knot. Could these be the same three who had attacked Lathso on Rat's hill? Evidenced by the stout shoulder-length cudgels they carried, they well could be.

"You cannot deceive us. We know all," one assassin declared. "You were guided by a young sorcerer to an iron-making. He came to you from the desert after salt traders found him and brought him to you. Using your knowledge, your slave cured his wounds. Now she walks the night naked with him. They couple in the dark like animals." He laughed as if incredulous. "She has even found her belly for this sorcerer's pup. Isn't what I say the truth?"

"You are better informed than I," Kaariba complained. "So long it was since I had a woman that way, I did not recognize the baby in her different smell."

One of the assassins guffawed, slapped an explosion from the outside of his thigh. At the news of Bisui with child, an aimless thrill snaked through M'nalo's essences. He made a rapid survey of nooks and caves about him, wondered if she, too, was peeping from the blackness of one.

"We have been straightforward," the easily humored fellow had continued. "Now, old man, you must do likewise and you will live to know the heat of another day." He laughed hearty as if he'd cracked a joke. "This man-child is dangerous unless returned to the sorcerers' guild. So tell me, old man. When is the traitor's pup returning?"

Answered Kaariba, "That I know not. With the freedom of youth and no scrutiny, he comes and goes as he pleases."

His eyes must have flooded, as another of the assassins interposed, "No need to weep, honorable one. You are in no peril. We do not disrespect the destinies of elders."

"In any case, old man," continued his bullying companion, "we have special use for you. It's a message to your slave and eyes. Since she has no place to go, she will return to you. We know this. We want her to understand that the boychild in her belly belongs to the guild of sorcerers. She might have keep of it for its first years, but we shall return when it comes of age!"

The third fellow, silent until now, stopped him with a gesture. He had been sniffing the air like a dog all the while. Now he lifted his arm, pointed straight up towards M'nalo's perch.

In the same moment, M'nalo was gone, softly padding away as fast as his familiarized feet dared through the dark caves. His heading was his bat-skin raft.

Chapter Three
ESCAPE

The current's speed had increased with deceptive constancy. What began as a soothing susurrus was now an extreme, high-pitched keening that rang in M'nalo's ears. Made him swallow spit to wet his dry throat. Cautious about the forceful flow, he undid his boubou, used its length to fasten his wrist through the cobbled side of his raft. Tethered so, the two would not be separated.

Then, wearing nothing but the splendid knife in its sheath strapped to his thigh, he bellied into the bottom of his cradling craft, grappled his hands into the spaces at its lip. He closed his eyes tight, thought a prayer to Yemoja and her sister river-rain goddesses who ruled the sweet waters. Then, not even attempting to steer, he consigned his àshe to the hurtling belly-close blackness that roiled and rippled beneath him.

Once, seeking some sense of his speed, M'nalo eased a tentative foot over the edge of his pillow raft, reached his toes down. But so fast, and like a hand, did the cold water grasp, he swiftly withdrew it. Felt relief as if close escaped.

The eerie hollow growl grew to a swishy hiss. Abrupt rolls and dips of his flexible raft continually doused him. These signs told M'nalo that the channel was narrowing. Then brisk against the unseen walls came a new sound suggesting openness.

Where had he heard such a sound before?

Yes! It was at the gorge where he and Bisui fished the evening air for bats.

Just at that moment his raft struck something hard, bounced away and veered giddily contrary to the current's terrific pull. M'nalo lurched close to capsizing around a curve as the raft spun and scraped against a wall. Then his head hit with a jolt that nearly tore free his hold.

But his strong hunter's hands held on despite the pain and dizziness. He adjusted his long frame middle of the raft so it could fold around him and better protect both body and balance. He blinked water from his eyes, snorted the sting from his nostrils, and turned his throbbing head to one side. And his every gulp of air was breathed as if it were his last.

Time, speed, and darkness commingled into a terrifying melee. His straining eyes saw nothing. He thought of where his blind passage might be taking him and shivered from dread. His heart pounded against his chest as if wanting out. It seemed that he was going too fast, sweeping past life itself, when with a swish like air escaping, the rushing channel plunged downward. Then, unready and breathless, he was dragged beneath the violent surface.

Instinct urging, his big hands grabbed at the water, his feet kicked for purchase. So long he had not swum. At his wrist, the tether to the raft pulled contrary, yanking him into a different consciousness...

...outside the slack floating frame of flesh and bones, M'nalo's essences swim free. The figures of the river-rain goddesses circle and hover, their dark visages frowning...

...his black àshe responds, "Oh great goddesses of rivers and rain, all praise to Oshun, and Yewa, and Ere, and Oya, and benevolent Yemoja. All respect. The breezes of your fans ripple the rivers and bring coolness to the land. Your swords wield destruction to the selfish."

"To whom do you plea, bit of man?"

"To the fierce crowned mistresses of wealth, of wind, of witchcraft. To the cool mistresses of sweetness, of ecstasy, of health. To the powerful mistresses of the dagger that wields black àshe."

The water goddesses wrap their slick green tresses about M'nalo's empty body, steadying it upright for parley. Nine times they wave their round fans.

"This bit has presumed our affection."

"That is the nature of a man."

"This man-child is minion of an outcast, an aberration created out of spite."

"His master enjoys Eshu's favor and protection."

"We who rule rivers and rain have defied Ifà himself. So what of his mischievous messenger? All judgment remains in our domain."

"One with a princess, one with a slave, this orphaned bit has fathered two in his own image."

"Which neither commends or condemns this bit of breath."

"We have always welcomed this speck of dirt as favorite."

"Indeed, he enjoys the coolness of our fans. So one more time we shall not abandon this pulse of life."

Warmth upon his face roused and recalled him to consciousness. He lay on his back up to his ears in water. His legs were spread apart, his feet dangling over the edge of the bat-skin raft. He remained with eyes closed while his essences commingled, became whole again. Then, gently, he clenched his muscles, testing himself for injury. Bruises complained with every flexing. Knees and elbows stung from abrasions. His forehead throbbed from a tender knot fingers wide. Nothing too bad, though. So he breathed deeply of relief, praised his orisha.

This air he breathed carried no scent of goats or stale cooking smoke. No sultry female flavor, or old man's mustiness, either. Pure and sweet in his nostrils, a zephyr on his naked skin, this air bore the sounds of lapping wavelets, calls of waterfowl. M'nalo relished each breath, memory already salvaging from his past and touching on longings that reminded of home. Like a fancy for the food and fruits of his compound. Like the thatched domes of zangalas under the ancient baobab. Like the happiness of his youthful freedom.

Melancholy tugged briefly, but couldn't restrain the delight at his fortune. And only then did he open his eyes. And had to jerk his face sideways from the bluish white glare from straight above. The sudden movement unbalanced his raft, and water slopped in. So he carefully clambered to a hands-and-knees crouch, looked about.

The raft lay entangled in tall shoots of grass edging a wide brown river. He saw that he could easily paddle the raft through to a stand of trees on what seemed more solid ground fifty or so paces distant.

The solid ground turned out to be grassy slush into which he sank to his knees when, too soon, he slid off the raft. Then, as he labored to pull it along, squelching through mud to firmer ground, a host of flying blood-hungry insects attacked. Remembering remedy against such an onslaught, M'nalo quickly smeared mud all over his exposed skin and thwarted the pests. Then he slogged on towards a grass-covered bank.

Partway there he came upon a nest with five dirty-white eggs. As he paused to suck down two of them, he noticed several other rude nests close by. Water fowl, he guessed, and felt a swell of contentment at these forgotten familiar creatures.

Solid ground beneath his feet at last, M'nalo braided long blades of grass through its lip spaces and secured his raft. He marked its location relative to three different landmarks—the dry trunk of a broken-off tree to his left; a small mud-hill in line with a distant bend in the river to his right; and straight on before him, a high tuft of specially light green marsh-grass.

Then detaching his soggy boubou from the lip of his raft, he tied up his muddy loins.

After the months of cool echoing caves, even the wet slurp of his footsteps was satisfying. M'nalo relished every non-desert sensation. The brush of bush against his skin. The calls of unfamiliar birds. Even the warm scent of dirt with life in it. Once on firmer ground, wasting no time beneath the sunshine, he set out to scout his marshland surroundings. He wanted to reacquaint himself with whisker-fish, and eagles, and herons. To observe snakes slither by on a search for eggs and chicks. To marvel again at the hard-diving pelicans plunging into the waters after surface fish. To smile as pesky gulls stole from the plenteous scoop of the pelicans' bills. To admire short-winged kestrels and kites riding valiant against the winds. To indulge himself and gawk at the magnificent cormorants as they spread their waterlogged wings to dry.

For hours he wandered, savoring this indescribable freedom that he had sorely missed.

Back on his raft, the whim of slow currents taking him southward and a little towards the setting sun, M'nalo drifted through a land nurtured by a mighty river. He slept lightly, dozed often. Each day he took communing dips with the river-rain goddesses. In turn, they blessed him regularly with fat, sleepy fish, whose sweet and tender tissues he ate raw. Sometimes, relaxed on his aimless float, he disturbed flocks of scarlet flamingos that rose from the river like shape-shifting mists. Some days, crouched low in his raft, he watched distant herdsmen following the high grey clouds that emptied life over the expansive plains, over the grazing lands and water holes, tantalizing the parched ground.

A naked speck adrift under an incurious sky, M'nalo watched many a dawn emerge bleary, glowing pink, fresh birthed from mysterious Night. He watched as it promised gentleness to the soft clouds in the cage of sky and watched again as these baby clouds hardened into thundering, gray-black violence. Many a time, from heavens such as these, M'nalo tried in vain to sense a pattern.

Often in this profound solitude, unexpected notions urged his oko to recollect particular scenes. The bat-skin of his craft reminded of the surprising crispy hair top of Jureyi's thighs. A misty morning recalled the tenderness of the lady Tebika's kisses. Star shine made him long for darkness and Bisui's passion. Haunted by the will of these fine ecstasies, he'd milk their memories to exhaustion and sigh. Then reassured that Life had loved him well enough, his àshe would lift and float aimless as his raft on the gentle currents.

Afloat in a half-sleep one afternoon after feasting on a careless fish, M'nalo's drifting recollections returned him to boyhood, to a story from a stranger at a neighbor's night fire. The man, in strong voice, had boasted, "Once I escaped a crocodile, in truth, a pair of them. They had taken to preying along Oguno riverbank. You know the place, that muddy bend downstream from the shallows where herd animals cross."

The stranger was of medium height, and brawny. He paused often, flashing a quick, baffled smile as if to support his incredible tale. When the squatting men grunted recognition of the place, he continued, "Two days straight I stalked them. Then I killed an olose, laid traps and waited. Dry season was at its limit, the river low, the bank sticky brown mud. For two days I became like a lump of that mud. It all paid off when these eyes saw the biggest pair of crocodiles crawling up on the bank at their leisure, setting themselves up nicely, nicely near my traps.

"They were happy, yes! The bull bellowing pleasure at the sunshine, making water droplets on his back jiggle and dance. With a great squelching of mud, he would roll over and touch the female's nose with his snout. Thus they played at the river's edge, heads slapping and splashing the water, beating an off-time rhythm to the water-birds' anxious calls.

"Not welcome in these displays, the cleaning birds were crying alarm. Too much danger, too little chance for picking through those open jaws of gnashing teeth. 'Aiee!' cried the hungry birds, calling their concerns to the wind. 'What of our hatchlings?' they complained. 'Where shall we feed?'

"Yet all the wind can do is bear a plight. Carry a cry over the endless brown earth and the endless green that covers it to that distant point where the sky greets a red-eyed sun…"

'Don't blame the wind!' interrupted a deep voice. 'Brother Breeze is merely a traveler, toting messages it cannot teach.

A wine-eyed man in front jumped up and blurted, 'Talk about your weapon…' but companions on either side grabbed his elbows and pulled him back down.

The storyteller grinned and continued, "Amazed at the size and intelligence of these marvelous beasts, I started to wonder if I could slay one. I assessed my weapons. Though it might cost one of my precious iron-tipped spears, I sang homage to Ogun and decided to try. Downwind, silent and with patient precaution, I began to creep close enough for a clear shot at that soft part behind the front leg.

"Well, the sun smiled on me, and I got a strike deep into the flesh of the female. At which her mate turned in attack, his stubby legs churning over the scrub and mud so fast that I thought for certain I was a dead man.

"Lucky for me he slipped on a patch of soft mud, which gave me a moment to stand and turn. Time enough to cast my last desperate spear. And by what magic, I can't say, this faithful weapon went straight in the snapping jaws, down into the gape of throat."

'What a strike!' exclaimed a listener at the edge of the circle.

"The crocodile stopped altogether and thrashed about," the storyteller pressed on, gesturing dramatic with his arms and hands. "It was trying to tear the spear from its throat even as it was beginning to cough up blood. A mad swipe of his vengeful tail slashed my leg here"—the man bent, showed off a jagged pink scar on his left calf—"as I tried to jump away. Then he rushed back into the water and joined his fatally struck mate.

"Two days I had to wait before their bodies floated up. But by this time their skins were too water-soaked to make quality hide."

M'nalo felt a soft touch on his thigh. So caught up in his memories, he turned expecting his mother's frown as she scolded him for staying so late from home. He realized, instead, that his raft had drifted onto a grassy sandbar. The touch was no more than a dried spray of windblown reeds. Still, it stirred up a melancholy that stung his eyes well past a bruised purple sunset.

All afternoon, clear to inaudible, then clear again, the messages had wafted on the sparkling air. As M'nalo drifted downriver the drum-talk became plain, and he could understand. No secret message this. An initial barrage announced joyful praise to the gods who lit the lamps of full moon. A second thanked the gods for their generosity. Third came a thumping invitation to each and all within earshot. Come gather and enjoy!

M'nalo, longing for company, chose welcome over wariness and, using his hands as now-for-now paddles, began steering toward the bank. Dusk was falling and lake flies beginning to swarm when he passed around a slow curve, saw the floating lights on the water ahead of him, and the single-manned small boats. It took him a moment to realize what they were about.

Despite the massing midge-flies, the fishermen were expertly pulling loaded nets from around the light baits, by which, it seemed, both flies and fish were fooled. The prospect of savories now equaling the promise of companionship, M'nalo quietly directed his raft toward a front of reeds short steps from a busy group of men sorting fish.

Safe landed, M'nalo found folks on shore netting other food. With thin cloths shielding their faces, men, women, and children moved into the clouds of lake flies. The gatherers raised flat, round nets, and spun in circles, each revolution snaring more of the hapless insects, which the folks then scraped off into large covered baskets.

Already some villagers were firing large pots. One heavyset woman, whose friendly manner achingly reminded of Ammaa, had made even more progress. She was busily mashing handfuls of the writhing mass into patties, and dropping them into her bubbling pot.

Watching from behind the gnarled trunk of an old almond tree, M'nalo hungrily swallowed his spit. Eventually putting trust in the woman's generosity, he approached, hopeful for a prepared portion.

Her welcome was abundant as her smiles. She handed him a cooked patty. Instantly he was an honored guest.

As expected, during the feasting he was met with queries. "Which village are you from?" "Who is your family?" "Where are you traveling?"

Hard questions indeed. For confused by the many days of travel with the Arab slaver, and his mysterious flight through the sandstorm, and the healing sojourn in the iron-master's caves, and his black underground escape, and most recently, the many days of river drifting, M'nalo could scarcely locate himself in place or time.

Other than the familiar language they spoke, he had no idea whether he was among friends or traditional enemies. So even if he had better than his wrecked whisper of a voice, he could not have answered properly. In response, he gestured first that he was mute, then pointed to the river, and supported with nods whatever banal suggestions the curious made.

Whatever else, these folks were generous, and accepted him at their cooking fires. But by the end of the feasting, before their storytelling began, M'nalo sneaked away. Nothing wrong with their company, except that after the long time passed in solitude, he was oppressed by so much of it.

Dawn breezed in slightly pink with a wisp of silver clouds about her face, beautiful to behold. But after one peek, wrapped against the chill in a long khanga stolen from a drying pole, M'nalo squinted away from the brightness to drowse in the comfort of his slow floating raft. Dozy memory stole him from last night's festive midge-fly gathering, smoothly returned him to savories of childhood...

...the air hot in the crisp bright day. In answer to the villagers' fervent prayers and offerings, the gods have sent the swarms of locusts flying past, safe and high over the ripening field, the crackle of their stubby wings like wind in dry leaves.

...the danger above clattering away, villagers are quickly scooping low-flying stragglers into covered baskets. Mere failures of the mighty flock, but still many, many of them. Quite enough for the communal roast that evening...

The juice of delicious memory dribbled from the corner of M'nalo's smile as he roused and turned, and relaxed again into sleep's embrace...

...no sunshine bathes this river basin...no audience is watching... yet with melancholy steps, his skeleton is dancing, graceful as a white snake in the murky water, it shapes a message of departure...

After this, no longer did M'nalo bask indifferent, the river his companion and driver. Now his indolent passage was disturbed by busy-ness. Instead of a tortoise exploring the warm surface waters, he felt more like a disgruntled crocodile out of pace on mankind's waterways, and forced into the riverside reeds. No more periods of delicious solitude along the currents. Even as he sought to laze in the eddies, distracting people were ever fleeting by: Enormous pole-punted rafts laden with baled and wrapped mysteries; longboats with sweaty ten-man teams racing the midstream; gardeners in make-do watercraft ferrying their toil towards merchants' purses.

In truth, the recent lake-fly feast had subtly touched his àshe, and revived simple longings. He craved food spiced in a fired pot. He missed a shared, spontaneous laugh at some quick-witted bit of humor. He yearned for the warmth and smells and colors of community. So at last weary of the solitude and security of his lonesome raft, one pleasant morning he pulled it high up the riverbank.

He used the splendid knife to cut Bisui's intricate stitching and, by tying together the round leather bottom of his raft, created a carry sack that slung comfortably across his shoulder. Next, from a suitable branch, he fashioned a stout staff. Then he strapped the knife in its sheath tied to his thigh and hidden under the stolen khanga. So equipped, M'nalo set off through the forests edging the river.

Late that afternoon, he came upon a smoldering fire belonging to a rude palm-leaf lean-to beneath which squatted two hard-faced young men. The long-limbed one flashed a shifty spokesman smile. His quiet partner was chubby as a porcupine. They shared a corrupt air, a look of shallow dignity. Yet M'nalo so longed for the salt of human company, he stood before their door with a plea on his face and bowed.

The rangy one crawled out, stood up. Nearly as tall as M'nalo, he worked a shrewd smile as he said, "Greetings, friend. I am Nhedu Femry, of the Ibo. Welcome to our door." With a grand wave of his hand, he indicated his heavyset companion who, save for a slow shifting of his gaze, had not moved. "Kajuna Dhu, here, is my true brother, and also welcomes you."

Kajuna Dhu fixed his eyes upon M'nalo and nodded casually.

M'nalo bowed again and gestured to his throat, indicating that he had no voice. Then, pulling a good-sized fish from his bag, he mimed a request to use their fire, make a meal for all to share.

Femry laughed and clapped his hands. "Your generosity humbles me," he declared. "Our fire is at your disposal." As he spoke, he shook his head side to side as if denying the worth of his words, a habit of which he seemed unaware.

M'nalo reached into his bag again, brought forth a handful of fat groundnuts, clumps of red dirt still soiling their cream crinkly shells. He stooped and placed them near the fire.

A fleshy mass of smooth-moving muscle, Kajuna Dhu emerged from the shelter, approached close to the fire. "I'll do that," he said, a fat under-lip sucked in.

"You see," said Femry, chuckling. "Already you've convinced Dhu's belly. It so loves roasted nuts."

M'nalo smiled and drew another handful from his bag, added it to the pile by the fire.

Humored by the gesture, Femry's giggle heightened in pitch. Busily blowing life into the fire, Kajuna Dhu paused to grunt his agreement.

They proceeded to make a pleasant meal.

In the quiet of evening after dinner, Femry and M'nalo sat on their heels, watching the fire, freshening it with twigs from time to time. Kajuna Dhu, curled up again under the lean-to, called out something to his friend in an unfamiliar dialect, which brought on an extended bout of ribald sniggers between the two. When Femry could collect himself enough to notice M'nalo's puzzlement, he spoke again in Ibo, "Forgive my rude laughter, my silent friend. Kajuna reminds me of a story. Maybe you'd like to hear it?"

Only now realizing how he had missed this pleasure, M'nalo smiled and nodded with vigor.

So Nhedu Femry began, "I have heard it said that one after another, our glorious African gods, being imperfect themselves, made and remade humans in their many attempts to figure out a workable model. I'll tell you straight away that they never succeeded. As I hear it, one particular model had the two sexes completely mixed up. Every person was a little bit male and a little bit female. How they managed the mixing of emotions never comes into this version, so I can't talk about that.

"As my story goes, in this mixed trial, a male might have an obo's nipple on each breast for his sex organs. A female might have a man's stones without the oko itself. Some persons might end up with both oko and obo; others, half of each. You see how I mean when I say it was romping confusion.

"But that was the manner of these hilarious gods. Tried all sorts of experiments for a laugh, they did. Although no major harm was done. Indeed, these early people were flexible and adjusted to the situation without embarrassment. Found many ways to enjoy their unusual endowments. No boring routines for them.

"So life was progressing evenly, the gods laugh-happy as ownerless jackasses, mankind ignorant as ever. Thus this confusing situation might have continued indefinitely. But then came the 'Wala' incident.

"'Wala,' as you would expect from its Bantu meaning, is that neutral bit of a female's body, that partition of the nether regions. One particular Wala had a troublemaker's personality out of proportion with its real function, which as I say, was to do nothing but be there. In a fit of whimsy, the gods had allowed this base separator the gift of eloquence and the distinction of having its own tuft of hair—finger-long, silvery curls.

"These gifts were the gods compensation to every Wala for work in an unpopular place. They sympathized with the assignment to unpleasant monotony when compared to its closest companions; which were organs always involved in goings-on, and thrills, and intrigues.

"With all that dull time to think—and not a little envious of its cruder but lively neighbors—eventually this reflective Wala concluded that it was somehow soiled by its immediate neighbors. So it instigated a campaign of bad feelings between the two. Within Caca's hearing, it began flattering Obo that she was soft and pink and juicy, while Caca was a common stinking worthless vent.

"For two weeks straight that was all Caca heard. Then in protest and deciding that Direct Action worked better than fancy statements, it tightened up its hole and stopped doing anything at all for the rest of the body united.

"So imagine the scandal! Within three days, the body Wala served became harrowed by demons without purpose. Belly, ever unsettled, complained strenuously and swelled up bloated. From Feet to Eyeballs, every other body part was reacting badly—headaches, fever, chill bumps, pimples, red eyes, foul breath.

"Yet Caca remained unmoved. Made no statements. Not a squeak. Not even a squeaky fart. Though privately, it jeered, 'Let the juicy Obo take over.'

"Even Obo herself began weeping blood, pleading for mercy. Yet Caca remained a cage of stone. 'My pride's hurting hard,' it allowed. 'I want amends.'

"Well, once they heard this, the rest of the body turned on Wala. 'Apologize now!' each part demanded, and with such a passion, Wala became intimidated and claimed regrets for the mischief it had made.

"Which was all that Caca really wanted. It relaxed its vent, and not too long, all body functions were back to normal. Full relations and good accord were once again in order.

"And that would have been the end of this story except for one detail. As usual, those inquisitive gods were watching all, and they took exception to the Wala's behavior. They decided to eliminate that particular model of humans. Although, off and on, here and there, a sample with a hairy tuft still might slip through.

"And about the troublemaker of this story? Well those meddlesome gods punished it fair. They took away its pretty hair, left it stuck in that same dull spot, still smart and curious, still neither here nor there. Still neither Wala Caca nor Wala Obo!"

Story done and it being obvious that the simple shelter could not sleep them all, M'nalo gestured to Femry that he preferred to remain outside. He'd stand guard a bit, he signed, then lay down in a nook among the roots of a big laurel tree whose beguiling aroma pervaded the camp. His new companions offered no objections.

Brief twilight turned to near-black night, and M'nalo, intending to impress, sat with his back against a buttress root. He flexed his shoulder muscles hard, adjusted for pokes that the bark roughed into his skin and sat resolute to protect his new friends' sleep. As the quiet, unruffled time slid by, his mind rambled between sayings of his village elders, all the pronouncements relating to a single theme.

"Trouble lurks at the only bend on a lonely road," he remembered, the very reason for M'nalo to be the appointed guardian.

"Trouble pounces during a single blink of the longest night," quoted the philosopher within.

"Not so when I am tense with effort in every muscle," M'nalo told himself.

He squeezed his eyes shut tight, then stretched them wide open, watchful of the grayish glow of the moonlit scene, alert to the wind like a creeping shadow trembling the treetops. Like everyone else, M'nalo had grown up with ideas of what these mysterious nighttime forests might hold. He had heard tales from family, village elders, childhood intimates. On one fact all the stories agreed: The dark beneath these tall trees was home to terrible secrets and close-concealed awesome power. The shadows were a realm where...

...a passionate female presence is challenging him with a promise of sexual ecstasy...a sultry scent reassures of her earthy fervor...yet her alluring presence remains at the edge of sight almost behind him and try as he might, he's unable to turn his head to see...

Day slyly dawning, M'nalo's insistent bladder awoke him.

One idle midmorning, M'nalo and his companions were wandering the dusty thoroughfare of a nearby harbor town. Unheeding of his friends' usual comments and jibes, M'nalo barely could tear his eyes from the dazzle and dance of the ocean. He still could not get used to its vastness, to the water stretching away to a horizon where no farther shore boundaried it, just as the jalis Anandan had described during his childhood.

A noisy band of strange fellows burst out of a compound nearby, and snatched his attention from the glittering sea. The foreigners stumbled about the public path as if drunk. They laughed at their excesses with faces red as baboons' backsides. Each face was partly covered with thick hair—reddish bronze or muddy brown, dried-grass yellow or gray-streaked black, even one with the scruffy white of an aged gorilla. Robust, scrawny, or short, the men all wore short loose khangas above coarse leggings held up by buttons and belts with brilliant buckles. In their own language they shouted rude-toned remarks to each other like children at play, rather than behaving like proper adults.

Taking advantage of the foreigners' childishness, some vendors and bead-sellers were misbehaving as well. Some ludicrously aped the fellows' antics as if bartering. Meanwhile, in fact, they stole the strangers' pretty buttons, and even their nice hats and helmets. Amazed and ashamed, M'nalo stood gawking at the locals' bold dishonesty. Were the foreigners this ignorant? Then one of them, a tall man with long yellow hair, turned pale eyes toward M'nalo's companions and halfway raised his hand in a gesture of recognition.

M'nalo glanced at his friends, but neither seemed to have noticed the fellow as they resumed their dusty saunter.

Late that day, poking sparks from the fire, Nhedu Femry held forth on how these strange-colored people came to be.

"They come from a distant place," he declared, "where the older one grows and the more wisdom he gathers into his skull, the darker and darker his skin becomes until he achieves the proper natural blackness. There are some folks in this faraway place who have grown so wise, they are indistinguishable from night itself. Some are even blacker than people from our great land..."

M'nalo nodded, but his mind drifted to remembering a man who one day had appeared and settled in as a squatter at the far end of his village. Neither M'nalo nor Izi nor any of their circle had actually seen the man, though most had heard from others of the white spots and blotches that covered his body. On his face, back, thighs, and even genitals—sightings made at the riverside while the disfigured fellow bathed.

Some folks opined that he was a ghost undecided whether to return to the other place, or to stay among the living. Needless to say, with all this unnaturalness about him, this fellow's hut was left severely alone by every boy who valued his black àshe. Then one day, the fellow was gone. He simply vanished and stirred up even more excited conjecture about whether he'd moved on in this world, or moved on to the next.

Now M'nalo glanced furtively at his own arms, relieved that his long days drifting on the river had warmed the pale blotches on his skin closer to their natural tones. His muteness was difference enough that set him apart.

The next afternoon the threesome went scrounging for food at the marketplace. M'nalo was a little way off from the others, salvaging overripe but firm-enough mangoes from a throwaway pile, when something—perhaps the hunter in him, perhaps Eshu, messenger of mischief—made him glance up. Through the throngs he spied Femry talking to a foreigner. It was the same tall, yellow-haired man of the other day. The sight made alarm sting through M'nalo's fugitive soul. More than the aloof stance of the white man, it was Femry's eloquent cower, a posture of betrayal, that alerted M'nalo. At once he noted a quartet of hard-eyed Lufembe mercenaries. They stood ready at the factor's beck and grasped impressive staves tipped with iron spearheads.

Then M'nalo saw Femry turn a scoundrel's smile his way and point a lanky hand. In the same instant he dropped his carry-bag and started through the market's throngs, running in the other direction, plunging through the crowd, dodging and shoving. His ears made plain the waste of looking back. Loud cries of "Runaway!" and the rising excitement of the yielding mass clamored how close was his pursuit.

Gathered khanga flying at his hips, M'nalo sprinted from the marketplace, heading toward openness. Blindly and swift he ran, until he found himself on a narrowing ledge of overhanging rock—and trapped! He had out-maneuvered himself, he realized with an empty feeling. Better aware of the lie of the shoreline, his chasers had quarried him down a ledge ending in rock-face. Not far behind him, he could hear the triumph in their shouts.

Except for the dusky sea far below, he had no options.

A breath of hesitation, but only that, M'nalo turned and jumped. Long heartbeats slipping through the air...then *splash!* into cool brine. He surfaced and quickly swam under the rocky overhang. The rough, salty water welcomed him wickedly, refreshing the stings and bruises of his getaway dash, yet energizing and buoying him up. Swimming easy, he slipped out of his khanga. He felt good, and with sunset imminent, was certain he could tread water longer than the pursuit's patience.

Confidently, M'nalo flipped onto his back to rest and paddling outstretched arms under the surface for quiet, listened to the noises of his hideout. Lapping wavelets, nowhere to go, lazily tripping over themselves. Gentle, lulling thuds from a flotilla of dried coconuts, their shells casually nudging his shoulders. Sloshes and gurgles of other bits of bobbing flotsam. High-pitched, rat-like squeaks.

Startled, M'nalo righted himself, grew even more alert as, suddenly, he became aware of other, more threatening sounds. A suppressed panting. An inadvertent splash. The cautious approach of a swimmer on the search?

M'nalo quietly sucked his chest full of air, let himself sink into the black water. He waited...and waited. Then after as long as he could manage, like brother Tortoise stealing a breath among a romp of alligators, M'nalo's head broke surface with barely a ripple.

Someone splashing close by spit out water and yelled, "I can't hear you."

"See him?" returned a faint shout.

"It's dark down here. Rats, too, I think...eeeiiik! Something bit me!"

A frantic swashing ensued.

As the foamy turmoil headed away from him, M'nalo allowed himself a long breath of relief. Then in the quiet the searcher had left behind, M'nalo heard the squeaks again and all at once every part of his body felt like rat bait.

Now close to M'nalo's right ear there was a particular squeak that set consternation competing with comfort in his mind. That teasing tone, that tinge of amused impatience.

Could a rat's squeak contain the essence of his master?

"Thought your oko was my next nibble, huh?"

"Uncle?" M'nalo spluttered, the water somehow fattening the timbre of his whisper. "Is it you?"

"Keep your breath, young leopard. This night we face a long journey, and maybe your river-rain goddesses sport with some other favorite."

"Where are we going, master?"

"To a place where the drum is safe. A distant place where you must teach the dance."

"Which drum, Uncle? Which dance is that?"

"The drum is you, young sorcerer. You will sound the dance, the message pulsing through your blood. The *opun* of knowledge drummed safe inside your souls..."

...M'nalo shivered on hearing the sorcerer word that meant 'a crossover into ancestral secrets of true power'. He kept treading water, and listened...

"...the special purpose for which I prepared you. Now, follow your Fà. Think defiance as I have taught. Practice my dance. Take sides with charity. Be strong for the weak. Act from intuition, move towards harmony. Live like a rat, like the survivor you are. But now, we swim," said the rat.

Outbound tide helping their way, they set off. M'nalo stayed two arm's-lengths behind with eyes fixed on the small whiskered head bobbing along the moonlit sea. Dip and pull and push and roll and breathe. Dip and kick and push and pull. Big hands against the yielding fluid. Big feet like paddles, strong legs kicking. Just so, M'nalo pushed through, comfortable in the warm sea. Dip and pull and roll and kick. Just so he worked to outdistance a nagging concern that he might lose sight of his extraordinary guide.

Then from close ahead, strange sounds assailed his ears. A heavy slack flapping. A thin insistent lashing. Creaks and squeaks as when tree branches rub against each other in the wind. A peculiar muted human grumble. Curiosity as energy, M'nalo dipped into the sea more strongly, followed in the rat's wake.

Suddenly looming out of the dark like a great rocking wall, the source of the noises was there—an enormous craft shakily balancing on the unsettled waves. From the shore he had seen several of them floating near the horizon like great dark birds with dingy white wings raised high to dry in sun and wind.

"Slave ships to the Caribbees," Nhedu Femry had told him. "They remain out there when they're laden up and ready for their long passage. They are awaiting good winds. Out there, also, they have space enough to flee if surprised by sea pirates. They're safe, too, from slave-raiders from land, and from the mosquitoes..." here a pause as Kajuna Dhu had grunted to add a point "...and from our local demons," Femry had interpreted and laughed slyly.

They are not safe from raiding rats, nor from such escapees as I, M'nalo now observed ruefully. His guide swam onto and mounted a thick tie-rope sloping into the sea from the ship's beak. Close copying the creature, M'nalo scrambled up the rope hand over hand, and heaved himself over a railing at the top. He landed on a wooden floor that thudded hollow under his feet. Then he scurried after the vanishing flash of the rat's tail that went through a raised hatch. Down a curved ladder went the two of them into the belly of the slave ship. Into a dim humid hollow stinking of storage and offal, a crowded cavern which sounded a misery of human moans and shrieks and prayer and protest.

The rat streaked into the darkness and disappeared. M'nalo slipped and twisted himself a passage through numerous fat barrels and bales and tall stacks. Finally, in the corner farthest from the open hatchway, he settled his back against the rough wall of the ship and peered about the dim space. His anxiety eased right away as he saw that, from ceiling to floor, from one side to the vague other, the considerable enclosure was crammed full of hiding places. He strained his eyes into nearby shadows and corners, but there was no sign of his master in the guise of a rat.

M'nalo prowled about the hold exploring. The din of human misery seemed to come from the aft end of the hold. He started in that direction to investigate. But the cargo was too tightly stacked, and bulky. Deciding instead, to check his immediate area, he jostled a way to the ship's hull, and located a small round glass window through which moonlight glowed. Come daylight, he could slide himself over a large roped-up bale and see outside.

Gentle snuffling animal grunts and clucks drew him to creep forward of the hatchway through which he had come. He found that this narrow part of the hold had been penned off for several pigs and roosting fowl. So contentedly at rest the animals seemed, M'nalo took wry example from them. He returned to his nook among the barrels and bales and stacks of he knew not what, and made himself comfortable for the night.

Chapter Four
SHIP'S PASSAGE

The red sun fell into the sea behind them as Night and its pale full moon returned. His eyes squinted against the brisk wind, Captain John Burnside of the *Princess Elene* stood beside his first mate, Sam Bowmon, and watched the proceedings on the quarterdeck below. Frowns briefly furrowed both their brows as a clumsy deckhand lost sequence in winding wet sail rope into a large spool. But the veterans on his team just patiently improved their stances, and with better efficiency, restarted the spooling.

Above them, the Captain and first mate nodded in unison. Rough reflections of each other, the two bearded men braced themselves against the sea's roll by holding the top-deck rail with one hand—the stout captain by his left, the shorter Sam Bowmon, his right.

In a voice suiting his bulkiness, Captain Burnside observed, "But fer the whip o' that damned jungle wind, we is a'right."

Familiar with the man's manner of speaking his thoughts, Sam Bowmon did not respond. In the nine years he had worked the seas with his captain, never once had Burnside uttered a statement meant for him without prefixing "Mr. Bowmon" to it.

Bowmon understood the captain's anxiety, though. In tropic waters, evenings brought fierce hot land winds rushing to cool off on the ocean's face. Sometimes so violent, they tossed the waves into bad humor, disrupting everything, which, of course, included the schedules of people like Captain Burnside, who lived by them.

Sam Bowmon did not share his captain's derogatory attitude toward Africa. He did not see the place as jungle, or its people simple. Indeed, over the seven, eight voyages of his sailing career, he had developed solid respect for the dark people, had found them to be canny sailors, wily businessmen and women. On his third trip down here, he had taken ill with dengue fever. Medicine from a marketplace witch-doctor—a green, bitter syrup—had delivered him from the abyss. And as for baser human needs, the most satisfying recess he'd ever experienced was one week with a tar-black woman. Never had a silver florin of his bargained such a profit.

"Mr. Bowmon," said the captain.

"Aye, sir," Bowmon responded.

"I'll be gaein' in now."

"Aye, aye, sir," said Sam Bowmon, unbalancing himself for a moment to briefly tip the brim of his floppy hat. Then he watched the captain stride off to his cabin on the foredeck.

Two weeks now they had been working the Slave Coast: anchoring the *Princess* out-stream; making day trips with barter goods by longboat to coast-side slave markets; loading up Africans and their special foods. Now the slave-traders' stocks were almost exhausted, and the ship's holds promisingly full. With this last group settled in, Sam Bowmon reckoned they were near ready to sail, which was close enough to Sam's rathers. The earlier in June they left, the better the chances that the six-to-seven week journey would be finished before summer hurricanes sprang up. This concern plagued and aged all slave ship captains. That worry, along with too many cargoes caught in these unforgiving storms, also sent their contractors to early graves.

It gave reason, too, why Sam Bowmon so appreciated his first mate's position. To his thinking, it was far more sensible to be chief order-taker than chief order-maker. Why hazard one's peace of mind with these weird winds and the waves they conjured up? Except for their destructive bent, who could depend on them?

As he entered his cabin, Captain Burnside clapped his hands sharp at the sound of scurrying inside the ceiling. The scurrying offender above was undeterred, though. It merely crept to a spy-hole in the woodwork, applied one red eye to the action beneath.

Captain Burnside took a silver timepiece from his fob pocket. He flicked it open with his thick thumb and squinted at it for a long moment. His chest rose with a deep breath as he replaced the watch, nodded like a man satisfied with small routines. Then he strode to his sideboard, took out a decanter and poured himself a brandy. With deft coordination of head and hand, he tossed the burning liquor down the lane of fond memories. Before long, gazing at his desk, the captain was musing on those childhood days when his hardest chore was practicing penmanship.

John Burnside had picked up the pen under the stern eyes of his father, a village schoolmaster who never at the same time had a dozen pupils in his school in the Scottish countryside. Mister Charleford Burnside believed in rigor. His son, an excellent student, made his father proud, at least until he succumbed to temptation and gambled higher education for the gold of a ship captain's life.

The captain sighed, dropped into the comfortable bentwood chair before his desk. After a moment, he struck his trusty flint and lit the hanging brass lantern against the growing dark. Then he pulled open the broad drawer, took out a leather-covered journal, a bottle of ink, and a long-handled whalebone pen with a fine-pointed silver nib. His father would never have dreamt it, but he still found sweet passion in the graceful forming of words. He still thrilled to the smooth flow of ink from pen to crisp paper, the delicate black lacing formed across the pale page.

Although expressing it remained beyond the childless Captain John Burnside, he found something akin to birth in the writing process. And this inkling of continuity refreshed his sense of heritage, soothed his crusty disposition.

During his life of long voyaging, diligent practice had pushed his competence only so far forward. He was able to execute a fair script just as fast as he could compose cogent sentences. If made to admit to a weakness about his performance, it would be his penchant for many unnecessary pauses, during which he pretended to powder and blot ink. While, in fact, he was admiring his notion of exceptional handiwork.

The burn of the brandy smoothly down his throat readied him for the serious task at hand. John Burnside drew his chair closer to the table and set to writing the day's entry in the ship's log.

13th June. The blessed Princess Elene is well-stocked, ready to set sail for the West Indies. Despite the infernal interferences of the Dutch and Portugee devils, our businesses have proceeded with reasonable facility and dispatch, and we now possess a full laden cargo.

In the forward third of the lower hold we are transporting to the colonies several implements and machineries for agricultural purposes. We also carry a dozen or so hens and two roosters, as well as a sounder of six common pigs, namely, one boar, three sows, and two yearlings. Ye shall discover among the ship's invoices a variety of cisterns and cauldrons and plows and long cutlasses, as well as garden hoes and pronged forks of first class iron. We also carry some forty barrels of potable water, a dozen barrels of strong spirits, five barrels of cured fruits, such as apples and plums and pears, eight barrels of fresh potatoes, eight barrels salted cod, as well as several bales of brocades and satin and also Dutch cotton and beeswax and pepper.

Especially for the Negroes, there are stores of their essential foods: their palm oil, yams, dried peas and beans, rice, bananas, breadfruits, and green cherries.

The remaining two-thirds of the hold has been duly rebuilt and palleted to accept seventy-eight Negroes. Solely males so as to avoid the complications of our last venture. There is a seventy-ninth Negro, a consignment which cost a full day's wait, although the fair amends of three healthy young males and a ten-foot length of good ivory were given. By especial request of an heathen royal representative, we have agreed to transport this particular Negro. And for the aforementioned sum we have promised to dispose of this man, said to be a most fearsome wizard, in deepest waters after three weeks passage. Though I find no reason why we should not deliver him to the slave market with the rest and augment our profits. Our go-between expressed great fear and demanded that we secure the man well, so he is chained and fastened apart from the others. Royal or no, these blackamoors are insistent about their superstitions.

Of the ship's crew, two seamen are disabled from fevers. Young Jim Miller is abed and fast failing. McCoy, our ship's bones, has bled him and augurs that he will not last a six-day week. Persuaded by such expert recommendations, this seaman's effects and estimated profits have been measured and made ready for postage home to his family in Tannery Lane, Liverpool. The likely bearer of these black tidings will be the good ship Antigua which shall arrive home during England's gleaming autumn. Thus may God have it be.

With tide and favorable wind, and the grace of our good Lord, this midnight we shall duly raise our sails and pray for a felicitous passage."

Captain John Burnside spent an indulgent moment decorating his plain signature. Then he went through his entry, elaborating his "l"s, tailing his "y"s, and adorning his "g"s with many extravagant curlicues and flourishes. Each a beauty to his eye, however commonplace they were.

M'nalo was startled awake by a commotion on the other side of the hold's barricade—a fence constructed from a double row of saplings lashed and nailed together, extending ceiling to floor. The fresh-cut wood was still green, its sap seeping yet another scent into the hold. Though impenetrable by a person, the fence offered gaps through which vision might steal.

M'nalo crept closer, peeked through and took an alarmed step back, so close was the activity beyond. By the light of a lantern hung on a post, crewmen were securing an unconscious prisoner against the other side. One sailor held a musket at ready, while four others stood the fellow's slumped body against the barricade and spread his arms out. Passing a long chain through the staves, they bound up all but his hands then attached locks to either end of the chain. And just so, his weight hanging on his arm sockets, they left the prisoner.

M'nalo searched and found a vantage through which he could study the man. Short and muscular, he had a big head made even larger by its enormous growth of hair. A glob of blood wobbled at his chin with each shuddering breath he took. Although M'nalo could see no wound, the poor light did reveal scars marking the fellow's cheeks—deep twinned whiskers of the Leopard guild, same as those M'nalo himself bore. Now he partly understood the special precautions for this fellow.

The captive sorcerer, uttering a fitful groan, slowly tested his weight to his legs. Then he threw his head back against the palisade as his body went slack again. Several of his thick braids jammed in between the fence's uprights, the end of one partly snaking through. A beam from the lantern glinted on the remarkable hair revealing its color gradation from black near the scalp to ends of reddish bronze. Such an intricately curled mass, with tiny bits of dirt and moss and seed entwined. Lint from his every bed was there, as was matted fluff from his traveled trails. All had left impression. M'nalo had a sense that within that mass of hair were remnants of every rainfall, every lightening, every darkness, every camp the sorcerer had known. Worn so lion proud, the great ropes of hair were an exceptional record of his complicated life.

A tingling nudged at the back of M'nalo's mind, a phantom urging. So he reached for the knife at his thigh, cut off one of the unconscious man's matted locks. He gazed at it for a moment then worked the braid close to the scalp under his own nappy mass. As he did this, all at once it came to him that a sorcerer cannot harm any part of himself. So M'nalo used both hands to twine and tuck in the stolen braid even more firmly.

Recovered from the bouts of dizziness and stomachaches from seasickness by the third day out, M'nalo began taking more than cursory notice of activities in the hold. On the slaves' side of the barricade, a party of crewmen took the Africans up on deck every midmorning. Others smoked out the hold and using broad brooms, washed out their captives' night soil with buckets of seawater. Kept up on deck for a good long while, the prisoners were then returned to their chains.

Late every afternoon, one particular fellow, stocky and authoritative, came and looked over each slave as if seeking out illness or disability. After being examined, most prisoners burst into prayers or pleas, or cries of protest and outrage, or dire threats and curses by dint of their several gods. They shouted in so many languages, M'nalo doubted their examiner understood. Certainly, from his demeanor, he hardly minded.

The sorcerer was treated specially—doused down where chained and occasionally hand-fed by a nervous crewman. He took scarcely of food, though he accepted water. Crewmen armed with muskets remained posted at the single hatchway, but they were usually relaxed, smoking and talking quietly.

On M'nalo's side of the hold, a grating squeak warned each time the hatch-door was opened, so he could slip into hiding. Twice each day, an older crewman came down and gathered food supplies from bales and boxes. A younger fellow made several trips to carefully fill and haul up buckets of water. Then there was another crewman who, morning and afternoon, climbed down to feed the livestock. Twice already, M'nalo had spied him with his clothes dropped loose at his ankles, his oko driving into a squealing sow's behind.

On the thirteenth day of the voyage, Captain John Burnside entered the following remarks in his journal:

"Whatever remarkable knowledge ye may possess of these infernal savages, they never cease even more to amaze. I duly acknowledge Mr. Bowmon, my standfast first mate, for the essentials of this report. Upright God-fearing Englishman that he is, still Mr. Bowmon has developed a rare sympathy with the Negroes. He has admirable facility with their languages. Indeed, these savages have speech in numerous tongues. There are reports from the cursed Spanishers that some savages can converse with animals and birds. I myself have encountered char-black Negro vendors in the marketplace who barter in a full score of separate tongues.

"Since Mr. Bowmon does not object to close contact with these dark peoples, I have seen to it that he, in my good name, facilitates any business to be engaged with them. And, as a linguister, he is most efficient in making new slaves follow the order of business aboard my command. I maintain that, except for the unfortunate business of our last voyage, (and there is question whether anyone can be held responsible against the devilish designs of a savage witch) Mr. Sam Bowmon is most adequate.

In the present instance, Mr. Bowmon reports that the dangerous Negro entrusted to us by the royal representative continues his diabolic influence even as we sail. The three slaves who were paid as compensation for his transport and destruction believe that this vile man owns their souls, and has control over their destinies. It appears that this black wizard has, even from his shackles, used his power over them and commanded these three savages to wound themselves most grievously by bruising away their ankle skin against their manacles. After several days of this self-brutality, their feet and legs have grown gangrenous and therefore a danger to the rest of the cargo. These poisonous Negroes have been removed and disposed to the sharks. This operation has given rise to many anxieties, as the other savages have threatened upheaval upon several occasions. The crewmen have been forced to quell their desperate behavior with use of belaying pins, stout cudgels, and rifle stocks. Pains have been taken not to fire on them, as bloodshed is always a wasteful expense. As best as can be expected, the crewmen have also avoided blows to teeth and groins and hands. Tincture of iodine has been applied in cases where skin was necessarily broken.

The loss of the three Negroes by self-murder voids all previous arrangements. It is now necessary to transport the Negro wizard to Barbadoes and obtain some value for him. Methinks he is strong enough to fetch some seventy pounds.

It must also be noted that young Jim Miller has passed and was buried at sea last sunset. God rest his soul. The men were given a nip of rum to jolly their spirits.

Safely ensconced in the prow of the galley store-hold, M'nalo twisted himself and put an eye to his porthole. His view was a world where the wind god commanded. The sea was roiling restless, white wave-tips skipping to an eager, whipping wind. The sky was fierce with flights of laden grey clouds. The flutter of blustering sails, unseen far above him, reminded of frightened fowl uncaged.

Blending with the keening wind was the more guttural misery from the human cargo in the vessel's bowels. M'nalo felt he could plumb the captives' despair within the well of their wailing. And as tears swelled, a great sorrow filled him. Just as the terrific rainstorm hit.

Up on deck, snapping an occasional order and watching critically as the men hurried about their various tasks securing the ship against the rising storm, Sam Bowmon, too, heard the chorus of hopelessness. "Poor black devils," he mused, his mood embittered, "let's hope they don't despair and kill off my profits. They must in truth be terrified. Them coming from such a vast solid country. A place where water is rivers or rain, flood or storm."

The ship lurched and seemed to fall into emptiness, making Sam Bowmon grab onto a fastened bale to maintain his balance, and maybe his mood. "These miserable chained wretches," he thought, "What do they know of the whims and fury of this sea? What of the raw force of a seventy-foot wall of water crashing down at the speed of a diving eagle? Aye! What do these wretched Africans know of the sea, except their awful fear? And what a fate to meet these monstrous elements confined in such a way. Hmmph! Poor devils."

He hunched his shoulders against the rain that had begun sheeting down and turned his attention back to his business. His dry berth and a jigger of rum would soon be his well-earned reward. Indeed, he'd be happy to see the end of this voyage. To be back in the West Indies with his pockets full and companions to share his good fortune.

After several days of wind and rain the storms finally abated, and once again the prisoners had been taken up on deck. M'nalo was scrounging for food, stealthy as a rat, when the sorcerer suddenly cried out in Twi, "Oh, hands and nimble fingers of Eshu-Elegba. Whatever form you have assumed, lower your fences and heed your servant's cry for help. My lobirs refuse to leave me for a journey through your masks. Now my appeal is shouted to your respect for our mighty ancestors. For surely we are of one people.

"See how many of our tribe suffer the chains of these pale-skinned slave merchants. Why must you close your powerful eyes to us?" On went his desperate plea.

The sorcerer's plaint strummed a response deep within M'nalo. He wormed his way along his side of the palisade to a spot directly behind the prisoner. Then, with the handle of his knife, he began tapping on one loop of the fellow's chains, a gentle rhythm of drumbeats offering support.

For a stunned moment, the chained man's chant faltered. Then, comprehending, the plea in his prayer grew to an exultant roar. A burst so rich in praise and confidence it suddenly was the only sound in the dismal hold. Ship's squeaks, the rattle of shifting chains above deck, the usual background chorus of hopelessness were drowned out altogether.

Startled and grasping their muskets tight, the two sailors guarding the hatch peered in. They searched the extent of the hold for activities that supported their sense of alarm. But for the spirited chanting of the chained prisoner, nothing seemed amiss.

"Maybe 'e's thanks us f'r 'is fine quarters," suggested one sailor, and received a nervous chuckle from his companion as they settled back to their sentry duty.

As that night fell, first mate Sam Bowmon came below to make his customary inspection. From the averted or fiercely staring-back face to the manacles at wrists and ankles, he examined each slave with tedious thoroughness. Made certain everything was shipshape. Whatever else he might feel, he well understood that spoiled merchandise brought poor prices, and this was, all said and done, a business venture.

When he was finished with the other prisoners, Bowmon went and stood before the chained-up African, silently studying him as he sometimes did. He had given up speaking to him, as the man never responded. Suddenly the fellow made a toss of his great head, one rope of his hair flicking close to the first mate's face. Yet Sam Bowmon seemed insensible to this and neither flinched nor reacted. He seemed unaffected until, selecting a key from a bunch hanging at his waist, he unlocked the sorcerer's shackles at both wrists. Then, turning smartly on his heel, he strode to the hatchway, climbed up the ladder, and disappeared out onto the deck. The guards returned to their posts atop the ladder.

"Help me unwrap these chains," came the sorcerer's urgent whisper to M'nalo, crouched watchful on his side of the barricade.

"The guards," M'nalo hissed back.

"True. Try with patience. Go slow."

Sticking his knife's blade between the saplings, and raising link by link, M'nalo began to loosen the chain extended around the sorcerer's left arm. Night was half done by the time the chain was free enough for the prisoner to slip out of its grasp. Which he did, though yet maintained his chained-captive pose.

"I must borrow your weapon," commanded the sorcerer.

Loath to part with his knife, M'nalo replied, "There are cutlasses stronger than my blade. Wait and I will pass one through to you." He crept off towards a particular chest, having long since scouted the contents of his hiding space.

The cutlasses located, M'nalo passed one through a space between floor and the bottom of the barricade. The nearest prisoners witnessed the exchange, and their excited murmuring grew steadily to a subdued roar.

"Hear me, fellow Africans," said the sorcerer in a low, calm voice. "If you are sensible, I can save us all. Return to your moans and groans. Keep these pale-skinned men unsuspecting and I shall take this vessel."

He had spoken in Yoruba dialect, and it took a few moments before his message was translated along the rows of manacled men. No sooner they understood, they all returned to spirited moans and lamentations. Although anyone with critical ears would surely have noticed their undertones of elation.

Screened by this chorus of false mourning, the freed sorcerer lowered himself to the floor, crept toward the torch. In one swift motion, he snatched it from its stand and smothered it on the floor, casting the hold into darkness.

The guards reacted immediately. "The torch has gone out!" shouted one. Then leaving his partner with the musket, he scrambled up on deck, perhaps to find another torch.

No sooner was the one guard alone than the sorcerer was at the foot of the hatchway. He commenced a clicking sound that teased, intrigued, invited investigation. The crewman peered in, paused. Then down the ladder he descended, and just as he stepped from the last rung, was beheaded with a single mighty stroke. His musket was snatched from his yet undead grasp.

Just then the other guard returned. One hand holding a lit torch high, he climbed through the open hatch, down the straight ladder. Two steps along the quiet floor, he called for his crewmate, "Hey, Tommy, where are yer, boy?"

Answer was a grunt and swishing sound. Then two soft thuds as the torch and another head fell to the hold's floor.

A hubbub of excitement filled the humid darkness.

From his place within it came the sorcerer's low voice once more. "Listen to me, Africans. Listen to me close. Let us be quiet as the darkness in which we bide. Let us be resolute. As we prepare to take this vessel, we must know our enemy. Know how many we must slay to claim victory. You who have been up on deck must now make count and assess the extent of the enemy."

Several voices spoke out. Seemed the best estimate was fourteen, perhaps sixteen crewmen. "And the captain," reminded one malicious voice.

"Two lie in pieces here," said the sorcerer. "Another has my lobir in his head, and will not resist us. Fellow Africans, I promise you that within one day the others will be finished."

There came a rousing shout and noisy celebration in a clanking of the prisoners' chains.

Then a lantern on a long pole was pushed down the hatchway, and a voice called out, "Hey y'all, Tommy. Hey thar, Vander. Are ye a'right down thar?"

A brief conference out of earshot, then the hatch door was slammed shut.

"I have noticed your scars, apprentice. I've heard our guild speak of a speechless one whose outcast master was defiant, and earned our enmity. Say quick, are you this one?"

"Me, an enemy?" M'nalo replied in his sibilant whisper. "I have freed your shackles. Is that not a truer answer?"

"Speak plain, leopard pup. Don't dare to bandy words with the right hand of Elegbara," the sorcerer answered, switching to *kuma* words in which M'nalo could hear tones of magical threat building up.

Before they could wield their weight, though, memory slid an answer to his tongue, and M'nalo hissed, "I am minion to the mischief messenger and have been punished into staying behind this fence of silence."

"Aha!" said the still wary magician. "A punished minion of the mischievous one. Then perhaps one day your rude wit will become as useful as your knife. On Eshu's mighty name, Amada Wasa Okapur is in your debt." He paused, and through the barricade, leveled a wary look at M'nalo "So long as our purposes are joined."

M'nalo nodded his head respectfully, dropped eyes to mask his feelings. Despite the protective lock of hair well tucked among his own, he felt no need to rile the wrath of the forceful sorcerer.

Wasa Okapur set to pulling apart the arm strips of the leather jerkin he wore. As he put each piece on the floor, by shifting and peering, M'nalo discerned that they were tubular, and concealed tiny balls and bits of matter. One after another, Wasa Okapur squeezed them out. His shining black face broke into a malevolent grin as he peered through the barricade to meet M'nalo's curious eyes. "This merchant's ship hold is now our pirate galley," Okapur declared.

He then pushed some bits from his jerkin through the space under the fence, and instructed, "Put the dried leaf to soak in the crew's drinking water. Crumble the other pieces and put it into their bread-meal and meat."

Easy enough, and knowing the crew's habits as he did, M'nalo did as he was told.

Morning come, the front hatchway creaked open as usual, and Captain Burnside, Sam Bowmon, and five crewmen armed with muskets descended into the galley hold. They shoved a passage through bulky cargo, got close to the barricade. They peered through, and spoke among themselves.

They had decided, it seemed, to starve the prisoners into submission and simply wait for the rebellion to die of hunger. So collecting their usual ration of supplies, they trouped back up the ladder.

Evening of that same day, directed by the sorcerer, M'nalo with knife gripped in hand, ventured up the hatchway and onto the main deck. There he saw disabled crewmen sprawled everywhere, asleep or worse. He had counted ten of them before he found Sam Bowmon's unconscious body, the bunch of keys on a rope around its waist.

He wasted no time in unlatching and opening the main hatch, sliding down the ladder, and handing freedom to the sorcerer, Amada Wasa Okapur.

Undisputed leader, the sorcerer unlocked the manacles of those nearby, then passed the keys to others so they could free themselves. Soon after, followed by the exuberant men, up the stairs he went. He examined the still unconscious slave-ship's crew, and without ceremony, condemned them to the sharks. Before his commands were carried out, though, the liberated slaves stripped the doomed crewmen of boots and clothes and weapons—useful and hard to come by as such were.

Among the Africans there were several able seamen. Although new to this extensive ocean, they had fair experience with lakes and wide rivers. They understood how a vessel reacted to the vagaries of wind over of water. They knew of lodestones and compasses, could handle knots and sails. So they had little difficulty managing the ship. Debate about returning to Africa soon dissipated when they assessed the food supplies. The need for fresh water, at least, they had no choice but continue westward. That decision made and announced by Okapur, the Africans grew sanguine and the mood of the ship relaxed. Men got busy and useful with hands and minds. Among the first at work were the fishermen, trying for sharks with unraveled sail rope. Then they went after the ever-playful dolphins. Wasn't long before they had improved the ship's meat rations. Groups formed based on common language, or tribe, or village geography. On nice evenings the starlit ship could become a creaky, floating place of nostalgic song and story telling.

M'nalo kept strictly to himself, out of the way. Maybe due to his role in their escape, the Africans were grateful but clearly uncomfortable in his company. Maybe it was his sorcerer scars. On the upper deck, in a nook behind the captain's cabin, he had made a bed of sailcloth. And during the half moon since they had captured the ship, this is mainly where he spent his time, daydreaming, dozing, wrestling with memories.

This morning he awoke prickly. Something nameless was gravely wrong. Rubbing the natural lines on his fingers together irritated. Tiny spots before his eyes had him seeing as if through a dirty brown veil. The precision of objects, the sharpness of the lines they marked against their backgrounds, became lost. At the same time, a brittle intolerance grew within him. Suddenly, as if it were a beaten drum, M'nalo was conscious of his heartbeat. He felt confused and oversensitive to an unnatural mixing of taste and sound and touch. This sense of ruinous disorder brought him close to vomiting. Trying for relief, M'nalo closed his eyes, but the fear still smothered. So he curled up on his sailcloth bed and suffered. In time he slept, and dreamt his three souls had fallen down the blackness of a well of loss.

Later that day, shade favoring his nook, M'nalo opened his eyes to a nudge at his shoulder. Wasa Okapur was crouched beside him. The grin that flashed from the black mat of his heavy beard was distracting in confidence. "Last night when I slept," he rumbled with grim amusement, "one of my essences returned from the homeland with news that the àshe of a certain outcast poisoner has fled to the other place."

His earlier strange edginess flashing to fore, M'nalo had to work hard at concealing distress. Terrible indeed was the idea of his master Lathso no longer watching over him. He summoned a whisper: "With the respect of a student to a master, I assume from your satisfaction that this departed one has been a rival."

Which seemed to give pause to the sorcerer's glee. He slowly nodded his leonine head and observed, "True, true. But maybe I share too much."

M'nalo did not respond right away. He felt as if an enormous chasm had wrenched itself between his being and his àshe. Yet, even as his essences quaked and grieved, another self remained within his mask of reverent student. As if innocent, that deceptive self asked, "How can a master share too much?"

Ten or so days later, pushed by spanking winds, morning found the ship surging through clear green waters teeming with fish. A lookout perched high in the sails' rigging shouted down that he could see land.

Scampered down, he gave them bearings. During the night, they had sailed through a channel. Behind them, to the right and the left, there were green islands. This news firmed Amada Wasa Okapur's decision. Despite the commotion and excitement, he chose to venture no further west lest he meet Europeans, and so steered his captured vessel southward. He had heard stories of a new Africa settled by the Garifuna, a black people like themselves, but native to this far side of the world. They would seek this land, Okapur promised his compliant and cheering companions.

Mind set firmly as well, M'nalo approached the sorcerer with a request.

"Great Master," he said. "I wish to face destiny in this new place alone by myself. I request of you a small boat equipped with a few essentials."

"As you wish, young sorcerer," replied Okapur. "You own the lives of all us free men on this ship. And in your special debt, I am foremost. If ever you should need my help, allow one of your souls to visit me. I shall always be open to you."

The ship was a diminishing spot on the horizon and with each dip into the sea and push of his paddle, M'nalo grinned pleasure. Triumph, too, at how his sly mask had out-maneuvered the mighty sorcerer. He hoped never to cross the man's path again. Still, he felt reassured to have the piece of braid hidden in his own thick curls. He'd make a bracelet of it, he decided, use it as a talisman. But now, heart buoyant as the bobbling boat, M'nalo stowed his paddle, took a look around. He breathed in deeply of the sweet air, strained his shoulders back until the muscles pained heady and good.

"Ahhh!" he sighed his happiness.

Setting once again to pushing water, M'nalo moved the small boat lightly over the afternoon sea. From a perfectly familiar blue sky, the sun beat down on his back. A steady breeze pleasantly cooled the burn. His intention was to make an unobtrusive landing on the green island, set up a camp close to the sea. With fish and fresh water, he felt certain he would survive. It would be that easy.

A sudden rushing sound compelled his attention, and M'nalo noticed that he was centered in a rippling oval patch of wavelets that extended perhaps ten paces away all around his boat. With a smile for the curious school of fish he anticipated, he balanced himself and halfway rose to better look into the clear ocean. But there were no fish. Just a broad murmuring ripple of wavelets staying apace around the drifting boat. Just a purposeful swath that seemed to reach little slivers of itself towards him. And slow as an idiot to reason, M'nalo realized it was a visitation. Although he yet remained without clue how to respond to the orishas declaring their presence.

Halfway squatting, awkward with his awe, he gaped at the tremble of water. At the evidence that he still moved within the cool fans of his river-rain goddesses. Yemoja's vibrant brilliance reflected from the sea into his eyes. Into his essence. Into the *blackness* of his àshe. And M'nalo's heart thrilled at a glimpse of his great destiny. His blood raced and his being thrummed as if to a powerful percussion, to a melody of bloodlines. A song of subtle wisdoms and survival.

Flexing his knees for balance, M'nalo stood tall in the little boat. He reached out his arms with hands palms up. "All praise and thanks," he sang out, and his voice came back to him forceful with *etutu*. "O sweet powerful Yemoja, and every divine one of you, Oshun, and Yewa, and Ere, and Oya. All ye whose fans bless me with breezes of *coolness*. O you mighty goddesses of health and wind and witchcraft, thank you for your attentions."

His àshe fitting to the ready rhythms of the sentient sea, M'nalo Fanta Bembo danced his independence.

M'nalo's adventures continue in the forthcoming
Web of Freedom.

Lightning Source UK Ltd.
Milton Keynes UK
18 September 2009

143881UK00003B/86/P